Good Deed

Steve Christie

Ringwood Publishing
Glasgow

First published in Great Britain in 2012 by
Ringwood Publishing
7 Kirklee Quadrant, Glasgow G12 0TS
www.ringwoodpublishing.com
e-mail mail@ringwoodpublishing.com

ISBN 978-1-901514-06-3

British Library Cataloguing-in Publication Data
A catalogue record for this book is available from
the British Library

DEDICATION

To Audrey, my wife and sometime therapist,
without whom I wouldn't exist.

ACKNOWLEDGEMENTS

Firstly I would like to remember three people important to me sadly no longer here. Angela my little sister, gone too soon, I know you would have loved this book sis, your star is still shining brightly in the night sky. My Dad Ronnie, you bestowed on me a love of literature and nature and inspired me more than you know, the evidence is sprinkled through this book and in my character Ronnie Buchanan. My Uncle Campbell always a gentleman, passionate about Celtic and an avid reader, you would have been blown away seeing your name here.

My Mum Bridget, life has been no picnic for you but you have always been there supporting and encouraging me no matter what else was going on, thanks Mum. My sons Lee and Marc for keeping me well and truly grounded and making me laugh (smegheads!). Teyah the long walks helped keep me sane. John, my father in law, for your support, despite the hassle you get from the rest of them, and my brother Andrew, bet you thought I'd forgotten, thanks for the occasional herbal remedies and memories.

Finally thanks to Ringwood Publishing for giving me this chance, in particular Sandy Jamieson the Ringwood M.D., who shares my love of real ales, thanks for introducing me to "Oscar Wilde", and especially Joanne Durning, my editor, for letting me do my own thing with only a little gentle nudge now and then.

Chapter One

Lucy Kennedy pulled off the motorway following the road signs to the Road Chef restaurant just outside Dundee. It was notoriously expensive but she had no choice. She was exhausted and in need of some caffeine. She had made good time despite the earlier mishap with the flat tyre. Thanks to a helpful stranger, she'd been back on the road in about ten minutes.

As she entered the restaurant, dazed from the long drive, she failed to notice Mark and Liam sitting outside in their parked car, but they noticed Lucy leaving hers, forgetting to lock up.

"Here we go!" said Liam.

Mark and Liam were two habitual criminals who prowled the country seeking victims at roadside restaurants and other such places. They never failed to be amazed by the amount of road users who, shattered from a long drive and in need of a coffee, would stumble into these restaurants leaving their cars unlocked, making their job so much easier. Once they had left their vehicle and entered the restaurant, Liam would pull alongside in his car, giving Mark cover to rummage through the car to see what bounty awaited them.

On this particular day they struck gold.

"Holy shit!" said Mark as he unzipped the tartan holdall lying in the back seat. What he'd found were two large packages of white powder well wrapped up in cling film. He knew they must contain a drug of some sort, smack, speed or coke it didn't really matter because judging by the quantity; it would be worth a whole load of cash on the street. He took the packages out of the bag, zipped it back up and jumped into Liam's car. "Wait till you see what I've got here, buddy." He showed Liam what he'd found.

"Check this, man! It's got to be worth a small fortune."

"Jesus!" said Liam. "What's a lassie like her doing carting all that shit about on her own?"

"No idea but it's our shit now, let's go."

They pulled out of the car park, re-joined the motorway and drove off under the grey, cloud covered sky towards the centre of Dundee.

Lucy, totally unaware of what had just happened, carried her overpriced espresso to the nearest table, sat down and peeled open the small stick shaped packets of brown sugar, poured them into her cup and began to stir her coffee for an inordinate amount of time. She had things preying on her mind, some bugging her more than others, the main thing of course being how the hell she had gotten herself involved as a drug courier. It had started off small time, a block of weed here and there. Her flat mate Julie had convinced her it was easy money and right enough it did help supplement her meagre university grant, but then she'd got greedy. She took on bigger and bigger amounts, and now four kilos of coke.

She reminisced on how it had all started. It was a typical students' night out, a meal at the local curry house, followed by a pub crawl round Newington. They were a party of six, a strange mix of people, Lucy, her flatmate Julie, Deborah, a mature student big on size and personality, Joe and Derek, two gay guys who shared a flat on the floor below, and Eric, the cause of all Lucy's troubles.

Eric was a strange guy, the cool student that no one really knew much about, Jim Morrison reincarnated. He picked up the tab for everything, the meal, the drinks, even the taxi home.

She remembered thinking, Jesus, this guy must have money coming out his ass. Only later on that night, back at her flat, did she find out where this money came from.

"I deliver a few packages," he told her as he skinned up a joint on one of Lucy's album covers, one of her favourites. "It's easy money," he said. "I could fix you up with the main man if you like?" And that was it! Lucy was in. No more shitty own brand label food from the local supermarket, no more eking out her meagre grant, life was looking up, or so she thought.

Due to her straight looking plain appearance she was perfect for the task. And because she was so perfect, she found herself getting all the bigger jobs. She was quite happy at first, let's face it, bigger job, bigger pay off. Then the paranoia set in, this couldn't last; eventually she'd get caught. What would her family say? What if she ended up in jail? All that studying would have gone to waste.

Well this would be the last, she wanted out and she'd tell them today as soon as she dropped off the package but she'd have to be careful how she went about it. It wasn't like packing in any normal job, a quick goodbye, a few drinks at the end of the last day and then you're off. These guys were scary so she would have to be tactful.

She bought another coffee to go, got her car keys out of her bag and returned to her car to complete the journey.

When she got to her car her heart skipped a beat. Shit! It's unlocked! Panicking she looked in the back seat, the holdall was still there. She caught her breath, tried to calm down a bit and got in her car and headed on her way.

*

"You have reached your destination," Lucy's satnav told her as she pulled in to Aberdeen's Whitemyres Industrial Estate, the same type of place as always, filled with commercial properties and warehouses, very soulless places Lucy always thought. As usual within minutes the dark car pulled alongside hers and the driver told her to follow. She was led to a small warehouse where heavy doors opened as if by magic. She drove in to the gloomy interior, feeling the hairs stand up on the back of her neck. She always felt like this, scared shitless when it came to the actual handover, but

3

she refused to let them see it.

Three men got out of the car in front and waited for Lucy to join them. "Bring the gear," she was told by the tall man who was obviously the leader of this motley bunch.

Lucy got out with the holdall in hand and walked towards them. "Where's my money?" Lucy asked, putting on a show of false bravado, which she hoped wasn't a mistake

"You'll get your money when we weigh the coke, you wouldn't be the first runner with sticky fingers." Lucy slid the bag towards him, impatient to get her money and leave for the last time. Puzzled, Lucy watched as one of the men unzipped the holdall and started pulling out her clothes and throwing them to the side. "What the hell are you doing?" asked Lucy. "The coke's on the top."

He turned towards the tall man.

"It's not here, boss."

"Where's my fucking coke?" the tall man asked as he grabbed Lucy in a vice like grip. As shocked as she was by the situation, she managed to stammer out a reply. "I, I know it was there. I packed it myself this morning!"

"So, it's just vanished, maybe snatched by the coke fairy while you were asleep huh?"

"I don't understand, it was definitely there," said Lucy.

"Well, looks like we have a serious problem, you have five minutes to decide your fate. Give me a thorough run down of your whole journey from Edinburgh to here, like your life depended on it, which it does!"

Panicking, Lucy's mind was blank.

"Four minutes!"

"Wait! I stopped twice, once in Edinburgh due to a flat tyre and once for a coffee in Dundee."

"Was anyone near your car?"

"No, no one! Well apart from the guy who changed the wheel."

"What!"

"The guy who changed the wheel, Donald something, I have his card."

Lucy fumbled in her purse. "Here take it!"

After studying the business card the tall man took off in discussion with the other two, before telling Lucy to get in the back of her car, shaking visibly she did as she was told.

As she bent over to get in the vehicle, a heavy blow floored her, sending her crashing to the floor in a heap.

Chapter Two

Vince was waiting when Terry and Dave got back to the warehouse.

They were a strange duo, thought Vince. Terry was huge, he looked like an overweight boxer who had lost far too many fights, whereas Dave was tall and thin, he looked fit, athletic even.

"Has it all been taken care of?" asked Vince.

"Done and dusted!" replied Terry in his nasal whine.

"Okay people, no point in hanging around all day feeling sorry for ourselves, let's get started. Terry, you and Dave check Lucy's flat, see what her flatmate can tell you. She could have taken the coke out the bag after Lucy had packed her things. Put the frighteners on her, do what it takes. I'm going to check out this Donald Campbell guy," said Vince. "As far as I can see they're the only two that had the opportunity to steal the coke. You two leave now, I have a few things to tie up before I set off, then I'll catch up with you in Edinburgh."

Vince produced two mobile phones. "Use these, leave your own mobiles here, you know the drill."

Terry and Dave left the warehouse heading for the A90 and the two and a half hour drive to Edinburgh.

Vince picked up his phone, opened the search engine and typed in, *Ramble On Outdoors Centre, Edinburgh*, under instructors and joint directors it had a picture of Glen Hughes and Donald Campbell. "Ah, there you are," Vince said to himself as he phoned the number.

"Hello, Ramble On!" the voice said.

"Hello, Phil Harris here, how are you today?"

"I'm fine, Mr Harris, how can I help you?"

"I'm interested in the outdoor tasters advertised on your website, what does that actually involve?"

"Well," she said. "Just a bit of everything really, trekking, abseiling, a spot of canoeing, we have a group on tomorrow if you can make it."

"That would be perfect, and who would be taking that?"

"It would be Donald Campbell," she said. "At ten am tomorrow."

"Brilliant, I'll be there," said Vince.

"Oh Mr Harris, before I forget, will you be hiring clothing and equipment, or do you have your own?"

"I have all the equipment I need," said Vince, looking at the firearm on the table.

Next he phoned Tony, the guy in charge of cutting the coke.

"Tony its Vince, there's been a delay; it should all be sorted out in a day or two."

"I hope so, there's a bit of a drought on so there's a lot of desperate people waiting."

"Tell them I'll raise the cut to fifteen per cent instead of their usual twelve, that should please their customers."

"Okay, I'll pass it on. Cheers Vince."

Vince picked up his bag and his laptop, holstered his gun, and left for Edinburgh.

*

Just as Vince left the outskirts of Aberdeen, Detective Inspector Ronnie Buchanan left the Grampian police headquarters on his way to a crime scene.

The fire brigade had been called out to a burning car in Hazlehead Woods. This car however, wasn't your routine stolen insurance job, this one contained a body in its boot.

He drove past the golf course and nearby park enveloped in frost covered rhododendrons.

He used to go there many years ago, mostly in the summer with a few of his mates. They'd sit in the Rose Gardens enjoying the sun and listening to music while their cans of beer stayed cool in the water surrounding the fountain.

He pulled into a clearing at the side of the road and thought back to earlier. The day had started off so great, a crisp frosty morning with the sun a lot warmer than it had a right to be this time of the year. He wasn't due in until later that day. He and Michelle had slept in, she wasn't due at work until two. They'd had a quick coffee then a long leisurely walk with the dog along the beach. Then, just as they were drying the dog off in the back of the car, he'd received the phone call. DI Wallace or Rennie as he was affectionately called due to his massive consumption of indigestion tablets had collapsed on duty, a burst stomach ulcer. "We need you, Ronnie." He'd have to fill in, forego his late start, he'd been told.

This didn't please Michelle, not one bit. She blamed him for ruining everything as usual. His ears were still burning from the tirade they'd received.

"You promised me a nice meal at La Lombarda, what happened to that then you bastard!, It'll finish off our walk nicely, you said." Well bugger it, she'd have to wait for her Italian.

The crime scene had been taped off and Ronnie could see the pathologist pull into the wooded area ahead. He got out his car and rubbed his hands together just as Joe Styles parked his car.

He was a huge bear of a man and he looked like something out of a Dickens novel. He was bald as a coot, had a huge walrus moustache and walked with a stoop. He had a strange habit of constantly looking at the antique pocket watch he kept attached to a chain hanging from his waistcoat pocket as if he was always running late for some important meeting.

"Hi Ronnie, a chilly morning don't you think? I believe we have a crispy one." Ronnie shook his head and sighed, a sigh visible in the cold morning air. "Sorry, pathologist humour!" said Joe.

Joe and Ronnie approached the crime scene heading for the burnt out car.

"I heard about Rennie," said Joe, "poor bastard, not a nice thing to happen at all."

"Is a burst stomach ulcer that serious, Doc?" said Buchanan. "Can be Ronnie. Stomach Ulcers, or Peptic Ulcers as they can be called sometimes, cause a hole or erosion in the stomach lining. Because of the stomach acid, they can be very painful. I have had ulcers on and off for years, it comes with the stress of the job. The trouble comes when they start to bleed, as in poor Rennie's case. A perforated ulcer usually causes sudden, sharp, severe pain often requiring immediate hospitalisation and surgery."

"Jesus, how do I stop myself getting one of these ulcer things?"

"Stay off the booze and fags, and try to relax more."

"Ah, but what if the booze and fags help me relax, what then?"

"Good point, Ronnie," said Joe patting Buchanan on the back. "I can't really argue with that."

As they got closer to the car Buchanan suddenly stopped dead, his feet crunching the heavily frosted grass below.

"Jesus, what's that sickly sweet smell?" said Ronnie.

"That would be the cooked flesh," said Joe. "Some liken it to barbecued pork."

"Do you know that cannibalism was rife in Polynesia up until fairly recent times? They called human flesh long pig."

"Well gee Doc, as interesting as that was, it wasn't exactly very fucking helpful to my case."

"Ha!" Joe laughed as they approached the body.

Joe put on his gloves and went to work, Buchanan watched him hover over the dried husk of the body poking and prodding with various instruments from his case, occasionally with a puzzled look on his face, sometimes with a knowing nod to himself.

Buchanan knew not to rush him, so he stood back and lit a cigarette, tapping the ash now and again into the portable ashtray he kept in his pocket. He always used it at a crime scene, the last thing he needed was to drop the dog end on the ground, only for it to be collected as evidence, and lead to wasted resources chasing up a saliva sample that belonged to him.

Joe finally stopped leaning over the boot, stretched his back with a sigh and looked at his pocket watch.

Looks like he's finished, thought Buchanan.

"Well Joe, can you tell me anything?"

"You'll have to wait for the Post Mortem for this to be confirmed, but from what I can see, there's a good chance that she is, or was, a young woman, maybe twenty to thirty years old. The body tissue as you can see is severely damaged, so much so, that we'll need to go on dental records, or possibly medical history for identity purposes, I'm afraid."

Ronnie pulled out a handkerchief to protect himself from gagging at the smell, "Anything else?"

"Well!, don't quote me on this, but judging by the body position, there's a good chance she was alive and frantically trying to get out when the car was set on fire."

"Heartless bastards!" said Ronnie.

"I'll make sure you get the P.M. results as soon as it's done tomorrow. In fact, I'll come in early and do it myself," said Joe as he left the scene.

"Thanks Doc!"

Phil Maxwell, a young sergeant approached Buchanan.

"Inspector, we have the vehicle check results."

"Well? Spit it out Max."

"According to the registration, the car was stolen just over two months ago from an old couple in the London area, sir. There's been no sign of it till now."

"Do you think they'll want it back, Sergeant? It'll need a hell of a paint job, and they could do with some new seat covers."

Max grinned, "I doubt it sir, it's not exactly a fixer upper is it."

Buchanan thanked him and returned to his car. He opened both front windows fully, despite the cold weather, to try and get rid of the burnt smell which seemed to be sticking to his clothing and drove a short distance to the Treetops Hotel on Springfield Road. He entered the bar, ordered himself a Guinness and sat down next to the huge open fire. Then, as he always did when starting something new, he took out his notebook and wrote down a quick list of the main points relating to the case so far.

Burn victim 20-30 year old female
More than likely alive when car set on fire
Burned vehicle stolen from London area
6 Mths ago
Not much chance of prints or trace due to fire
Murder

Buchanan underlined the word murder, put away his notebook and ordered himself another Guinness, a drink as black as the charred flesh on the mystery woman in the boot of the car.
I wonder what her name is, he thought to himself as he sipped his pint, relishing the heat given off by the flames of the fire.

Chapter Three

This was turning out to be some shitty day, thought Julie as she had already been woken up at six am with the drilling going on in the street outside the flat in Newington, an area popular with students like herself. Lucy, her flatmate, had forgotten to buy the breakfast cereal and the rest of the weekly shop, and to top it all, the nice warm relaxing bath she had just ran for herself, wasn't warm as the water heater was on the blink again.

She took a deep breath.

Calm down Julie, she told herself, the take away you ordered should be arriving soon.

She managed to wash her hair at least, with the help of the kettle, and had just wrapped a towel around her head when she heard the door.

Julie answered the door expecting to see the pizza delivery guy with her double pepperoni, not a man with a sawn off shotgun and a face straight out of an old Hammer Horror movie.

"Inside, bitch!"

Julie did what the scary man asked.

"What's your name?"

"Wh…' what?" stammered Julie.

"I said, what's your name?"

"Julie Tarrant."

"Well Julie, why don't you sit yourself down on that chair over there like a good girl until a good friend of mine arrives and we can all have a little chat."

Julie did as she was told.

"What's this all about?" asked Julie.

"It's all about questions, questions and answers. You answer correctly, and you can go back to your normal life in this shit hole of a flat. What is that god-awful smell?" asked Terry.

"That'll be the guinea pigs, they belong to my flatmate but she usually cleans them out before it gets this bad."

Dave entered the room with Julie's pizza under his arm.

"Check this man, she must have known we were coming, she ordered pizza, extra pepperoni no less, and a stuffed crust to boot."

"Right first things first, we'll have something to eat then we discuss a few things." said Terry.

"You got any beer?" asked Dave.

"There are a few bottles in the fridge," said Julie, "you can help yourself."

"I'll go get the beers Dave, you can stick on some music, I'm sure Julie here must have some CDs. Oh! And make it nice and loud." Dave put on some music while a scared and trembling Julie sat quietly, watching them eat her pizza. She'd lost her appetite so she had none herself. She heard some old blues guy from one of her flatmates' CDs singing something in the background about bad luck and trouble as she stared at the shotgun on the table next to Terry.

*

Approaching the Forth Road Bridge Vince took a call on his mobile.

"Vince, it's Harry, what the fuck's going on?"

Shit! Vince thought to himself.

"She turned up without the coke Harry, insisted she had it when she left, but don't worry I'm on it. I just have a few leads to follow up and should have it back in a couple of days."

"You know me better than anyone Vince. I won't tolerate such fuck ups, so I hope she was shown the error of her ways?"

"She's been taken care of," said Vince. "Now let me get on with my job. You pay me to fix things, and it'll be fixed."

Vince disconnected the call, threw his phone down on the passenger seat, and drove on towards Edinburgh.

About halfway across the bridge he found himself in a situation he could have done without. The guy in front braked too fast, his rusty car had no brake lights, hence no warning.

Fuck! This is all I need, thought Vince. Both cars slowed down and pulled over to the left.

The stick thin driver opened his door, Country and Western music blaring out the car. He prised himself out of the driver's seat and headed towards Vince's car.

He was dressed like a cowboy, his huge brimmed Stetson making his thin frame look ridiculous. "Hey asshole, you just fucked up my motor."

Vince got out his car.

"I think you'll find you're the asshole, that piece of shit's got no brake lights. What are other road users supposed to do, just guess when you're about to slow down or stop?"

"Piece of shit! I'll have you know that car's a classic."

"Ok, sorry, that classic piece of shit, partner."

"Fuck you! Give me your insurance details."

Vince thought about throwing the guy over the side of the bridge, he couldn't have weighed more than eight stone but now their little crash was causing a scene, people were slowing down to try and get an eyeful of what was going on.

"Look calm down," said Vince. "Here's two hundred quid, get the bumper fixed and keep the change."

"I don't want your money; I want your insurance details. That is if you've got any. I've heard about people like you driving without insurance, that's what puts the premiums up for honest people like me."

"You tell him Bob," said the woman who had just got out of the passenger side dressed in a ludicrous multi-coloured smock. Maybe I should just shoot them both, thought Vince, do the world a favour. "Three hundred?" said Vince removing a thick wad of cash from his inside pocket, "then we can both be on our way."

"Oh, so you're one of these rich guys, think you can go driving about in your fancy suit and your fancy Merc paying everyone off. I'll ask again, insurance details?"

Then smock woman got herself involved.

"I think you're compensating for something," said the woman pointing at Vince.

"Fancy cars are phallic symbols. I read that in Cosmo. You know what that means?"

"Enlighten me," said Vince.

"It means in all likelihood you probably have an extremely small penis."

Vince was close to losing it and was just about to grab the guy by the neck when he heard the police car approach from behind. Vince leaned against the half open back window of the guy's car as the man and woman moved towards the police vehicle. The two officers approached Vince.

"What's the problem here then?" said the first policeman.

"I just told you, that asshole ran into my car and he refuses to give me his insurance details," said the thin man from behind.

"That right, sir?"

"Far from it," said Vince wiping his hand on the handkerchief he had seemingly magically produced from nowhere.

"I'll just go and get them now, but first could I have a word?" said Vince, lighting himself a cigarette from his antique silver cigarette case.

The police officer followed Vince to his car.

Vince nodded towards the other man, "I think you have a more pressing problem than a slight bump between two cars," said Vince quietly.

"This guy's unstable, officer and very dangerous I believe. Have a look in the back seat of his car; you'll see what I mean." The officer approached the other car taking time to glance at the back seat. His eyes immediately fell on the handgun, the barrel glinting in the low winter sun. The hand gun that had just recently been wiped of prints and thrown through the half opened window a couple of minutes ago, by Vince, as he leaned against the car. It was a spare; he could afford to lose it.

After having a quick word with his partner, the first officer moved towards the other man, his baton extended as his partner made a grab for the woman.

"Get down on your knees," he shouted to the now extremely confused man as he struck him heavily across the back of the legs. As this was all taking place, unnoticed by all in the on-going melee, Vince got back in his car, turned on the ignition and gunned it towards the other side of the bridge.

Time to change the car I think.

*

Terry had been questioning Julie in the bedroom for half an hour while Dave had searched the flat from top to bottom. He had heard her muffled screams but doubted anyone else could, thanks to the loud music.

He hated this side of things, the beatings and the killings but for some reason known only to him, Terry seemed to enjoy them. "I just love to hear folk scream," he'd once told Dave.

Just then Terry came out the bedroom covered in sweat, his face red as a beetroot. "She hasn't got the coke; I take it you found nothing?"

"Bugger all!" said Dave.

"Right I'm going down to the car to phone Vince. I've taken care of the girl, leave the body, nothing ties her to us. You can tidy up as usual. Don't forget to wipe everything down, turn off the music and lock the door on the way out, I'll see you downstairs, don't take too long."

Terry took out his mobile and phoned Vince.

"Turned out to be a dead end, Vince. She knew about the drug runs but sod all about the missing coke."

"Fuck!" said Vince, "I hope you tied up any loose ends?"

"Yes, I've seen to that, no worries there."

"Good man," said Vince. "Listen, meet me tonight at the Stable Bar, it's in the middle of a Caravan Park at Mortonhall, it's a bit out of the way, perfect for our meeting, make it nine pm."

"Ok Vince, we'll see you there."

Dave got in the car.

"What next, Terry?"

"We're meeting Vince tonight, somewhere in the middle of fucking nowhere as usual so that leaves us a couple of hours to kill, let's go for a pint."

*

Buchanan sat at his desk looking at the photos from the crime scene, pretty gruesome he thought to himself.

It reminded him of a documentary he'd watched recently. The bog man they'd called him. Some peat workers were loading cut blocks of peat into a lorry in the eighties. When they looked more closely at one block they saw a body, no one could tell by looking how old the body was until they had done a post mortem and carbon dated it. As it turned out, he had died between A.D.50 and A.D. 100. The scientists learned, after further examination, that the man had been murdered. He'd met a horrific death. He was struck on the top of his head twice with a heavy object, he also received a vicious blow to the back breaking one of his ribs. He had a thin cord tied around his neck, probably used to strangle him and break his neck. By then he must have been dead but then his throat was cut. Finally he was placed face down in a pool in the bog lying there until the peat workers had found him so many years later. Talk about overkill. The peat had preserved him, turned him brown and dried him out, turning him in to a shrunken mummy. Looking at the photo of his victim's burned remains, they could have been twins.

He picked up the phone and called Steve Kershaw in the lab to see what the SOCOs had come up with.

The SOCOs, or Scene of Crime Officers, could break a case by diligently searching a crime scene for any evidence available.

"Do you have anything of interest to tell me, Steve?"

"Not that much Ronnie. A couple of footprints have been cast, no chance of trace or prints due to the fire, one thing might be quite helpful though, some sort of ID was found in the burnt holdall, can't make out much of it at all but let us work on it a while and hopefully we can enhance it and see what we can find."

"That sounds promising Steve, it would be great if we could give the victim a name," said Ronnie. "Keep me informed."

Buchanan walked to the office next door looking for Sergeant Maxwell. There was no sign of him. Further along the corridor he found him at the coffee machine deep in conversation with a young WPC.

"Get me one of those Max, with plenty of sugar and bring it through to my office."

*

Max arrived with the coffee.

"Here you go, sir."

"Any news for me?" said Buchanan.

"Not much sir, local enquiries are on-going but due to the fact the car was dumped in the woods apart from a few cyclists and dog walkers no one much goes out there unless they're going for a picnic, and it's a bit cold for that this time of the year."

"Who phoned it in?" said Buchanan.

Max took out his notebook, "That was a Mr Davies, out walking his dog."

"Did you get a statement?"

"Yes sir, doesn't help us much though, he saw no one else in the area."

"Well thanks sergeant, let's call it a day shall we?"

"Fine by me sir, I'll see you tomorrow."

*

He had just got in his car when his mobile rang.

"Ronnie, you fancy going for a curry tonight?"

"To be honest Michelle I've had a hell of a day, I quite fancy a night in."

"Suits me, how about I nip into the supermarket and pick up a couple of curries on the way home?"

"That sounds great but don't forget the beer," said Ronnie.

"Like I would!"

"How was your day anyway?" asked Buchanan.

"Could have been better, the kids in the nursery were doing my head in, I'm not sure what was up with them today."

"Could be the full moon, it's meant to drive them nuts isn't it?"

"That's lunatics Ronnie, not kids."

"Lunatics, kids, same thing isn't it?"

Michelle laughed. "You're nuts!" she said.

"See you at home, hun," said Buchanan.

Ronnie drove home, haunted by the burnt woman and wondering what tomorrow would bring.

Chapter Four

Vince locked himself in the washroom, unzipped his bag and removed the blonde wig, false beard and the spirit gum. He washed and dried his face then carefully applied the gum, rubbing it in until it became tacky then carefully applied the goatee and put on the wig.

It was a skill he'd perfected many years ago, the art of disguise. He'd learned it from an old girlfriend who used to work in the film industry as a makeup artist, and it had got him out of more scrapes and dodgy situations than he cared to remember. Her name was Greta, a German woman with blonde hair and blue eyes. He hadn't thought of her in years. He'd loved her accent.

She'd lived in a house-boat, a Dutch Barge situated in an idyllic spot in a canal in West London. He'd enjoyed the months he'd spent there, he'd found it relaxing. He remembered vividly lying in bed with Greta, the gentle undulation of the canal rocking them from below as they listened to her favourite jazz station on the ancient looking radio she kept by the side of her bed.

Vince forced himself from his reverie. He didn't have time for such thoughts, he had work to do.

He looked at himself in the mirror.

"Well hello Mr Harris, nice to meet you!"

He jumped into his car and joined the line of traffic heading onto to the city bypass on his way to the Ramble On Centre and his encounter with Donald Campbell.

At around about the same time, Terry and Dave approached Campbell's house on Old Dalkeith Road, as had been planned the night before when Vince had supplied them with the address. They passed several protestors waving placards and singing hymns by the side of the road.

"Who the fuck are they?" asked Terry.

"Anti-abortionists," said Dave.

"What are they doing here?"

"There's a hospital across the road, must do abortions there I imagine. Stop here, this is it."

They left the car and headed towards the house.

It was an old miner's house built in 1887 according to the weather beaten plaque on the wall. It was quite small and recently white washed. Set back slightly from the road, the garden was full of overgrown shrubs, which suited them fine as it gave them some cover from prying eyes and nosey neighbours.

They slowly opened the rusty gate, had a quick glance around to make sure they weren't being watched and approached the door.

Dave picked the Yale lock in about five seconds and they both entered the premises to begin the search. Whether they found the coke or not, they had to contact Vince by ten thirty am, hopefully saving him a messy interrogation job at his end.

*

"Think it's going to rain, Bill?"

Donald Campbell carried his coffee and bacon roll into his office where Bill Briggs, one of the Junior Outdoor Instructors was already waiting.

"Could do I suppose, it is kind of cloudy out there. What time do we leave today anyway?"

"The clients should all be here by ten, say ten fifteen to allow for late comers, so we should be heading out about twelve, after they've completed the training."

"I'll go see to the transport and pack the equipment then," said Bill, "and leave you to your breakfast."

"Before you go, any calls for me?"

"You mean from that woman you helped out, the one with the

puncture don't you?"

"Not necessarily."

"Oh come off it, she's all you've talked about since yesterday."

"Well," said Donald. "I thought we really hit it off, she asked for my mobile number and said she'd phone me as soon as she got back last night, she left me a message at home saying as much."

"Well don't give up yet," said Bill. "She might phone today, you never know. Catch you later."

Donald Campbell went back to his breakfast and a quick look at the day's paper.

*

Terry and Dave had searched the house thoroughly; in fact they'd ripped it apart and found nothing. While Terry went through to the kitchen to phone Vince, Dave, on the spur of the moment decided to check Campbell's answer machine. There was one saved message so he hit the play button.

"Donald, its Lucy, the girl with the puncture."

Dave was frozen to the spot, the voice from the grave making him break out in a cold sweat.

"I'd like to thank you properly for your knight in shining armour routine, we could go for a drink, maybe a meal or something if that's ok. I've just stopped for a quick coffee so I'll have to make up some time, I'd better go. I'll phone you later tonight, bye."

Taking a few deep breaths to calm himself down, Dave ripped the machine from the wall and stashed it under his jacket.

*

Vince parked his car and got his backpack out of the boot. Entering the building he approached the reception desk.

"Hi, my name's Phil Harris. I'm booked on to this morning's taster session."

"Oh, hi Mr Harris, I believe I took your booking yesterday, if you could just take a seat the instructors shouldn't be too long. Feel free to help yourself to a coffee."

Vince had just introduced himself to the others and sat down when Campbell appeared with another younger guy in tow.

"Good morning folks! My name's Donald Campbell and this is my assistant Bill Briggs. As we will be doing a bit of abseiling today we should all put in a bit of practice in the training room, nothing too difficult, just a quick run through of the basics. Then you can apply what you learn on the actual rock face later on today."

"Excuse me, Mr Campbell, but do you mind if I catch you up? I'm waiting on a very important phone call, it should only take five minutes," said Vince.

"Try not to be too long then, you really have to complete the training as it's a health and safety requirement."

"No problem, like I said five minutes tops."

Vince walked outside just as his phone rang.

"Terry, about time you phoned, how did it go?"

"We searched his house from top to bottom; if he has the stuff there's no way it's here."

"Shit, that's not what I wanted to hear. I've emailed you a few things that need seeing to, take care of them and then you and Dave can take the rest of the day off, but make sure you keep your mobiles on, and keep them charged. I'll be in touch when I've taken care of Campbell."

Vince disconnected the call and entered the centre.

*

Stifling a huge yawn Buchanan walked into the autopsy room with a croissant in one hand and a coffee in the other.

He usually tried to give this room a wide berth, he usually sent another officer off for the P.M. results. The room gave him the creeps. He hated the sterile look of the place, all the stainless steel cupboards and white tiled walls. He hated the antiseptic smell and the vibrations created by the huge air extraction system, he could feel it through his feet. Then there was the autopsy table itself, a huge, perforated work space, the holes there to facilitate the down draught ventilation, removing most, but not all of the smells. It had fluid drainage chambers at the side, not that this burnt out husk of a body had much body fluids left. Add to that the various medical instruments in the drawers to the left, some he knew about, some he definitely didn't want to. This was somewhere he didn't want to be. And to top it all his cheese and ham croissant suddenly didn't seem so appetising, the smoked ham reminding him of human flesh. He threw it in the bin.

"Morning doc, how's the stiff?"

 "Still dead I'm afraid to say Ronnie."

"P.M. been done?"

 "Yep, first thing this morning" said Joe.

Buchanan put down his coffee.

"Well what have you got for me?"

"I did the blood gas analysis. CO-HB is over fifty per cent, what does that tell you?"

"It tells me that you are trying to be a smart arse. Put it in layman's terms, eh doc."

"CO-HB, or Carboxyhaemoglobin to give its full name could possibly be found in levels of up to ten per cent in a heavy smoker but levels as high as this can only mean that she was alive and breathing during the fire. Also, there's evidence of a hairline fracture at the back of the skull and a ligature mark round her neck."

Just like the bog man Ronnie thought to himself.

"So," said Buchanan. "She was cracked on the back of the head, throttled and then chucked in the boot and the car set on fire."

"Exactly!" said Joe.

"Can I ask you something doc? It's totally unrelated to the case."

"Fire away," said Joe.

"In your expert opinion, is there a way to kill someone and totally get away with their murder?"

"A few ways actually,"

"What are they?"

"An injection of potassium,"

"What does that do?" asked Buchanan.

"Potassium in large amounts causes a huge heart attack. If you were to give such an injection and then you kept the body somewhere for a couple of days before you dumped it, it's almost impossible to prove."

"Why impossible?"

"Ah, that's the clever part, you see when a body starts to decompose lots of different chemicals and gasses are released, one of which is potassium so a person that's been dead for a while will naturally have raised levels of potassium."

"That's brilliant," said Buchanan.

"Why do you ask Ronnie? Are you getting sick of Michelle?"

"No, no, no, it's just something we were discussing last night, she's thinking of writing a novel."

"Well if I ever find her laid out on my table, I'll remember this conversation."

"Bye Joe."

"Oh! And if she gets it published, I want a credit."

*

Next on the Agenda for Buchanan were the forensic labs on Nelson Street.

As soon as he walked in, Steve Kershaw ran up to him unable to contain his excitement.

"We've done it Ronnie, we got a name from the burnt ID, Lucy Kennedy, it's her student ID from Napier University in Edinburgh."

"Don't get too excited son," said Buchanan. "She could have just borrowed someone's ID, did you manage to clean up the photo part?"

"That was impossible I'm afraid, it was too badly damaged in the fire," said Steve.

"Not to worry," said Buchanan. "I'll arrange to get hold of her dental records and get Doc Styles to see if they match up with the body."

Next Buchanan phoned Sergeant Maxwell. "I want you to do a bit of digging for me Sergeant, a young woman by the name of Lucy Kennedy, a student at Napier University in Edinburgh, see what you can find out."

"Is that the dead woman, sir?"

"Possibly Max, and while you're at it find the address of her dentist. I'll meet you in The Prince of Wales for lunch and we can go over your findings, at say, twelve o clock?"

"That should be fine, sir, see you there."

*

Buchanan drove out to Hazlehead; he always liked to revisit a murder site when it was a bit quieter. He liked to try and picture himself in the killer's shoes, see if he could zone in to their way of thinking.

He spent a good half hour pacing the murder scene, occasionally kneeling down and looking at it from various angles. There must have been at least two of them, he thought to himself. It was a gut instinct. The killers drove out here with the body in the boot, torched the car then left the scene. They'd chosen the dump site well, plenty of cover from the mature pine trees all around. No one here to see them except for a few crows hiding in the branches above, he could hear them cawing now. The killers must be used to finding secluded spots. They needed transport away from here and it's very doubtful they left on foot or flagged down a taxi, too easy to be spotted and they'd have been stinking of smoke, easily remembered.

No. Far more likely two guys in two cars, one car dumped, one used for the getaway. Or it could be a man and woman of course. And why pick here? They must have had some local knowledge, it's not somewhere you would just come across, and they must have known the area. He finished his cigarette, took one last look around the crime scene and walked back towards his car.

*

26

Walking down the cobbles of St Nicholas Lane, Buchanan entered The Prince Of Wales and couldn't help thinking; this must be the closest thing you could get to going back in time.

The interior was what you would expect from a "classic" pub. Old, beat up wooden chairs and tables, plenty of space at the bar and well-marked wooden floors, a direct contrast to the many so called "trendy" bars that had sprung up in Aberdeen. It had the usual lunchtime clientele, students here for the reasonably priced food mingled with shoppers in need of a rest with a few businessmen dotted around with their laptops perched precariously next to their drinks on their tables.

"The usual, Ronnie?" asked the barman.

Buchanan nodded his head, "Cheers Ted."

"That'll be two pounds twenty."

"What! I'll have you up on a robbery charge son; you do know I'm a copper?"

Ted laughed, as Buchanan carried his pint over to a table in the corner, his usual place of choice. Taking out his notebook he began to write.

Killer had knowledge of area

Possible identification, Lucy Kennedy, student at Napier's

Skull bashed in and strangled with ligature (neither causing her death) before she was thrown in boot of car

At least two people involved killer needed lift from scene

Sergeant Maxwell approached the table.

"Would you like another one, sir?"

"Why not" said Buchanan, "and while you're there, grab a couple of menus, will you Max."

When Sergeant Maxwell came back with the drinks he pulled out his own notebook and proceeded to go over what he'd managed to find out about Lucy.

"Lucy Kennedy, 21 years old, only child of Jane and Jim Kennedy, parents stay in Birmingham, where Lucy was born.

She left home and moved to Edinburgh two years ago to take a place on a Software Engineering course at Napier University.

Her home now is a flat in the Newington area of Edinburgh which she shares with another student called Julie Tarrant.

Oh! And her dentist is The Southside Dental Practice."

"Well done Max, I think I'll get on to an old friend of mine, John Brannigan at the Lothian and Borders, see if he can send round a couple of uniforms to her flat and see if there's any sign of Lucy, or at least talk to the flatmate to confirm if she's missing. Now let's eat, I'm starving."

Chapter Five

The two constables knocked on the door yet again; they had been trying to get an answer for a good few minutes to no avail. They looked around the grubby hallway. It couldn't have been painted in years and for some reason the whole place seemed to smell of curry. Just then the door across the hall opened slightly, an old woman peered through the gap between the edge of the door and the security chain, her claw like fingers poking through to the outside. She opened the door fully and stepped out into the hallway, her hands holding her grubby pink dressing gown closed at the neck.

"I have a spare key you know, got it from Lucy a while ago, just in case she or Julie ever needed it."

"And you are?"

"Mrs Webb, I've lived here over thirty years you know."

She pointed over to the girls flat and shook her head from side to side, reminding PC Jones of one of those dogs you used to see in T.V. adverts.

"I take it it's something to do with drugs. Is it?"

"What?"

"Drugs, well they are students."

"No it's not drugs, we're just making enquiries," said PC Jones.

"Are you going to let us in then?"

Mrs Webb went back into her house and returned with the key to let the police officers into the flat.

"Don't you need a warrant for this?"

"No we don't, not if we believe a crime might have been

committed on the premises," said PC Jones.

After Mrs Webb taking about five minutes to line the key up with the keyhole, the exasperated officers finally entered the flat.

*

"Tim, see if you can find anything in the living area to explain their absence, I'll take a look in the bedrooms," said Jones.

The sight that met him as he entered the first bedroom would haunt PC Jones for the rest of his life. The dead girl's milky white eyes stared at him through a mask of dark, dried blood; her blonde hair plastered to the side of her face, naked from the waist up her torso was a mass of deep cuts. She was tied to a chair with a large blood pool gathered around her feet.

Then the smell hit him, a metallic rotten meat kind of smell that clawed at his nostrils.

PC Jones ran into the bathroom to throw up while Tim, the other officer, who didn't look too well himself, took a few deep breaths. Gaining control of himself he used his radio to call in the murder.

*

Back in Aberdeen, Buchanan picked up the phone in his office.

"Ronnie, what sort of shit have you dragged us into?"

"What do you mean, John?"

"That flat you sent us round to, you remember? Well we found the flatmate but she's not saying too much, possibly due to the fact that someone's sliced her up and strangled her."

"Jesus!" said Buchanan. "Do you think the two murders are connected?"

"Well gee Sherlock, what's your guess? I'll tell you one thing though, since you opened this can of worms you can get your ass down here and help us out, call it a joint investigation. I'll square it up with the higher ups at both ends."

"Fair enough John, I'll leave right away, as soon as I've been home to pack a bag. I'll take Sergeant Maxwell with me, see you soon."

He phoned Max to let him know what was happening, told him to pack a bag and asked him to pick him up from home in about half an hour.

*

Engrossed in the loud music coming through his headphones and trying his best to ignore the stale urine smell in the landing, the young man didn't so much walk as shimmy up the stairs to the third floor of the block of flats in Dundee. He knocked loudly on the paint stained door. Totally ignoring the crudely drawn hand with the raised middle finger and the words written in marker pen telling him to fuck off, he patiently waited for it to open. Eventually he heard someone inside sliding back the cover of the spy hole and then turning the latch.

"Hi Jimmy, c'mon through."

Liam led Jimmy through the dingy flat to the living room where Mark sat staring at the two bags of white powder lying on the coffee table. "Hi man, look what we got," he said with a big grin on his face.

"What the fuck is that?" said Jimmy.

"We were hoping you could tell us," said Liam. "You're the drug dealer."

"Look guys, I sell a wee bit of weed now and again that's it, but this, fuck, its way out of my league, man."

"Can't you at least tell us what it is?"

Jimmy pulled out a pen knife and cut a slit in the corner of one of the packages, "Liam, rub some of that on your gums."

"Like in the movies, does that work?"

"It should tell you if it's cocaine or not," said Jimmy. "It should freeze your gums, just like an injection at the dentist."

Liam did as he was asked. "Jesus, that's fuckin' weird man."

"Did it work?" asked Mark.

"Too right it did. I can't feel fuck all of my mouth."

"Where did you get it?" asked Jimmy.

"We boosted it from a car at the Road Chef. Some daft lassie

31

forgot to lock her door."

"She was a looker too, eh Mark?"

"Aye, she was gorgeous."

"Any chance of a coffee?" asked Jimmy.

"I'll get it," said Mark as he went through to the kitchen, leaving Jimmy alone with Liam.

"While we're alone there's something I need to say, Liam."

"I know exactly what you're going to say," interrupted Liam. "Tell Mark to keep his mouth shut."

"Well we both know what a gob shite he is, he can't keep anything secret."

"We've discussed it, he'll be ok with this, trust me."

"Coffee up," said Mark appearing with the tray in hand.

"Listen," said Jimmy. "This is a shit load of coke, I don't know who it belongs to, I don't want to know, but you can rest assured that someone is going to be looking for this big time. You can't sell it here in Dundee, so for a small cut of the proceeds I'll ask Uncle Frank if he maybe knows someone in Glasgow or Edinburgh who'll take it off your hands. Give me a few hours; I'll be in touch later."

Chapter Six

"The Pentland Hills are about twenty five miles in length, most of the land is used for sheep farming but the public does have a right of way on all paths. Today we're going to be hiking up Scald Law which rises up to almost six hundred metres."

Jeez, thought Vince, does this guy ever shut the fuck up? He had been sitting in the Land Rover for about twenty minutes now, heading uphill with the other five people in his group.

Luckily he was in Campbell's group so all he had to do was bide his time until the opportunity arose to separate himself and Campbell from the rest. It shouldn't be too hard because, if there's one thing he was good at, it was thinking on his feet and taking advantage of the situation. It had served him well over the years.

It was almost five years ago now since Vince had got involved with the drugs scene. He'd started off small time buying smallish amounts and overseeing the cutting and selling of the gear. He'd made a name for himself, always coming across with the goods well on time and making sure it was always top quality. Then he'd come to the attention of Harry Black, a top Glasgow gangster, because of his reputation of always getting the job done. He came into Harry's employ as his nationwide distributor, whether it be firearms, dodgy money or drugs, he was "the" man for the job and he'd done the job perfectly, always overseeing every big drop off personally.

He'd always worked the same way, he employed local muscle like Terry and Dave and their ilk to take care of the messy stuff, and employed, through a third party, a complex network of couriers to deliver the goods from A to B. Any cock ups along the way and he always seemed to have the talent to fix it, no matter how big or small the problem. He was even known in some circles as "The Fixer," so how had this job gone so wrong? It had been perfectly planned as usual. They had used a courier that had been used many times before yet the coke had miraculously disappeared and now he'd been left with the job of seeing to Donald Campbell personally, something he never usually got involved in.

He couldn't possibly have left the task in the hands of Dave or Terry, they were at best adequate but bereft of the brains to interrogate Campbell, possibly having to eliminate him in front of so many witnesses, and make their getaway, hence the disguise. No matter what he had to do, all the witnesses would see is a blonde haired and bearded Phil Harris not Vince Mackie.

The Land Rover came to a sudden stop.

"Ok folks, stretch your legs for five minutes until Bill catches up, we'll hike over the hill, have a bit of lunch and then carry on to the lake for a bit of kayaking. We have a great day for it so everyone should enjoy themselves."

Vince got out and went over to join his fellow hikers. "Hi, I'm Monica Ray," said a woman smoking a cigarette. "I'm a Doctor, and you are?"

"Phil Harris, chemical supplies."

"Is this your first time on anything like this Phil?" she asked.

"I've done a bit of hill walking before, but the rest of it is new to me."

"Yeah, it's new to me too," said Monica. "My daughter said I should do something to get fit, so I thought I'd give this a bash. If I like the taster session maybe I'll sign up to something more substantial."

"I take it they give you a hard time over the smoking?"

"Jesus, don't they just. You're not going to get all preachy on me are you?"

"No, quite the opposite in fact, I was going to ask you for one. I've left mine back at the car."

The woman handed over the packet of cigarettes and Vince lit one up.

"Don't you think that kind of defeats the purpose?" said a loud voice from behind.

Vince swung round to confront the owner of the voice. He was a middle aged weasely looking man with the type of face that just screamed out to be punched. He was doing stretching exercises against a huge boulder.

"What are you talking about?" said Vince.

"We've all came up here for the fresh air and exercise and the two of you are smoking," he replied, waving his hand in front of his face as if the smoke was encroaching on his space. "It's not exactly good for your health now is it?"

"Neither is two broken wrists," replied Vince purposely blowing smoke in his direction. "And if you don't stop waving that right hand of yours, that one will be the first to go."

Monica and the rest of the group sniggered as the man slowly slunk off towards the jeep.

"What an asshole!" said Monica.

"Yeah, you seem to get them everywhere nowadays," said Vince. He looked to the distance. "Here's the other Land Rover arriving so I suppose we'd better get going. Thanks for the smoke."

*

Max picked Buchanan up at his home on Kings Gate and headed down Anderson Drive towards the A90.

"Ever wondered how many roundabouts are on this stretch of road Max? Go on, have a guess."

"I would say, three!"

"No, six, six fucking roundabouts in about what, maybe two miles of road? Who the fuck planned that? Is that a coffee you have, son?"

"Yes, why?"

"Can I have a sip?"

"Help yourself, sir."

"Man that's a good coffee, how much that set you back then?"

"About three quid, I bought it from that new coffee shop across from the station, Costa something. I can't remember the name."

"Three bloody quid! I could get a whole jar for less than that, enough to make what, twenty, twenty five cups maybe."

"Sir, don't take this the wrong way but could you stop the moaning maybe?"

"Sorry son, I get like this on long car journeys. I'll go for a nap, wake me up when we hit Dundee, I'll buy you another coffee. Not if it's three quid mind you."

He was asleep in minutes.

Peace at last thought Max as he drove across the bridge of Dee, his eyes glancing over at two swans that almost seemed to glow on the cold grey water of the river. He turned right at the roundabout which was thankfully quiet at this time of the day, turned on the radio making sure the volume was low, and continued on his way.

*

Approaching Dundee, Buchanan woke up just in time to receive an email on his phone from DCI Brannigan with the attached Post-Mortem report. Julie had been beaten badly, cut over forty times and strangled to death, it had occurred recently, round about midday yesterday.

John had told him to phone when they reached Edinburgh and they could meet up for a drink. It would give them time to go over a few things before driving to the crime scene.

"Pull into this garage Max; I'll get you that coffee I promised you. Do you want anything to go with it, a biscuit or a cake or anything?"

"Get me a Kit Kat, sir."

"Good choice," said Buchanan. "I think I'll have one myself. I wonder if they have any of those double ones."

Buchanan entered the garage; he decided to go to the loo before buying the coffees. The door was locked. It had a handwritten sign attached. Please see staff for key, Deposit required.

Is anything straight forward nowadays, he thought to himself.

He walked to the front of the queue.

"Excuse me; can I have the key to the loo?"

"You'll have to take your turn," answered the spotty youth behind the counter.

"Hold it right there son, I'm planning on buying a couple of cups of coffee when I come out. Now, I'm not planning on queuing up twice. So just give me the key before I end up embarrassing you, me and everyone else in here by pissing all over your nice clean floor."

The young man at the till sighed, bent down under the counter and picked up the key which was attached to a huge block of wood. "£10 deposit!"

"You taking the piss?" asked Buchanan.

"That's the rules, the bogs been vandalised recently so it's £10 deposit for the key."

Buchanan looked at the change in his hand.

"I only have £6.50."

"Well you can't have the key then," he said smirking to himself, "Sorry, sir!"

Right, change of tact thought Buchanan. He reached into his pocket and produced his ID card.

"DI Buchanan, I have reason to believe there's been a suspicious package dumped in your toilet, I need your key to check it out." The guy was struck dumb, he looked at the ID.

"Just give him the bloody key," said the customer from behind. Reluctantly the youth handed the key over.

"Thanks son, and by the way, you can pour me out a couple of those fancy Mocha-chinos, super-size and throw in a couple of those Kit Kats. I'll have them on the house, that is unless you want your boss to find out how you wasted police time."

"Yes sir," said the assistant through gritted teeth.

Max watched Buchanan leaving the garage with the two huge coffees in hand and opened the passenger door for him.

"Thought you didn't like fancy coffees sir. You said they weren't worth the money."

"Ah but these are special coffees Max," said Buchanan with a big grin on his face. "Costa-fuckalls I call them."

*

After following John's directions, they met up with him in Deacon Brodie's, a pub on Edinburgh's busy Royal Mile, so called because the distance from Holyrood Palace at the bottom to Edinburgh Castle at the top was approximately one mile. Buchanan spotted his old friend sitting at a table at the back of the pub. They ordered a pint each and went over to join him.

"Good to see you Ronnie, how was the trip down?"

"Not too bad John, but finding a parking place round here was a bit of a nightmare."

"Tell me about it. Here take this." John handed him a card which stated, Lothian and Borders Police Official Business. "You can park anywhere now, believe me you'll need that around here. I take it this is Sergeant Maxwell?"

"Nice to meet you, sir," said Max.

"Likewise Sergeant, is this your first time in Auld Reekie?"

Max looked perplexed.

"He means Edinburgh, son, it's an old local nickname for the place."

"Oh I see. This is a nice pub though, who is Deacon Brodie, the owner?"

Brannigan laughed, "Not exactly, grab a seat and I'll tell you all about him."

"You had to ask, Max, now we'll get one of his bloody history lessons."

"Shush Ronnie!"

"A respected member of society, Deacon Brodie was a cabinet maker and town councillor in eighteenth century Edinburgh. Unknown to most folk however, at night time he had an unusual hobby. He prowled the city with his gang of burglars. Part of his daytime job involved the repair and manufacturing of all sorts of security locks and mechanisms, however while working in his customers houses he would copy their door keys, allowing him to gain access to these premises at will. He did all this to support his lavish lifestyle and gambling habit."

"What became of him?" asked Max.

"One of his accomplices, a man named Ainslie turned King's Evidence on the gang. Brodie escaped though, scarpered off to Amsterdam but was caught and returned to Edinburgh to face trial. He was sentenced to death and hung from a gibbet which, believe it or not, he himself had designed."

"Some things never change," said Buchanan.

"What do you mean Ronnie?"

"Well at the end of the day he was just a robbing bastard councillor, same as we have nowadays. He robbed the affluent people of Edinburgh, whereas today's councillors rip off the public purse with their lavish expenses."

"No arguments there, my friend. Now, let's eat, and then we can visit the crime scene."

*

They drove the short journey to Newington and climbed the stairs to the flat, a young PC guarding the door jumped to attention when he saw the approaching DCI.

"At ease Constable, have you seen DI McLean?"

"He's in the flat, sir."

"Well stand aside man. Let us past. Ah, there you are McLean, this is an old friend of mine, DI Buchanan and his colleague Sergeant Maxwell. As I mentioned before, they're working on the death of her flatmate Lucy, hopefully we can work together and help clear this bloody mess up."

They all shook hands.

"Right bring us up to date with what we've got."

"Door to doors been done, the woman across the hall gave a sketchy description of 'two well-dressed friends' who visited her yesterday afternoon."

"How did she know they were friendly with the victim?" asked Buchanan.

"She said one of them turned up with a pizza."

"Killers that deliver lunch, pretty unlikely I'd have thought," said DCI Brannigan. "Get her to talk to Mike, see if he can come up with a sketch of them, anything else?"

"Yes, just over twenty grand, found locked in a case under the bed in Lucy's room."

"Christ and I thought students were always skint. Do some digging Mclean and see if you can find out where the money came from, see if she was on the game or worked for an escort agency or the like and report back to me later."

"Will do, sir," said McLean.

"Oh, and find out if forensics picked up a pizza box. If so, get them to check it out for prints and the usual evidence."

Buchanan turned to the DCI, "How can we help John?"

"You and Max could get yourselves over to Napier University and talk to their friends and classmates. I took the liberty of phoning ahead and arranging a room for interviews, the classmates have been told someone would be along to talk to them later today so it's all been arranged."

"Ok John, we'll get onto it right away. Come on Max, let's see what the intelligent people look like down here."

*

Just as Buchanan got in the car his phone rang and flashed up crime lab.

"Ronnie, it's Steve Kershaw, thought you should know, we were going through the various items found at the crime scene, one of the SOCOs found a discarded cigarette packet with a print, and get this it's a match to one lifted from an unsolved murder in Summerhill, a guy beaten to death in his flat last February."

"I remember that" said Buchanan. "A small time dealer in Stronsay Drive, damn near decapitated if I remember rightly. Great work Joe, keep me informed if anything else turns up."

Buchanan phoned Brannigan and relayed the information to the DCI.

"Looks to me like there could be a drug connection, what do you think Ronnie?"

"Well if you take the twenty grand into account, there could be."

"I take it we don't know who the print belongs to?"

"I doubt it John, it threw up nothing when we put it through the database last year but I'll get Steve to check it again just in case."

Buchanan ended the phone call, brought Max up to date and they headed off to Napier University.

*

The rain started falling as soon as they set off. Donald Campbell led the group with his assistant at the rear. Vince, who had always kept himself fit, had no problem keeping up but already some of the less able members were beginning to lag behind.

"What happens if someone gets injured?" Vince asked Campbell.

"How do you mean?"

"Well say someone twisted their ankle or broke their leg for instance, how would you deal with such a thing?"

"I'm afraid the whole of the day's activities would have to end."

"Why's that?" asked Vince.

"For health and safety reasons we must have two guides on each excursion, one in front and one behind for hiking, one at the top of the cliff and one holding the safety rope for the abseiling and one upfront and one at the rear for the kayaking, why the interest?"

"The company I work for Mr Campbell."

"Call me Donald."

"The company I work for, Donald, is looking for somewhere to use for team building weekends, I did a bit of research on the net, found your centre, and it seemed to fit all the criteria we're looking for so I booked myself on to this day trip to test the waters so to speak."

"Well I must admit Mr…?"

"Harris, but you can call me Phil."

"Any clients you can throw my way, Phil, would be much appreciated, and I don't mind telling you the money wouldn't go amiss either."

"I take it business is slow at the moment?"

"Could be better," said Donald, "but then again, I suppose it could be worse, lots of small businesses are going under, the way the economy is at the moment. At least we're managing to stay afloat."

"A sudden windfall would come in handy then?"

"What do you mean?" said Donald.

"I mean if you get our contract, of course."

As they got higher up the hill, the sky cleared and the rain was slowly replaced by sunshine.

Chapter Seven

They stopped for a break halfway down the other side of the hill, Campbell took a large thermos out of his backpack, while Bill checked the various ropes and harnesses they would need to abseil down the rocky cliff.

"Anyone for coffee?" asked Campbell.

"Yes please," the group answered, almost in unison.

"Next on the agenda, is a quick scramble down some scree for half a mile or so until we reach the platform above the cliff, from there you can use your newly learned abseiling skills to rappel down to the base. After that a few miles hike to the reservoir and a bit of Kayaking that should round off the day nicely."

"Excuse me?" said a young man in the group. "It's all very well abseiling from the platforms in your training room but doing the same off a rock face with our back packs on, isn't that a bit dangerous?"

"Not a problem," said Campbell. "I designed the cliff platform myself. I incorporated a steel basket attached to a pulley, and your backpacks can be lowered first. As for being dangerous, it's just as safe as the training room. I'll stay at the top to control the safety rope while Bill holds your guide rope at the bottom. It's a piece of cake. Of course we don't want to force anyone into it so anyone who wants out let me know now, the basket can be used to lower people as well as equipment."

They all agreed to give it a go and headed down the scree covered slope towards their destination.

When they reached the platform Bill went round gathering all the backpacks.

"Hold on a sec, I need something out of there," said Vince.

Making sure no one was looking; Vince quickly removed the handgun and tucked it into his belt before handing his backpack to Bill.

"Right, any questions before we start?" said Campbell.

"I have one," said Vince, "we must have travelled quite a few miles so far, I can't see us having time to travel all the way back to our transport before dark."

"We don't travel back," said Campbell. "We have another two vehicles stashed with the kayaks in the boat hut for the return journey."

Very handy indeed, Vince thought to himself.

Most of the group took it slow, not Vince though; he rappelled down the cliff like he was born to do it.

"Who the fuck is this guy, James Bond?" said the man next in line.

At the foot of the cliff they all gathered together after their descent. "Well done folks," said Campbell. He turned to Vince, "You've obviously done this before Phil, where was it, the Army or maybe the Navy?"

"Somewhere like that," replied Vince.

"Wow! What a view!" said one of the group.

"Exceptional isn't it? If you look along to the right you can see the Glencourse Reservoir, built in the eighteen twenties to provide water for the mills of Auchendinny, Milton Bridge and Glencourse. It's a very popular boat fishing spot, perfect for a spot of kayaking."

"If everyone could grab their backpacks, and be ready to head off we should have time for a quick coffee before we get down to the last of today's activities."

*

Bill washed the cups in the water at the side of the reservoir while Campbell opened the padlock on the heavy door of the wooden shed.

The door, like the rest of the shed, was old and weather beaten. It had seen better days. The edge was slightly askew and Campbell had to lift it up slightly to get it to open.

It finally moved with an unhealthily loud creak.

The inside was large and gloomy with a musty smell of old damp rotten wood. The vibration of the door opening sent dust mites, visible in the encroaching sunlight falling down towards the bare earth floor, where a dozen orange kayaks lay off to the right hand side just in front of the land rovers in three rows of four. Another three larger ones, covered in cobwebs were strung up from the beams on the roof. The roof itself was patched in places with old tarpaulins obviously put there to stop the rain leaking in.

Campbell walked towards an old wooden box on the left, opened the lid and removed some lifejackets and helmets. He handed them to Bill Briggs and then turned to face his clients.

"If you could all help yourselves to a Kayak and drag it down to the shoreline. I'll go over a few quick pointers with you and then we can get going. First, Bill will provide each of you with a life jacket and a helmet for protection. Bill will leave alongside the leaders and I'll stay at the back with the rest. Remember, if you capsize grab hold of your kayak, the life jackets will keep your heads above water but the kayak is far more buoyant, just stay afloat till either Bill or myself comes to give you a hand."

As the first few members of the group entered the water Vince bent down, checked no one was looking, and made a small hole in the side of his kayak with the knife he'd removed from his pocket. After making sure he was last in line he entered the water alongside Campbell.

"Keep up Mr Harris, you're lagging way behind," said Campbell.
"That's because my fucking canoe is leaking!"
"It shouldn't be. Bill checked them all before we took off and he said they were all fine."

"Well that might be true, but I can assure you I'm taking on water."

"Hold on!"

Campbell pulled out his mobile.

"Bill, it's Donald, Mr Harris has sprung a leak. I'll have to go back to the hut and get him another kayak. You take the others across and we'll meet you there."

"No problem!" said Bill.

*

Donald Campbell opened the padlock of the boat shed for the second time that day, got a spare kayak from behind the Land Rover and turned round, straight in to the barrel of Vince's gun.

*

Buchanan stood outside the university and lit up a cigarette. The stuffy room combined with the myriad of interviews had given him a headache. Most of the girls' peers said the same thing, they kept themselves to themselves, were very friendly with each other, but they didn't socialise much with anyone else.

Just then his phone rang.

"DI Buchanan, it's DI McLean, we have a partial registration for the car the two suspects from the girls' flat were using. DCI Brannigan thought I should let you know."

"Let me guess, the nosey cow across the hall?"

"Yep, she came in for the artist's sketch and suddenly remembered."

"How is she getting on with the likenesses anyway?"

"Well according to her we're looking for a tall burly boxer type and the other one looks like a young Tom Jones."

Buchanan laughed. "It's quite common for folk to liken people to celebrities they know, in fact 'it's not unusual.'"

"Very fucking funny," said McLean.

"Did she get the make and model of the car?"

"Not quite, all we got off her was, a beat up black BMW starting with the letters SKO."

Buchanan walked back in to the University to see Max waiting
for him with a huge grin on his face.

"What you looking so bloody happy about, son?"

"I managed to take advantage of all the computer geeks in here,
sir, got one of them to do a bit of hacking and find me Lucy's
password for her email account."

"And…?"

"She kept her inbox quite clean but I found an email that should
be of some interest."

Max showed Buchanan the printout.

AB15 6XH at ten a.m. "That was sent the night before we found
her body sir."

"Whereabouts in Aberdeen is it?"

"It's Whitemyres Industrial Estate sir."

"Well done Max, I'll get on to Queen Street and get them to look
into it."

After phoning Aberdeen, Buchanan phoned the DCI to let him
know what they'd found.

"Cheers for keeping me informed Ronnie, I'll have to get going,
the Superintendent has set up a public appeal, Press, TV, the usual,
see if we can find anyone who recognises the e-fits the nosey old
bugger next door put together. He knows how I hate doing those
bloody things but the bastard is still putting me in front of the
cameras."

"Alright if I have another look at the crime scene?" asked
Buchanan.

"If you want, I'd almost forgotten about your solo walkabouts,
knock yourself out."

"Cheers John!"

Buchanan ended the phone call and told Max to drive him to the
crime scene.

When they arrived, Buchanan sent Max further down the road to check their belongings into the hotel and asked him to pick him up in about half an hour.

*

Approaching the door he flashed his warrant card at the young PC and was ushered through.

He turned on the light and stood in the living room, looked around and thought to himself. Could they have made a mistake and possibly killed the wrong girl? Both girls were blonde, a similar height and weight. After realising their error they could have come down to Edinburgh for the intended target.

But what about the money under Lucy's bed, that had to play some part in the girls' killings and, as the DCI had mentioned, taking that into account with the partial print, which had turned up at, not only last year's unsolved murder in Summerhill, but also near the burned car in Hazelhead, there could be a possible drug connection.

Leaving the flat, Buchanan asked the Constable which door belonged to Mrs Webb.

"It's the red door across the hall, sir."

He rang the doorbell, and the door was opened by a very small, extremely wrinkled old woman.

Jesus thought Buchanan, stick a light sabre in her hand and she could be Yoda.

"Hello Mrs Webb, I'm DI Buchanan, I'm investigating the murder next door, I wonder if I could talk to you for a few minutes?"

"Do you have identification?"

"Of course!"

Buchanan handed over his ID.

"You can't be too careful, not with murderers running amok."

"Quite right, Mrs Webb."

"Well, come in then, would you like a cup of tea?"

"That would be great, I'm parched."

"Well sit down Inspector, what would you like to know?"

"The two men you saw arriving, one carrying a pizza, had you seen either of them before?"

"Not at all, the girls had very few visitors, they were very quiet for students, not like some we've had in here, loud music, party's going on till all hours of the morning."

"So no one came to see them on a regular basis then?" asked Buchanan.

"Not that I've noticed, I did see someone putting something through their letterbox."

"When was this?"

"A couple of days ago, the night before Lucy left for Aberdeen."

"She told you she was going to Aberdeen?" said Buchanan.

"Yes, visiting a sick relative. She said that she was going to stay overnight and she would be back today. I thought she'd be home by now. I wonder where she is? The poor girl will be distraught when she finds out about Julie."

*

"How long you going to be on that laptop, Dave?" asked Terry.

"Two minutes, what's the hurry?"

"I thought we might do a bit of sightseeing while we're here, then hit the pub. Not much else to do until Vince gets in touch."

"Just let me finish off these e-mails and we can go wherever you want buddy."

Dave sent the last of the dozen or so messages he had sent that afternoon, the same message had been sent to all the recipients whose names Vince had supplied.

It simply said "*For Your Immediate Attention*" and contained a coded link to a file hosting site.

Dave, out of curiosity, had gone to the site to see what the message was, but it had been encrypted, meaning that anyone wanting to open the file needed a special password to access it.

He's a clever bastard, thought Dave.

With a last click on the send button, Dave closed the laptop.

"Right Terry, grab your coat, we're off, I think we'll forgo the sightseeing though and go straight to the pub, there's one just down the road a bit.

*

They drove into the car park and got out of the car.

"You just go in, Terry," said Dave. "I'll hang about out here and have a smoke."

Dave lit up his cigarette and surveyed his surroundings. The Robins Nest Inn it was called. It was situated just in front of a golf course on Gilmerton Road. He looked through the windows.

It looked a strange pub, it had a small bar to the left hand side whereas to the right, where you would expect a normal lounge, it was more like a restaurant, pleasantly decorated and from what he could see of it very busy. The bar was earthier, it had a pool table set amidst a few mismatched tables and chairs but it looked tidy enough. He watched as one of the bar staff, a small bald headed man wandered over to a display board outside the bar and changed one of the posters.

'Two for £5.00 choice of eight meals' it declared. Sounds reasonable thought Dave as he entertained the thought of buying Terry lunch.

"You're not meant to smoke there; we've had complaints from some of the residents about fag ends blowing into their garden," said the bald man. "We have a smoking area round the back though; you just go through to the end of the bar, past the toilets and down the stairs."

"Cheers for that," replied Dave. "I'll remember next time." He extinguished his cigarette and followed the barman in.

*

"Any change on you, Dave?"

"Aye, but you're not getting it. You've probably put enough in that bandit to buy the bloody thing. Grab a seat, I'll get you another pint how much you down anyway?"

"Thirty quid," replied Terry.

"What the hell is the fascination with them things anyway?" asked Dave nodding towards the bandit. "Is it the flashy lights, the noises, the bright colours, or what?"

"It's the thrill of winning the money. That machine there pays out up to seventy five quid right. That means if I hit it at the right time I could get seventy five quid for an initial investment of twenty pence. You can't get better odds than that."

"But you never win Terry, you always fucking lose."

"Yeah but there's always the chance I could win, that's where the excitement comes from," replied Terry with a huge grin on his face.

Dave shook his head and made a mental note.

Never try to talk sense to a gambler.

As he carried their drinks over to the table Dave received a text from

Vince – *"don't drink too much"*-

He showed it to Terry.

"Looks like we can add psychic to Vince's list of skills," Dave said.

Terry looked around the bar.

"You reckon he's put a tail on us? What about that old woman in the corner over there, that could be Vince himself, he does like his disguises."

Dave looked at the woman and laughed.

"Doubt it, he'd have to shave about a foot and a half off his height and go on a crash diet, she's a skeleton. Anyway, he gives us the afternoon off, where else we gonna go? It's not exactly hard to work out is it?

"Aye, you're right enough Dave."

"I wonder how he's getting on anyway?" said Dave.

"He'll have it under control; Campbell won't know what's hit him," replied Terry. "It's not like him though, taking on something like that himself; he usually likes to keep his hands clean. That's usually where we come in."

"What do you know about him anyway, Terry?" asked Dave. "Not a lot, he pays well, and anyway, I don't want to know too much. People that stick their noses into his business have a habit of disappearing."

"How do you mean?" asked Dave.

"Just a rumour I heard a while back. Supposedly, some copper didn't like the look of him, started doing a bit of digging into his background, questioning his associates and the like, you know how it is. Anyway, word got back to Vince and the next thing you know the guy goes salmon fishing up north somewhere and he never comes back."

"What happened to him?"

"No one knows, he's never been found. They found his car at the side of the river but no sign of him. It was like he'd just dropped off the face of the earth. The cops interviewed anyone who was likely to have had a grievance against him. He was a real bastard supposedly so it was a long list. A list that included Vince but he had an alibi, cast iron it was."

"What was it?" asked Dave.

Terry leaned closer.

"Get this; he was playing in a charity golf tournament all weekend at some exclusive golf club. Half the golfers were members of the legal profession, lawyers, judges and the like. When asked, they all said the same thing; he'd never left the place. He was either playing golf or sitting most of the night in the residents bar in the hotel with the rest of them."

"Jesus, that's what you call an alibi," said Dave.

"So," said Terry, "a word to the wise. Don't go poking your nose into Vince's business."

"I'll drink to that," said Dave. "It's your round Terry, try and stay away from that bandit on the way back with the pints."

Chapter Eight

What the hell's all this about?" asked Donald Campbell.

"Give me your phone," said Vince.

"What? All you want's my phone?"

"Yeah that's right, I hiked six miles, abseiled down a cliff face, separated you from the rest of the group and I'm now holding you at gunpoint because I wanted your fucking phone."

"Well what is it you want?"

"A few answers to start off with. Where do you keep the keys for the Land Rovers?"

"I have them here."

"Give them to me. Next, what's the quickest way back to the main road?"

"There's a dirt track behind this boathouse, take it for a couple of miles and it leads on to the A70."

"You're doing well Mr Campbell, now there's one more thing you can help me with. Cast your mind back to yesterday morning, Lucy Kennedy... Name mean anything to you?"

"Yes, I stopped and helped her with a flat tyre."

"What else did you help her with?"

"Nothing, Jesus! If you're her husband, I didn't even know she was married, I wouldn't have given her my number if I'd known."

"I'm not her husband Campbell, now stop freaking out and tell me the whole story from the beginning."

"There is no fucking story. I stopped to help a fellow motorist in trouble that's it."

"What about the coke?" asked Vince.

"Coke… You mean drugs?"

"No, I mean the sweet refreshing sugary drink. Of course I mean fucking drugs."

"I have no fucking idea what you're talking about," said Campbell. The white hot shooting pain travelled up Campbell's leg to just below the knee when Vince shot him through the foot with the silenced gun.

"You bastard!" he screamed.

"Painful as that may seem Mr Campbell, it's nothing to the pain I'll inflict with my next shot, so I'll ask you once again, where's my fucking coke?"

The survival instinct taking over Donald Campbell's mind quickly took in Vince's position, the large two man kayaks above his head and the pulley system for lowering them. Quick as a flash he dived for the hook attached to the rope that suspended the two boats above Vince. Just as the second bullet grazed the top of his left shoulder the two kayaks with the support netting pinned his enemy to the dusty floor of the boatshed.

Hobbling in excruciating pain Donald Campbell made it to the boatshed door padlocking it behind him.

He crawled to his kayak, leaving a trail of blood behind him and set off for the other side of the reservoir.

*

A dazed and confused Vince untangled himself from the netting and found the boatshed door shut fast.

Shit, thought Vince, how could I have been so fucking stupid? Know your surroundings, a credo he'd always adhered to well, until now. He should have scoped out the boat shed, maybe then he'd have seen the danger above him. Checking the perimeter, he found what he was looking for, a weak spot.

A large area at the back of the shed was damp, the wood rotted over time.

Vince started up the Land Rover, manoeuvred it into position, and reversed at great speed through the weakened wall. He found the track and headed off towards the A70, stopping only to get rid of his disguise and gun down the nearest rabbit hole. He pushed them down as far as possible with a long branch he found nearby and used the other end as a makeshift broom to sweep away any footprints he'd left in the surrounding earth.

*

Across the other side of the reservoir Donald Campbell used every last ounce of energy he had to reach the shore,
"Jesus Donald! What the hell happened to you? You look like you've been in a car wreck."
"I've been shot, phone the police!" he murmured as he collapsed on the shoreline and oblivion took over.

*

DCI Brannigan sat in his office with the whisky bottle from his desk drawer in front of him.
It was a particularly fine malt he'd received as a gift from someone. He couldn't remember exactly who. It was one of the best he'd tried, smooth and slightly peaty. It came from the Isle of Skye. The label was in Gaelic and hard to pronounce. '*Poit Dhubh*'. He'd look up its meaning when he had some time on his hands.
Bugger it, one more won't do any harm, he thought and besides he needed it. He always did when it came to these murder appeals. Dutch courage, that's what they called it, named so because in the seventeenth century a Dutch doctor used Dutch gin as a medicine. This was then used by English troops in the thirty year war and became very popular for its warming effect and the way it calmed them down before battle, hence the name Dutch Courage.
Of course the name applied to all alcohol nowadays not just gin.
"The TV crew are all set up John, time to make the statement."
"Five minutes," said Brannigan, as he poured himself the whisky and downed it in one.

"Julie Tarrant was found dead in her flat in Newington this afternoon not long after her flatmate Lucy Kennedy was found murdered in the boot of a burned out car in Aberdeen."

"Post mortems have been carried out on both girls showing that they were the victims of particularly grisly murders."

"I'm speaking to you today as I'm sure someone in the local community either here in Edinburgh or in Aberdeen must know something about these incidents. I'm appealing to them or indeed anyone else who may have any information either on the two men whose photo fits you see behind me, or on Lucy or Julie. A joint investigation between Lothian and Borders and Grampian Police Forces is underway and we are now currently in the process of trying to piece together Lucy's recent movements prior to her body being found up in Aberdeen. It's possible someone may have vital information which could help us in identifying the person or persons who committed these terrible acts and I appeal to them to come forward. Our phone number can be seen below me. Of course any information we receive will be dealt with in the strictest confidence. Anyone have any questions?"

"How were the girls killed?" asked a voice from the back.

"Both killings were particularly messy and both victims showed signs of strangulation but I'd rather not go into too much detail at the moment."

"Is it true that Lucy was still alive when the car was set on fire up in Aberdeen?"

"Where did you get that from?" asked an irate Brannigan, staring daggers at the petite blonde sat in the second row.

"I have my sources," replied the woman with a smirk on her face. "Yes! Yes, she was still alive."

"Were there drugs involved, them being students and all?"

Jesus, not another one thought Brannigan.

"Contrary to what some people seem to think, not all students take drugs. Next question?"

"You never answered my question."

56

"No drugs involved as far as we're aware," replied Brannigan. "Anyone else?"

"Is there any truth to the rumour that the killings were ritualistic, that there were satanic symbols left at both murder scenes?"

"Where in the name of God did you hear that?"

"It's just a rumour that's going around."

"Well Mr…?"

"Fred Barry, Evening News."

"Well Mr Barry, I suggest you check your sources, they're talking rubbish. Believe me, I've been to the second crime scene and I've seen the photos from the first, nothing ritualistic, no satanic symbols. In fact, you can do me a favour and quote me on that. If these types of rumours are doing the rounds I'd like to nip them in the bud right now."

A man in the front stood up.

"Don't you think Julie should have been put under some sort of protection?"

"How do you mean?" asked Brannigan.

"Well, let's see, her flatmate was found murdered up in Aberdeen. Didn't anyone think that maybe someone had it in for the girls, and she could be the next victim?"

"Listen," said Brannigan. "Lucy was found in the boot of a burned out car, it took a while to formally identify her. When that identification came to light, Grampian Police informed us. As soon as we received this information we acted upon it. We visited her flat but it was too late, her flatmate was already dead. I'll take one more question."

"What was Lucy doing up in Aberdeen?"

"According to one of her neighbours, she was off seeing a sick relative. However, other information has now come to light, information I'm afraid I can't share with you at the moment. That leads us to believe that this was no more than a cover story."

"Thank you!"

*

Donald Campbell opened his eyes and looked around the hospital ward. He felt like he'd been run over by a bus. He tried to sit up, the dizziness forcing him to give up on his efforts. He winced at the drip in his arm as he moved on to his side to try and get a bit more comfortable. His mouth was as dry as a bone and he felt as if someone had glued his lips together.

"Mr Campbell?" said a voice from the side of the bed.

"Mr Campbell, my name's Ronnie Buchanan, DI Ronnie Buchanan, do you feel up to talking?"

"Sure, if you get me some water."

Buchanan poured some water into a glass, handed it to Donald Campbell and pulled a chair over to the side of the bed.

"The reason I'm here Mr Campbell is because the Inspector who responded to your shooting heard you muttering the name Lucy as you flitted in and out of consciousness. That wouldn't be Lucy Kennedy would it?"

"Yes it would, why?"

"Mr Campbell I'm part of the investigation team looking in to the murders of Lucy and her flatmate."

"She's dead?"

"I'm afraid so. That's why when the DI heard you mention her name he put two and two together and thought it might tie into our case."

"Well he wasn't wrong there."

"How do you mean sir?"

"The guy who shot me asked about Lucy as well."

"What did he want to know?

"I hardly knew Lucy, Inspector. Yesterday on the way to work I stopped to help a young woman put on her spare wheel as she had a puncture, that woman was Lucy Kennedy. Phil Harris, the guy who shot me somehow knew about that and seemed to think I'd stolen something from her car."

"Stolen what exactly?" said Buchanan.

"He was convinced I'd stolen a large amount of cocaine, his cocaine from the vehicle."

Jesus, I knew it, or at least I had my suspicions, Buchanan thought to himself. "If you don't mind, sir, is it okay with you if my Sergeant takes your statement and your description of the assailant?"

"Well make it quick, I'm bloody knackered. Before you go Inspector, how was Lucy killed?"

"She was burned to death in the boot of a stolen car."

"Heartless bastards!" said Campbell.

"Exactly what I said sir, exactly!"

Buchanan left the ward and approached Max.

"Get his statement son, he seems on the level to me but dig a bit deeper see what you can find out, then meet me in the hospital cafe."

Buchanan phoned the Aberdeen crime lab.

"Steve, do me a favour, check if the burnt out car had its spare wheel on."

"I'm looking at it now, it has, on the front passenger side, how's Edinburgh?"

"Full of bloody tourists, what you expect?"

Buchanan ended the call and headed off looking for the hospital cafe. When he got there he ordered a coffee, grabbed a rather limp looking egg mayonnaise sandwich, wandered over to a table in the corner and began to write.

Murders linked

Drug connection

Campbell's story checks out

Print found at two murder scenes

One of the men bears a striking resemblance to Tom Jones

Who is Phil Harris???

He put his notebook away just as Max entered the cafe.

"What you think Max?" said Buchanan.

"Well, I'd put money on the shooter's name not being Phil Harris, but his story is plausible."

"More than plausible Max, I phoned Steve at the lab, the car did have the spare on. Taking all the evidence into consideration I see it playing out like this. Lucy' been doing a bit of drug running in her spare time. I'm not sure about Julie; remember the twenty grand was in Lucy's bedroom. Somewhere between here and Aberdeen the drugs have gone missing, lost, stolen, whatever and now these guys are hunting down anyone who had the opportunity to take them."

"That's a good theory," said Max.

"Yeah but that's all it is a theory, but it's also all we've got."

"Come on, let's go see DCI Brannigan and keep him in the loop."

"Could we nip in past Campbell's home first? It's just across the road. I said I'd get him a few things."

"Well make it quick Max."

*

Buchanan half closed his eyes in the car as he waited outside Donald Campbell's home. It had been a long day he thought as he drifted off.

He was walking along the beach, heading toward the Donmouth; a local nature reserve near Old Aberdeen where the River Don meets the sea. It was one of his favourite walks, usually ending with a cold beer for him and a cold bowl of water for the dog at one of the tables outside the nearby pub. The dog was slightly ahead of him, dashing through the waves in search of the ball he'd just thrown. It was a bright sunny day, the brilliant blue of the sky reflecting off the water below. The lapping of the waves mixed with the calls of the Terns from the nearby colony, providing a pleasant sound track to his journey. Squinting, he could just make out a large boat in the distance; it looked like a supply boat heading out to the rigs with some much needed supplies.

The dog returned with the ball, his tail wagging and his black and white coat dripping water onto his feet, eager for him to throw it once more, which he did.

As he carried his shoes and socks in his hands, feeling the hot gritty sand beneath him, he watched an angler cast his line, the hook at the end flashing in the sunlight before it disappeared below the water. He thought he recognised the guy and just as he was approaching him he was awakened with a start by the knocking on the window.

"Sir, his place has been done over. It's a right mess."

"Christ, I was miles away there. Phone it in Max and we'll get it processed. Surely to fuck between here, the boathouse and the girls' flat they'll come up with something."

Chapter Nine

Vince knew that the longer he stayed on the road in the vehicle, the more time it gave the police to set up their road blocks. He'd dumped the disguise and changed into the spare set of clothes from his backpack so any description that Campbell could give them was next to useless.

He'd spotted a small country pub about half a mile back and was now driving up a small farm road looking for somewhere to dump the vehicle.

A small track on the left led into some thick woodland. Perfect, thought Vince. He drove in and when he thought he was far enough along the track he drove in amongst the trees as far as he could go and abandoned the vehicle, stopping to cover it with some loose pine tree branches. Once he was satisfied with the result, he then set off to walk the half mile back to the pub.

*

Vince calmly walked to the bar, ordered himself a beer and phoned Terry to come and pick him up.

"Would you like anything to eat?"

Vince looked up at the pretty waitress standing at the side of his table. She must have only been about four foot six.

"What do you recommend?" asked Vince.

"Today's special is chilli, with handmade tortilla chips, just the thing for such a cold evening."

"Ok, you've talked me into it; bring me a large bowl, along with some chips and another beer please."

"My pleasure!" she replied.

The elfin like waitress left to get Vince's order.

*

DI McLean approached the car that had been left behind by the shooter.

"I've never seen such a clean car" said Ritchie Briars from forensics. "No prints whatsoever. Not even on the steering wheel. Whoever drove this car was a ghost."

"Tell me about it" said McLean. "The car was stolen from a couple in Gilmerton who, according to the neighbours, won't even know about it as they're half-way through a fortnight's holiday in Spain. How are they getting on at the boat house?"

"They found some blood, most likely from the victim and a .22 bullet they managed to prise out the wall, it's already on the way to the lab."

"Cheers Ritchie, I'm off to meet the DCI. I'll let him know."

*

"Hurry up Ronnie, what you having?"

Buchanan eyed up the dozen or so taps of real ale on offer at the Guildford Arms as he pondered what one to go for.

"Make it a pint of eighty shilling John, cheers."

They both took their drinks over to the table where DI McLean and Max were sitting in animated conversation.

"Right guys; let's get up to date with what we have. We've already heard Ronnie's drug courier theory which sounds bloody good to me. When we worked together at Strathclyde, his hunches were always on the money."

"I never realised you both worked together in the past," said Max.

"What, he never told you? I owe my career to this guy. When we worked in Glasgow together, the DCI vacancy came up here in Edinburgh. Ronnie was a shoe in for the job and he knew it, but

63

he pulled out of the race and I got the job."

"It was no big deal," said Buchanan. "You had a young family, it was a better move for you, besides I couldn't be arsed with the paperwork that came with the job, I'm happy as a DI, far less responsibility and far less people to answer to."

"I'll give you that Ronnie, the paperwork's a real pain right enough."

Brannigan drank what was left of his pint in one big gulp.

"Right, DI McLean, what have you got for us?"

"DI McLean, how come no one round here seems to call you by your first name?" asked Max. "You do have one don't you?"

"Will you tell them or shall I?" asked Brannigan.

"It's all right sir, I'll tell them."

He turned to Buchanan and Max. "I never use my first name if I can get away with it. Most of the folk I work with know that so that's why they all tend to call me McLean."

"Well spit it out then," said Buchanan. "What is your name?"

McLean's face turned red.

"It's Tiberius!"

The table erupted in laughter.

"Give him his due though it's a noble name. Tiberius Gracchus was an officer in the Roman Army. He eventually went into politics, became a tribune and stood up for the poorer folk in Rome. Helped them get their lands back if I remember correctly," said Brannigan.

"Yes, I've heard all that" said McLean, "but the trouble is I was named after Star Trek, both my parents were big fans."

"Star Trek!" said Buchanan looking perplexed.

"After Captain James T Kirk, guess what the T stands for?"

"Tiberius," shouted the table in unison, drawing strange looks from the other patrons of the pub.

"Right the fun's over, what do you have McLean?" asked Brannigan.

The DI opened his notebook and checked that he had everyone's attention.

"Julie was cut over twenty times and beaten very methodically.

Ritchie at the lab says it's a safe bet she was tortured. The car stolen from the outdoor centre and left in the woods was scrupulously clean, no forensics from there at all. But they did find a bullet in the boat hut which we can match up to the firearm if we find it. One other thing, the assailant was using a false name, a name he lifted off the cloned credit card he used to pay the outdoor centre this morning. I've put a trace on the card, just in case he uses it again."

"He won't use it again," said Buchanan as he stood up. "He's too methodical. I'll go get a round in and let Max bring you up to date with what's happening in Aberdeen."

"The e-mail we found on Lucy's account," said Max, "led us to a warehouse in Whitemyres Industrial Estate. Forensics has confirmed they found Lucy's blood on the premises. The warehouse was taken on a short term lease and paid for with; you guessed it, another cloned credit card."

Buchanan arrived with the drinks.

"What the fuck's that you're drinking this time Ronnie?" said Brannigan.

"It's Heather Ale!"

"What's that when it's at home?"

"It's been brewed in Scotland since 2000 B.C from an ancient Gaelic recipe for "Leann Fraoich". Fraoich being the Gaelic word for heather. It's one of the oldest beers on record."

"Ok, real ale lesson over, let's get back to business," said Brannigan. "I have some breaking news. You remember the pizza box? Well, we found it, not in the flat but outside in the bin."

"No offence sir, but how do we know it's the same one?" said Max.

"We know it's the same one Sergeant, because it had two prints on it, one of them matches up with the partial from Aberdeen......"

"The elusive partial print once again," said Buchanan.

The DCI ignored the interruption. "And one belongs to this guy." Brannigan took a folder out of his briefcase.

"Terry Watt!"

"Not fucking Watty!" said Buchanan.

"You know him then Ronnie?"

"I've had a few run-ins with him. He's an evil bastard, quite capable of the girls' murders from what I've seen in the past."

"He's a strange one, started off offering his services to "protect" some of the small fish houses in Torry, seeing that no harm would come to them, for a small price of course. Then he progressed to a few bars and local businesses in the same area. He's a scary looking guy, tall, muscular, with a real ugly looking broken nose."

"He likes to do his threatening with a machete or sometimes a shotgun and because he always works the same small area he's gained a fearsome reputation. No one will bear witness against him so any charges we manage to put his way will go nowhere."

"Make sure we get this guy's photo to the press. I want it in the first edition tomorrow, McLean," said Brannigan.

"Will do sir!"

"Now, I don't know about you lot but I'm bloody dead on my feet so I'm off home for some kip," said Brannigan. "I'll see you all bright and early at headquarters tomorrow."

"What are we doing lads?" said Buchanan, "early night, or another round?"

"Another beer for me." said DI McLean.

"What about you Max?" asked Buchanan.

"Yeah, why not?"

"I was hoping you'd both say that, it gives me a good excuse to try a pint of that IPA I seen earlier."

McLean slapped his hand down on the table.

"I know that one, India Pale Ale."

"Very good McLean, do you want one? Educate your palate so to speak."

"Fuck it, why not."

"How about you Max?"

"I'm game!"

"That's decided then, IPAs all around."

Just as Buchanan approached the table with the drinks, Max nudged DI McLean in the ribs.

"Watch this!"

He waited until Buchanan had sat down and taken a mouthful of his beer.

"Ronnie, do your beer thing."

Buchanan looked between Max and McLean with a smile on his face, sniffed his pint and then took another drink, swirling the beer around his mouth.

"A bit over carbonated, it has a pleasant smell of butterscotch vanilla and an ever so slight touch of raspberries. Very smooth and refreshing, with the butterscotch by far being the predominant flavour."

He took another drink.

"It's a bit light-bodied for an IPA, though a refreshing dryness lingers on the palate. Very smooth and malty and finishes well."

"Wow!" said McLean. "The man knows his beers."

Chapter Ten

As dawn rose on the south side of Edinburgh, Vince approached the small guest house on Gilmerton Road. He barged straight past the woman who opened the door and walked straight to Dave and Terry's room and knocked on the door. A bleary eyed Terry appeared, not expecting to be woken up at such an ungodly time in the morning by the explosive punch that knocked him off his feet.

"Put these on asshole," said Vince as he threw him the baseball hat and sunglasses.

"Dave, grab your stuff and let's go."

"What's up Vince?" asked Dave.

"Just go outside and get in the car," said Vince.

The three of them left the guest house watched by the owner who was hiding behind the kitchen door.

"What the fuck's this all about Vince?" said Terry.

"Look at the paper on the back seat and check the front page."

Terry looked at the headline.

'POLICE SEEK MAN IN DOUBLE MURDER CASE, PRINTS FOUND AT SCENE,' and below staring back at him was his own face.

"Shit!" said Terry.

"How many times have I told you never to take off your gloves till you leave the scene?"

"My gloves were on, we even took the beers we drunk and the pizza to the bin outside."

"Were your gloves still on when you dumped the rubbish?"

"I… I think so," said Terry.

"You think so! That's just fucking great."

Vince drove towards the town centre heading for Morrison Street.

*

"I have a safe house here Terry, don't move one fucking foot out the door until I say so. Try growing a beard or something, and you need a disguise."

"I could shave my head."

"Ok, you do that, here's the keys flat 9A, and don't get seen by anyone on the way up the stairs. If anyone's hanging about, wait until they're gone, do I make myself clear?"

"Yes, cheers Vince!"

Leaving Terry at the side of the road Vince got out and moved to the passenger side of the car.

"You drive, Dave; I have a few phone calls to make."

*

Mrs Grimes the owner of the Grand Vista Guest House picked up her phone and called the police about the man whose picture she'd just seen in her morning paper.

*

Arriving at the guest house Buchanan decided to look round the fugitive's room while Max interviewed Mrs Grimes.

The room was dark and extremely hot, the heating must have been on full tilt and there was a slight smell of sweat mixed with stale beer hanging in the air. Buchanan drew back the curtains and opened a window letting some much needed light and fresh air in. A dozen empty beer cans stood on the chest of drawers between the two beds next to a half full ashtray. They'd obviously chosen to ignore the no smoking sign on the wall. They'd even disconnected the smoke alarm; it lay on its side in the waste paper basket.

Very enterprising of them he thought to himself. He laughed the sound breaking the silence, enterprising, it brought to his mind all the times he'd spent Googling for the picture of Captain Kirk.

He could see they had obviously left in a hurry by the clothes strewn around the room. Under one of the beds he found a shotgun, Terry's weapon of choice he thought, and a large hunting knife.

Hopefully forensics could tell him if this was the knife used on Julie, although he felt he already knew the answer to that one.

According to the owner, Terry and the other guy, who she was pretty sure was called Dave, were quickly ushered out first thing in the morning by another taller man wearing a hooded sweatshirt. Terry she said was nursing a bloody nose.

It must have been a brave man that gave him that, thought Buchanan.

But who was this third guy? Going by the description supplied by the landlady, he looked bugger all like the guy described by Campbell.

*

Driving back to HQ, Buchanan suddenly asked Max to pull over. "Wait here, son, I'll be five minutes." Buchanan left the car and entered a small gift shop, and came back to the car with a box under his arm.

"What have you got there, sir?" said Max.

"It's an ornament, a Border Collie, Michelle collects them. Not just ornaments, paintings, calendars, postcards, she even sends everyone Border Collie Christmas cards, you ought to see my house it's like living at Crufts."

"Do you have a dog, sir?"

"Yes I do, Max."

"What kind?"

"Take a wild guess, Sergeant!"

"It's a Border Collie?"

"Well done Max, we'll make a detective of you yet."

Max laughed. "Fancy a coffee, sir? It's my shout."

"Oh, go on then. You've twisted my arm."

Expensive coffees in hand, Buchanan and Max headed to the briefing room where DCI Brannigan had just given the task force their morning briefing. Hopefully with as many officers as could be spared let loose on the streets with the photo of Terry, his apprehension shouldn't take too long.

"So we're looking for at least four guys?" said Brannigan.

"The three seen at the guest house this morning and the guy who tried to shoot Campbell."

"I think three!" said Buchanan.

"Why do you say that?"

"The guy who spirited the other two away this morning is obviously in charge. He must have seen the paper this morning, and got them out of there before Terry was recognised. The guy at the centre arrived in a stolen car, wiped it down and managed to separate Campbell from the rest of the group so he could interrogate him. Both these incidents are the acts of a man on top of his game. Such a methodical person, knowing the rest of the group could easily identify him, would go there in some sort of disguise. Add to that the guest house owners description, even although because of the hood and dark glasses she couldn't make out what he looked like, she did say he was tall, well over six feet. Campbell said the same thing, I think the guy in the hooded sweatshirt and Campbell's assailant could be one and the same, call it a hunch."

"Bloody hell are you psychic Ronnie. It's more than a hunch, we found the Land Rover dumped in woods near a farm. McLean hand me over the report."

"Here you go, sir."

"The Land Rover was wiped down, we couldn't even find Campbell's prints and he drove the bloody thing up the Pentlands. We did find a sticky residue on the steering wheel though. Forensics analysed it and it turned out to be spirit gum, a substance used to adhere prosthetics and the like, but, even though that seems to support your hunch, don't turn it into an assumption, because……"

"Assumption is the mother of all fuckups!!" said Ronnie. "I haven't heard you use that phrase in years, John."

"I've heard that somewhere before," said Max. "Off a movie if I'm not mistaken."

"You're probably right," said Buchanan. "John's a huge action movie buff."

"Right less chit chat, it's all hands on deck. Ronnie and Max, I want the two of you in the incident room to help man the phones. Hopefully we'll be under siege with reports of sightings of Terry Watt and have the bastard in custody by lunchtime. McLean, see if you can coax a better description of the guy who booked in to the guest house with Terry out of Mrs Grimes. She hasn't given us much so far. Her memory's not too hot but it's worth a bash. Now get on with your chores, gentlemen."

"Before you go Ronnie, can I have a quick word?"

"Sure John, what is it?"

"Have you been fucking about with the staff noticeboard in the entrance hall?"

"No idea what you're talking about, why what's happened?"

"Someone's replaced McLean's photo with one of William Shatner, he's not very happy. Everyone's making Spock signs at him and telling him to live long and prosper."

*

"What the fuck's that pile of shit?" said Liam.

"That's our transport," said Jimmy.

"You really expect us to drive around in that? Everyone's going to think we're a bunch of twats."

"What are you talking about?" asked Jimmy.

"You mean you don't see it?"

"What does it say on the side?" asked Liam.

"Bert Watson, Electrician."

"No, no, no, read the letters that are still clear."

"What do you mean?" asked Jimmy.

"Stand back a bit and take a look, the t from Bert and the first four letters from Watson are clear but the rest are faded," Jimmy laughed.

"Oh aye, I see it now. We'll call it the twat mobile."

"Where did you get it anyway?" asked Liam shaking his head.

"From Bert's widow, it's been lying in their garage for two years. I changed the oil, put in some fuel and it started first time."

"What about road tax?" asked Liam.

"Not a problem, I got a dodgy one off of Bent Barry, only cost me a couple of pints. I'll go and put it on now."

"We'll be lucky if that makes it out of Dundee, let alone all the way to Peebles."

"It's not that bad Liam, besides we'll be changing it for something far more impressive soon. So let's get going."

"Can you run through the plan again?" said Mark.

"Right for the last time, Uncle Frank has contacted as much of his old cronies as he can. Remember Frank was a major player in the drug trade, that's where he got the money to retire to Madrid. He's set up a sort of online auction for the coke, think E-Bay for drugs, word will soon get round about some top grade gear going cheap, bidders have three days to bid, the coke going to the highest bidder."

"How will they get access to the site?" said Mark.

"By phoning a special phone number. That phone number belongs to an unregistered mobile, the sole purpose of which is to relay a recorded message giving further instructions."

"Each bidder receives a password, so we know who bids the most, at the end of the auction we contact them and arrange the drop."

"What about whoever owns the coke, the folk we ripped of? Say they get to hear of this, say they win the bid, when we go to hand it over, they'll fucking kill us."

"That's immaterial!"

"The people who will be bidding for the coke will all be pretty fucking dangerous, it's not your normal E-Bay punters we're talking about here, we're talking about ruthless drug dealing gangsters. Let's face it, whoever wins the auction, they're going to have the contacts to cut it and sell it on for a profit, they'll all be major players. So taking that into account, it doesn't matter a shit whether it's the people you ripped off or some other gangsters, any of them are quite capable of turning up at the drop off point and putting a bullet in our ass and buggering off with the coke without paying anything."

"How the fuck are we going to stop that happening then, them just turning up and taking the stuff?" said Liam.

"It's all to do with how we plan the drop off. When they win the bid we tell them to come to a hotel located somewhere near us but not too close, either Glasgow or Edinburgh or possibly Aberdeen. When they get there, we tell them to await further instructions. Then we give them the final instructions and give them no time to plan ahead or prepare an ambush or whatever. It'll be a case of 'be there alone in five minutes or the deal is off'. One of us follows them from the hotel to make sure they are alone, and the rest of the plan I'll finalise in the next couple of days."

"You'll what? Am I hearing right; the next fucking couple of days! You mean you don't have the plan finalised?"

"Trust me I have a few ideas, look, all we have to do just now is babysit the coke until the auction's over, while pampering ourselves for three days in the lap of luxury. So let's go and enjoy ourselves with Uncle Frank's advance."

"Don't forget to add, and formulate the rest of the plan to stop ourselves getting wiped out at the drop off," said Liam.

"Calm down man, three days from now we'll be sitting on a plane, with plenty of cash, on the way to Uncle Frank's villa in Spain."

"One last thing, what makes you think that word of this won't filter down to the cops?" said Liam.

"Everything has a risk but we're pretty sure that taking into account the short span of the auction and the fact that only major dealers are being informed, that risk is kept to a bare minimum and remember it's a risk worth up to an estimated hundred and fifty to two hundred grand, possibly more. Now let's get going, we have to pick up some odds and ends before we book into the hotel."

Chapter Eleven

Vince listened to the recorded message once again, he couldn't believe his ears.

"You have found yourself here because you obviously want to take advantage of a unique opportunity to purchase four kilos of our clients' uncut quality merchandise.

This offer will be open until twelve pm on this coming Thursday, the winner being the highest bidder.

The web address of this once in a lifetime offer is www.cokebid.co.uk. When you reach our web site you will be issued with a password which we will use to verify your bid should you win this unique auction.

For your security, as well as our own, we would advise you to only make bids from an anonymously purchased internet enabled phone, using an anonymous email account. Don't specify any of your real personal information when you set up the account. Then use it only for this.

Then if things turn sour, you simply stop checking this account for new e-mail. That way there shouldn't be any repercussions for either yourselves or our clients.

One other thing, we have had an independent test done on the goods, the result of that test is displayed on our website.

Happy bidding people, may the best man win."

"Fuck!"

He knew when he'd got Dave to e-mail his contacts to be on the lookout for a large quantity of coke going up for sale he would eventually receive an answer. He also knew, by a process of elimination, the coke had likely been stolen from Lucy in Dundee. But no one on earth could have predicted this, not in a million years.

Another call came through.

"Vince, who the fuck are these bastards who think they can auction off my coke?"

"No idea Harry, but at least now we know we'll have it in three days."

"And, how the fuck you going to manage that?"

"Simple, I make sure I win the auction, deliver the cash in a bag with a tracer in it, retrieve the coke: then retrieve the money."

"Simple as fucking that?"

"Simple as that, Harry!" said Vince.

"You want some extra back up? I could send Sid over, he's a good man."

"Are you checking up on me?"

"Not at all, as I said he's here if you need him, just let me know."

"Bye Harry!"

Vince ended the call.

Psycho Sid that's all he needed. Vince had worked with him before. He was a drug addict, smack being his drug of choice but he wasn't shy at taking anything he could get his hands on. He was thin, some would say emaciated, with the biggest bulging eyes you're ever likely to see outside a cartoon character and he didn't wear clothes as much as allow them to hang from him. He was totally unreliable. He never took anything in. You could ask him to do something then, half an hour later he'd forgotten what you told him. He would take these fugues regularly. Add that to his frequent bouts of the noddies as he called them and you had the most useless bastard possible to take along on any job.

The noddies were the strangest thing Vince had ever seen. You could be having a conversation with Sid and he'd nod off halfway through. Unbelievable, as it seemed he could be talking to you and he'd nod off for a couple of minutes mid conversation and then waken up and carry on where he'd left off. Vince had once seen him do it during his breakfast, he'd nodded off over a bowl of cornflakes Vince had just watched him, dumbstruck, hoping he might drown in the milk but alas no, he just woke up and carried on as if nothing had happened, continuing his conversation with the corn flakes stuck to his face. Harry seemed to like him however. Fuck knows why. If anyone else fucked up as much as Sid, they'd end up in a car crusher, no doubt about it.

It was rumoured he was family, a distant cousin of Harry's ex-wife. That explained a lot.

And anyway what was Harry thinking of. Using a well-known addict with a voracious appetite for any drug going to help him get his drugs back, he must be taking the piss. That would be akin to getting a fox to guard your chicken farm.

"Dave, get your ass through here."

"Yes Boss!"

"Bring me the laptop and find me a pub close by with free Wi-Fi access. I need to check out a website."

*

Located within an area of unspoiled beauty and just over twenty miles south of Edinburgh, sits the quiet border town of Peebles.

In the centre of town, three scruffy youths approached the gent's outfitters, opened the door and went in. They moved towards the well-dressed man at the counter.

"Hello my good man, we would like to purchase three of your best business suits please," said Jimmy.

The well-dressed man looked down his nose at them.

"Sure you've come to the right place?"

"Positive my dear fellow," said Liam, getting into the tone of the conversation.

"Very well sirs, follow me."

They each picked a suit, a pair of expensive shoes, a tie and a couple of shirts.

"How shall you be paying for your purchases?" asked the assistant.

"With cash of course, what's the damage?"

The well-dressed man tallied up their purchases on an ancient looking till.

"That will be seven hundred and eighty pounds please," he said as he smirked to himself.

"No problem my dear fellow," said Jimmy as he took out the bundle of new crisp bank notes from his backpack.

"Now dear boy, could you possibly be as kind as to direct us to this lovely town's premier car hire establishment, tout suite."

The assistant removed his jaw from the floor and gave them the directions they'd asked for.

*

The three well-dressed youths walked into the Enterprise Car Hire office.

"What sort of car do you fancy, Mark?" asked Jimmy.

"Something big and fancy," replied Mark.

"Excuse me sir," said Jimmy. "I would like to hire a big bastard car."

*

With Mark and Liam in the back watching a movie on the screens built into the back of the front headrests, Jimmy drove along the private road to the castle hotel in the four litre, black Range Rover.

"Jesus, look at that," said Liam as they approached the magnificent Scottish Baronial Castle just north of Peebles.

"Remember we're three young business men, with our own online trading company," said Jimmy.

"And what do we trade?" he asked the others.

"Stocks and shares," they replied in unison.

"Just remember that, like Uncle Frank says, if things go tits up and someone comes looking for the coke, they'll be looking for three scruffy bastards from Dundee, not three wealthy young business men staying at a luxury hotel."

"Right, let's go enjoy ourselves, I'm dying for a beer."

They felt refreshed; they'd each had a shave and haircut at the barbers, followed by a quick swim and shower at the local swimming baths. They also smelled better than usual thanks to the liberal amounts of designer aftershave from the strange shaped bottle Jimmy had bought from Boots.

They got their holdalls containing their old clothes and not much else out the car, their new designer shoes crunching on the gravel of the car park. Dressed in their fancy suits and all three wearing designer sunglasses, even though it was the middle of winter, they looked up at the huge turret of the hotel.

"Jesus, who owns this pile - Victor Frankenstein?" asked Liam.

"Aye, it is a bit gothic right enough," replied Jimmy. "Now remember lads, act cultured."

"What's that supposed to mean?" asked Liam.

"Just act like this is the sort of shit we're used to. Basically act less like a Ned."

"I thoroughly intend to do just that, môn ami."

Jimmy laughed and shook his head.

Mark had remained silent throughout their conversation.

"You okay, Mark?" asked Jimmy.

Mark answered with a huge grin on his face.

"I could get used to this."

The three well-dressed men entered the hotel.

"Leave things to me," said Jimmy adjusting his tie and clearing his throat.

He approached the desk with Liam and Mark following side by side behind him like two well attired body guards.

"Yes gentlemen," said the man behind the reception desk.

"We have a suite reserved," said Jimmy, "in the name of Abraham Jackson."

The man checked the computer, "Ah yes, Mr Jackson, I'll get someone to show you up right away."

"Thank you sir," replied Jimmy, "and once we've seen our accommodation perhaps you could give us directions to your much talked about a la carte restaurant. I've been looking at it online and I must admit I'm well impressed and besides I'm fucking starving, I could eat a horse, bollocks "n" all."

Liam and Mark did their best to stop themselves creasing with laughter.

"I doubt that's on the menu," whispered Liam.

*

Terry was bored. How fucking long am I going to be stuck here, he thought to himself, no television, no food, I'd be as well in jail? Fuck it, I'm going for a drink.

He walked round the corner to Lothian Road and entered the nearest pub.

"Pint of lager please and could I have some change for the bandit?" He picked up his pint and began feeding the change into the slot machine, totally unaware of the barman picking up the phone and phoning the police.

*

"Hold the first two and use your two nudges on the others."

Terry took the guy's advice, his eyes fixed on the machine.

The animated noises and the flashing lights told him he'd won something.

"Forty quid, you beauty, I owe you a pint my friend."

"Oh fuck!"

"Hello Terry," said Buchanan, "another pint?"

"Aye, please, a pint of lager."

"By the way, we have armed officers front and back, so don't be a stupid bastard, okay."

"I get the message, I'm not going anywhere."

"A pint of lager and a Guinness please" said Buchanan.

"Enjoy that Terry, it'll be the last you have for a while, if not forever."

"Why are the cops not storming the place, I mean you have me in the frame for the two lassies murders."

"This is Edinburgh son, very tourist friendly, the last thing they want is a bunch of Japanese tourists snapping away on their cameras as you go down in a hail of bullets, so I persuaded them to give me fifteen minutes to talk you into coming quietly."

"Who recognised me? I mean I never thought I'd be spotted with the disguise."

"The barman phoned it in about thirty seconds after you walked in, the thing with disguises you see Terry is they only work when you hide your prominent features. I mean there's no point in wearing a baseball hat and sunglasses if you have a nose that looks like it's been chewed by a dog."

Terry laughed.

"I didn't kill the lassies you know, that was Dave's doing. You know me Mr Buchanan, I may be an evil vicious bastard but I'm not a killer."

"Aye and no doubt if we collar him he'll put the finger on you. Now finish your pint son, looks like we have a lot of talking to do." Buchanan stood outside the pub and watched as Terry was handcuffed and whisked away to St Leonard's police station to be held for questioning.

*

Liam, Mark and Jimmy sat at the corner of the bar deep in conversation.

"Check it again," said Liam.

Jimmy sighed, "I just checked it five minutes ago and I told you three offers so far, the highest is fifty grand, It's only been going eight hours, now try and forget about it. We're here to enjoy ourselves. Chuck us over a menu, Mark. I'm bloody starving."

Mark handed over the menu.

"What we going to do while we're here?" asked Liam.

"I know what I fancy," said Mark. "A bit of hill walking. According to this brochure there's a walk called the John Buchan Way, thirteen miles in total including an eight hundred metre climb."

"Sounds pretty good," said Liam, "but I don't fancy doing it in my new suit, it'll get wrecked."

"We could always drive back into town and get ourselves some outdoor gear after we've eaten, then we could grab a few beers and stuff them in a backpack."

"Sounds like a great day out," said Jimmy.

"Better leaving it till tomorrow though," said Mark. "According to this, the walk takes most of the day."

The other two agreed.

"By the way," said Jimmy, "who's John Buchan? The name rings a bell."

Mark looked at the brochure.

"Ever seen that Hitchcock movie, The Thirty Nine Steps?"

"No, but I saw the remake, it was on a couple of weeks ago, had that guy in it, him that played Jesus."

"Who played Jesus?" asked Liam, joining in the conversation.

"The guy we're talking about, him in the Thirty Nine Steps, Robert somebody or other."

"Robert Powell," said Mark. "It was on last Easter, Jesus of Nazareth, it was made years ago. It's one of those mini-series things; it had about three parts."

"Is that the same guy that was in that detective thing with Jasper Carrot, funny as fuck that programme. Mind you I can't see him as Jesus though."

"Aye that's him," replied Mark. "He looked the part, they hippied him up, gave him long hair, a beard and a robe."

"What's the Thirty Nine Steps about?" asked Liam. "Some guy gets his ass chased all over the shop by German spies," replied Mark.

"Sounds good, maybe we could hire it, watch it in the fancy car."

"Anyway, before we get any further off track, John Buchan is the guy who wrote the book that they made the film from," said Mark. "It tells you in the brochure."

"So why did they name the walk after him then?"

"Doesn't tell you that here, it just says he had many associations with the area, whatever the hell they mean by that."

"Oh well, back to the menu, what you lot having?" said Jimmy.

"I'll have a burger," said Mark.

"Me too!" chirped Liam.

"A burger!" shouted Jimmy. "This is a fancy assed place with a top class restaurant, not a fucking burger joint, they won't do burgers."

"Check the menu asshole, item seven under main courses."

Jimmy scanned the menu.

'Chef's homemade 6oz burger served with cheese, bacon and crisp salad, coleslaw and Chunky chips £9.95'

"That actually sounds pretty good." He called over the waitress.

"Could we have another three beers please and three of the home made burgers, cheers?"

*

After their burgers, a dessert each and a dish of select Scottish cheeses and crackers, Jimmy asked for the bill.

"Jimmy," said Liam, "we're spending money like water, not to say I'm not enjoying it but what's happening? We've had new suits, hired an expensive car and we're staying at a top notch country hotel, what's going on man?"

"I told you Uncle Frank gave us an advance."

"How much?" said Liam.

"Ten grand," said Jimmy. "When we get the money from the coke, we pay him his cash back, plus ten per cent for setting the auction up and split the rest three ways. Here!" Jimmy handed Liam two grand. "Give half to Mark and we can go get some outdoor gear for our walk tomorrow. Keep the rest for spending money."

"Anyone watched that programme 'Banged up Abroad' on the Discovery Channel?" said Mark.

"I've seen it," said Jimmy.

Liam shook his head.

"It's a series about real life stories of people who smuggled drugs; it tells you how they got caught and shows you the prisons they got sent to."

"What the fuck's that got to do with anything?" said Liam.

"I'm coming to that, the last one I saw was about this couple who were on holiday in Spain when some dodgy bastard came up to them and asked them if they would fly to the Canaries and pick up a package for him and fly back .They got a couple of grand upfront and a free week's holiday in a top resort before they had to carry the drugs back."

"For fuck's sake, get to the point," said Liam.

"The point is, although they tried to enjoy the free holiday they couldn't because of what they knew was to come. They knew they could get caught going through customs with the dope so it constantly preyed on their mind. That's exactly how I feel, I should be enjoying myself but how can I, when I know this whole episode could go tits up and we end up in jail, or even worse we could end up dead."

"Jesus, listen to Mr glass half empty. For fuck's sake, cheer up would you, that's bringing me down, man."

"Listen, both of you," said Jimmy. "I'm not going to let that happen, I have a fool proof plan about ninety nine point nine percent complete in here."

Jimmy tapped his head, "So try and put it out your mind and enjoy yourselves. I know it's hard but I guar-an-damn-tee three days from now we'll be sitting in the sun, a cold beer in hand and about fifty grand in our pockets. Now who wants another beer?"

"Bugger it, let's get pissed," said Mark.

Liam downed the rest of his pint.

"I'm with you there buddy. Waitress, three more beers and a round of tequilas."

*

Vince fired up his laptop and logged on to the GSM tracking site. The site had served him well in the past, he always made a point of handing out the phones he had registered online with them to whatever lackeys he was using at the time. Web sites such as these are really meant to be used for parents checking up on their kids or companies keeping tabs on drivers delivering goods, but for a small price you could register as many phones as you wanted to.

Which meant, whenever you wanted to know where a particular phone was, you just logged in and checked its location to within a few metres.

"What's that you're doing?" asked Dave.

"Watch and learn. This website will show me exactly where Terry is by displaying his phone's location. I don't trust that bastard to stay put."

When he input Terry's number he froze, staring at the location on the screen of his laptop as it displayed a map showing St Leonard's Police Station.

"Dave, listen very carefully. It looks like Terry has gone and gotten himself nicked, which means the cops will have his phone. This creates problems for us because it means they can find our numbers and trace where we are. They could be on their way here now for all we know, so we'll have to get out of here."

"He could have just lost the phone and someone's handed it in to lost property."

"Possible I suppose. We'll soon find out."

They left the pub and walked down the road to their car. Once inside Vince removed the sim card from his phone and replaced it with a new one. He asked Dave to do the same but not before he got him to phone Terry.

*

Just as DI Buchanan was about to check Terry's contacts list the phone rang.

"Hello, DI Buchanan!"

"Shit!" Dave disconnected the call.

"Looks like you're right, Vince."

"Better double check."

Vince looked up St Leonards and made the call.

"St Leonard's police department, enquiries" said the voice at the other end.

"Hello, PC Flannigan here. I was at the murder suspect's arrest this morning but the thing is I forgot to hand in some evidence to the DI, I take it the suspect is still there?"

"Of course he's still here, where else would he be?"

Vince hung up. "Can your mate keep his mouth shut?"

"I couldn't answer that, and he's not my mate, he's just a guy that throws some work my way now and again," said Dave.

"Just to be safe, I think we'll get out of here for a few days. It's not like I can't keep an eye on that auction from anywhere. Finish your drink and well get moving."

Vince and Dave started heading towards Fife leaving the centre of Edinburgh and Terry far behind them.

Chapter Twelve

DCI Brannigan looked up from his desk. "Problems, Ronnie?"

"That was the other suspect on Terry's phone; I shouldn't have answered it. Now they know we have Terry."

"Don't let it bother you; the press have wind of it already, they would have found out soon enough. Give the phone to McLean and get him to put a trace on the numbers. If the phones are switched on, we'll soon have a location."

"There are only two entries in his contacts, Dave and Vince," said Buchanan. "Dave just phoned."

"Should be easy enough to trace then, shouldn't it."

"You don't get it John, do you?"

"Get what?" said the DCI.

"Now that they know we have Terry's mobile, they'll also know that we have access to their numbers and that we can trace them, so all they have to do is lose the phones or change the sim cards and we're fucked. In fact if this other guy Vince, is as half as smart as we think he is, he's probably done it already."

Buchanan put the mobile onto speaker phone and called both numbers, both were out of service.

He looked to Brannigan.

"See! I told you."

*

"Where's my fucking solicitor?"

"You're being denied legal representation at the moment, son," said Buchanan.

"You can't do that; I know my rights," said Terry.

"Actually we can son, with special permission from the Superintendent. Due to the fact that waiting for your solicitor is likely to delay our investigation and apprehension of other suspects, we're quite within our rights. Now tell us from the beginning what happened to the two lassies?"

"You'd better ask Dave about that, I was only the lookout."

"The first murder in Aberdeen, you kept a lookout while your partner set fire to the car with the girl alive in the boot. That's what you're telling me!"

"I never knew she was in the boot, so don't try sticking an accessory charge on me, I've been through this sort of shit before, I know how this works."

DI McLean entered the room with a plastic bag.

"For the benefit of the tape, DI McLean has just joined the interview," said Buchanan.

"What about the second murder Terry, care to tell us the part you played in that? And before you deny even being there I must tell you we have a witness that saw you, and this Dave guy, enter the flat not long before the murder."

"All I did was keep a lookout from the living room window while Dave asked her some questions, I had no idea there would be any violence involved, or I wouldn't have taken any part in the whole affair."

"You telling me you abhor violence, you..., with seventeen assault charges under your belt?"

"Ah but that was the old me Mr Buchanan, I've become a different person since I rediscovered religion, my last offence was over two years ago, check my record."

Buchanan laughed. "You expect me to believe you're a born again Christian, that's your defence?"

"As God is my witness," said Terry, as he crossed himself, giving Buchanan a smirk.

"Well you're the first bible thumper I've seen who keeps a shotgun under his bed. When did this miraculous change come about then. I'd be fascinated to know?"

"Two years ago I got myself re-baptised online, at a virtual church site called Reborn Again, and since then I live my life according to God's word."

The interview room erupted into laughter.

"What?" asked Terry. "It has a real priest and everything."

"Did you have to pour some holy water over your head?" asked Buchanan.

"No, because I did it in the bath, I just sort of slipped under the water for a bit when the online priest guy told me to and that was it, job done."

"For the benefit of the recording" said Buchanan, "DI McLean has just left the interview room due to him pissing himself laughing."

*

McLean took the tray containing the bacon rolls and coffees over to the table where Buchanan and Max were seated.

"We never got round to showing him the knife we found," said McLean holding up the plastic bag.

"Plenty of time for that, we'll let him know we have his prints on the murder weapon when we have another go after we've eaten, but we'll have to take a different approach this time, maybe come down a bit harder on him."

"Do you think he really is one of those born again Christians like he says?" asked Max.

"Don't make me laugh son," said Buchanan, "he's an evil bastard, always has been."

*

The two DI's entered the interview room just as before, this time however Terry had his solicitor present.

"Before we start this interview," said the solicitor, "I think some credence should be given to how my client has changed his life around, as he has already told you he's a changed man and as his record shows he hasn't been on the wrong side of the law for over two years."

"If you say so, sir," said Buchanan.

"Terry, earlier on we mentioned the shotgun we found under your bed with your prints on it, care to explain?"

"It belongs to Dave; I just took it off him so that no one else would get hurt."

Buchanan picked up the bag.

"You recognise this knife? It has the blood of one of the girl's on it and again your prints."

"That knife also belongs to Dave; I must have touched it at one time or another."

"Do you seriously expect me to believe that **A**, the gun belonged to Dave, yet the only prints on it belong to you and **B**, the knife which forensics have proved was used in Julie's murder, also belonged to Dave but was found to have no other prints except your own. Do you really expect anyone to believe that shit?"

"Inspector, my client has given a reasonable explanation for why his prints were on these items, I suggest you calm down."

Buchanan banged his fist on the table.

"Reasonable my arse!"

"He always wears gloves."

"What!"

"Dave, he always wears gloves, practically sleeps with the things on, due to some sort of skin condition, I think," said Terry. "That's why he never leaves any prints."

Buchanan shook his head.

"Right, let's try something else. Tell me who Dave and Vince are?"

"Vince, now he's a strange guy, as far as I'm aware he oversees the smooth running of large shipments of merchandise up and down the country."

"What sort of merchandise?" asked McLean.

"Drugs mostly, I've only worked with him for the past year or so. When he has a shipment to a specific area, say Aberdeen, he employs local muscle like me and Dave to see to any problems, help split it into smaller amounts and distribute it to the local dealers."

"If he employs you to see to things in a local capacity, what the hell are you doing down here in Edinburgh?"

"The courier turned up as usual but she didn't have the coke, she swore she had it when she left, she said she packed it herself the night before."

McLean looked up from his notebook. "The courier? That would be Lucy?"

"Aye, nice looking lassie."

"Well she was, till you cremated her," said Buchanan.

"Inspector I must protest," said the solicitor.

"Sorry," said Buchanan. "Carry on, Terry."

"Vince learned from her that she'd stopped twice on the way from Edinburgh to Aberdeen, once due to a burst tyre and once for a coffee at the Road Chef in Dundee. He figured that either the coke could have been taken out the bag by the flatmate before she left, or the guy who helped her with the flat tyre had helped himself to it or, it had been stolen in Dundee."

"So he sent the two of you to put the frighteners on Donald Campbell and the flatmate," said Buchanan.

"The flatmate, yes, but Campbell he seen to himself."

"Scaring the shit out of people, hardly the best job for a born again Christian is it?"

"A man has to eat Mr Buchanan; it's all I know how to do."

"Right, let's try Dave shall we, what information do you have on him?"

"I've only worked with him a few times. I met him in a bar in Aberdeen, The Blue Lamp, there was some Hungarian Folk Band playing that night and they sounded good so we must have been pissed. He'd heard of my reputation and he was looking for some work so he gave me his phone number and I told him I'd be in touch if I could chuck anything his way. I mentioned this to Vince and when Jake done a runner, Vince told me to get him on-board. Well after he'd been thoroughly checked out of course. Vince is very thorough."

"Back up a bit," said Buchanan, "who the hell's Jake?"

"Jake Burns! I suppose you could call him my partner in crime, at least he was for a while. Vince teamed us up to help with the drug runs but he disappeared, no phone calls, bugger all. Seemed strange to me, that he wouldn't stay in touch, we were tight."

"What makes you think he ran off as you put it?" asked Buchanan.

"Well, according to Vince, he delivered a package but according to the buyer the package was short, so Vince reckoned Jake must have helped himself and buggered off with some of the gear to sell for himself. He's never been seen since, never even contacted his wife and kid."

"What was his address?"

"He stays, stayed, in a flat in Kincorth Circle, I'm not sure of the number."

"Back to Dave, what's his full name and address?"

"That I can't help you with, I only know him as Dave, no idea where he lives, although I'd guess it was somewhere around the Gallowgate as that's where the Blue Lamp is, and I can remember him saying that was his local."

Buchanan rubbed his eyes and sighed.

"Let's return to Vince, where's he been staying while you've been here?"

"No idea, he's a very secretive guy, every time he employs us it's the same. He takes our phones, gives us new ones, we can't make any private calls for the duration of the job. If the job leads us to other places he pre-books somewhere for me and Dave to stay and sees to his own accommodation. We never get to know."

"I take it you haven't recovered the coke yet?"

"Not as far as I'm aware."

"Do you have a second name or an address for Vince?"

"No. Sorry."

"Terry, you're not really helping yourself here, I'm sure your solicitor will tell you, the more you help us, the better it is for you."

The solicitor looked at Terry and nodded his head.

"I have a name, I think he's Vince's boss. I'm not positive, but the way their phone conversations go, he seems to be."

"Cough it up then!"

"Not until you promise to give me some sort of protection when I'm put in remand, this guy's a heavy dude."

"We must insist on this," said Terry's solicitor.

"Can you see to some segregation for our friend here, please McLean," said Buchanan.

"Consider it done."

"Well?" said Buchanan.

"His name's Harry, Harry Black, works out of Glasgow."

"Stop the recording McLean, we'll have a recess."

Buchanan walked to the coffee machine where he found Max.

"How's it going boss?"

"Could be better Max, could you do a few things for me?"

"Sure sir," replied Max taking out his notebook.

"Check into a guy called Jake Burns, he stays somewhere in Kincorth Circle. Terry says he's done a disappearing act. Check with his wife and see if he's resurfaced, he might be able to shed some light on this Vince character. Then get on to our lot back home, ask them to show the photo fit of Dave to the regulars at the Blue Lamp; see if anyone recognises him. And finally, get on to the Road Chef in Dundee and see if they've had any cars broken into lately and while you're at it, see if they have CCTV covering the car park."

Buchanan picked up his coffee and went to find the DCI. He was on a roll. He raised his voice, "John, do you have any contacts in the Strathclyde drug squad? We could have a breakthrough."

Chapter Thirteen

In the centre of St Andrews, a small town on the east coast of Fife, Dave walked into the hairdressers.

"Any chance of a haircut, I'm afraid I don't have an appointment?"

"We could see to you now, sir if you want, it's quite quiet at the moment," said the assistant.

"Cool," said Dave. "I'd like the beard off and maybe go bleached blonde with the hair, what you think?"

"I think that would work for you, any particular reason for the new look?"

"Yes, I'm an actor and I think I'd have a much better chance of the part I'm going for, if I changed my image."

"An actor, wow, would I have seen you in anything?" she asked.

"Maybe a few adverts," said Dave, "but I mostly do stage work."

Dave relaxed in the chair as the hairdresser went to work.

*

The bald bearded man pulled up to the side of the road beside Dave in a black four by four and wound down the driver's window.

"Waiting for someone?"

"Vince?" Dave did a double take. "Jesus man! It is you! I would never have recognised you."

"That's the plan!" said Vince.

"New wheels as well, a four by four no less."

"Well let's face it," said Vince, "we have no idea what Terry's telling the cops but we have to assume he's given them a description of some sort so we need to stay ahead of the game."

"Nice disguise, by the way, you look like one of Hitler's master race. Now hop in, I'll buy you a late lunch, I saw a bar along here with free Wi-Fi."

*

Dave took the drinks over to the table at the side of the bar where Vince sat with the laptop.

"What's our next move, Vince?"

"We're taking a trip through to Dundee, check this out."

Vince turned the laptop round so Dave could see the screen, which had the photo of two young men on it.

"I had an acquaintance of mine, who has contacts in the Dundee police, look into likely candidates who could have stolen the coke from Lucy's car. Dundee must be where the stuff disappeared. Every other possibility has been exhausted."

"Who are they?" said Dave.

Vince opened the attached file.

"Mark Douglas and Liam McGregor, they've been done for stealing from cars before and get this, both crimes occurred at roadside restaurants, seems to be their thing."

"I must admit they look good for it," said Dave.

"It's worth looking into, I might be barking up the wrong tree but we've got two days to kill till this auction's over, so we might as well see what we can find out. Finish your pint and we'll get going."

*

Buchanan turned on the laptop and opened the files he'd been sent from Strathclyde Police on Harry Black and Vince. No second name, just Vince.

Harry Black was into all sorts of illegal dealings, drugs being just one of them.

In brackets next to his name was the word "Road Kill", a name given to him by a Strathclyde Detective because on the couple of occasions that anyone was willing to finger him, they had both been victims of a deadly hit and run, no witnesses of course.

According to the file most of his success in never getting caught was down to one man, Vince.

They knew Vince was heavily involved in Harry's operation, knew he practically oversaw everything, from the stuff coming in to the country to the distribution of the goods, but the guy was like a ghost, and seemed to have nine lives.

Every time they got close to him, he was always ahead of the game, changing drop offs at the last minute while the police had the original scene under surveillance. This of course led to rumours that he must have some police officers on his pay roll. This had never been substantiated, but he was getting his information from somewhere. Even on the very odd occasion that they'd caught him on camera, or at least they thought it was him, he looked entirely different, bearded, bald, blonde, wearing glasses, not wearing glasses, if it wasn't for his noticeable height there'd be no reason to think this was the same guy.

"Fucking useless!" Buchanan said aloud, causing a young WPC to drop her coffee.

"Sorry love, let me get you another."

Buchanan returned with two coffees, one for the WPC and one for himself. He took his own over to the desk and began to write.

Drugs must have been stolen in Dundee, Road Chef?

Could Dave have killed girls and not Terry? Doubtful

Who is Dave? Obviously from Aberdeen but not on file.

Where are the drugs now?

Buchanan's phone rang.

"DI Buchanan? This is DI Prentice, Strathclyde. I heard something that might interest you. There's a rumour on the street that someone's trying to auction off a large amount of coke on the cheap."

"You're joking?"

"The information's from a good source, whoever puts in the highest bid gets it, but get this, my snitch says it's all being done online."

"Hold on," said Buchanan. "Nope, I just put cocaine into the for sale items on E-Bay and it's not there."

"Very funny!" said Prentice. "I'll tell you though, whoever is selling it, I wouldn't like to be in their shoes. If that is Harry Black's coke, their life won't be worth shit. Anyway, if I can find out any more I'll let you know."

"Cheers!" said Buchanan.

Just then Max walked in.

"Another coffee, sir?"

"Cheers Max, any luck with the Road Chef?"

"Yep, there have been a few thefts from cars there recently so I phoned Tayside Police and get this, they're getting the whole of the day's footage we need, burning it to DVD and hand delivering it to us. We should get it sometime tonight."

"Any excuse to leave Dundee, eh!" said Buchanan. "Good work Max, let me know when it arrives."

*

Just as the young officer left Dundee with the CCTV footage Vince and Dave arrived heading for Mark and Liam's flat.

"Why is Dundee called the city of discovery?" asked Dave.

"Because of the boat."

"What boat?"

"HMS Discovery, the one Captain Scott used to get him to the Antarctic, it was built here in the 1900's and now it's berthed here down at the docks."

"I'd like to see that," said Dave.

"Maybe later, but first we have to check this flat out."

*

"This place looks like Beirut, what a shit hole," said Dave. "Folk used to be embarrassed even to be associated with places like this at one time. Now they make TV programmes out of them and make stars out of the folk who live in them," said Vince. The housing estate was dilapidated; they passed a rusty car with no wheels lying by the side of the road. Next to it lay a wheelie bin, it was lying on its side, its contents spilling out into the street. Two dogs were eagerly gobbling up the old rotten food that lay around it. The gardens in front of the flats were all overgrown with weeds, some with fences around them but most without.

As they approached the flat they were looking for, three youths, all dressed in track suits, all with cans of cheap lager in hand, stopped their conversation and eyeballed the car as it passed. "You ever wondered why so many teenagers wear sports gear nowadays when they have no intention what-so-ever of participating in any sport?" asked Vince.

"It's the uniform of the street," said Dave. "I blame all those American Rappers. That's the sort of shit they like to wear." They parked outside the flat and got out the vehicle. There was a plump woman with a pushchair coming out of the gate. She wore a pair of tight Day-Glo pink leggings, her ample belly hanging over the waist band.

"How the fuck did she squeeze herself into them?" asked Dave.

"She is a bit Rubenesque," replied Vince.

"Ruby who?"

"Fat, Dave, she's a bit fat."

"Watch your car, mister?" said one of the youths who had put down his can of lager and came running over. "You don't want to leave a smart motor like that lying around here unprotected man." Vince handed him £20.

"You better do a good job lad. If I come out and find one scratch on it I'll shoot you."

Something told the youth this was no idle threat.

Careful to avoid the dog shit on the path, the two men entered the scruffy tenement. They walked up the stairs to flat 3F and knocked on the door.

No answer.

Dave picked the lock and in less than a minute they were in.

"Check this out," said Dave pointing to the many bolts on the inside of the door.

"These guys aren't half paranoid, just as well these aren't locked or we would never have got in."

The living room was quite small, and decorated with copious amounts of empty beer bottles, the odd pizza box and a sprinkling of pornographic magazines.

The furniture was simply the basics, a three piece threadbare suite, an old coffee table, an electric fire and an ancient looking television.

"Check the bedroom Dave. I'll give this room a quick going over."

Between Busty Asian Beauties and Hot Naked Housewives, Vince found a Scottish Hotels Guide. Flicking through, he noticed a lot of the hotels had been circled, some with question marks next to them.

Just then the front door opened and a young woman walked in with a cat carrier.

"Who the hell are you?" she asked Vince.

Vince drew out his weapon. "I'm the guy who's going to put a bullet in your skull if you don't shut that fucking door behind you."

The woman shut the door and the room instantly smelled of patchouli oil. She had on a white dress and had beads in her hair. Every time she moved she jangled, thanks to the huge charm bracelets on each wrist.

"Now get your ass through here."

She dropped the carrier and raised her hands above her head.

"I'm just here for Mark's cat, I don't want any trouble. I'll just pick him up and be on my way."

"Dave," shouted Vince. "You see a cat through there?"

"Yeah, the little bastard's under the bed, at least I think it's a cat, it could be a Tasmanian devil judging by the mess it's made of my hands."

"Right, go through and get the cat," said Vince. "Before you go, what's your name?"

"Summer, Summer Deveraux."

She returned with the cat under her arm and set it down on the floor.

"Unusual looking cat," said Vince "what breed is it?"

"It's a Ragdoll. Watch this!"

She held the cat up in both hands and it flopped over in her arms as if it had just died.

"They were first bred in California and are known for being very affectionate."

The cat purred loudly as she stroked its ears.

"They get their name from the way they go limp and relaxed when picked up, just like a rag doll."

"What's it doing prowling about this dump?" asked Dave.

"Mark got it from his Aunt, she had to go into hospital and he said he'd watch it for her. Thing is she never came back out, some complication with her surgery, she snuffed it, so he was left with Schwarzenegger here."

"That's a strange name for a cat."

"His Aunt liked action movies," Summer explained. "They tried to shorten it to Schwarzy but it didn't work. He just ignored you when you called his name and sat there looking at you with a pissed off look on his face."

The three occupants of 3F sat down in the living room with their freshly made coffees.

"So Summer, where exactly are your two friends?" asked Vince.

"All I know is that they're off somewhere and don't want to be found for a few days. In fact they said if things go to plan, they wouldn't be back at all. That's why I'm taking the cat home with me."

Vince held out his hand.

"Mobile!"

"What?" Summer asked.

"Give me your mobile!" said Vince.

"That won't help you, they left their phones here. They told me they didn't want to be disturbed on their trip."

"Give me it anyway."

Summer did as she was asked.

Vince flicked through the phone book.

"Summer, where's your mother at? Wait, don't answer that, I'll tell you."

Vince logged on to his phone tracker.

"She's at the local community centre, isn't she?"

"How the hell do you know that?"

"Thanks to your phone and the help of a favourite web site of mine, I can track down you, your parents or anyone else I find on here."

He tried the entries for Liam and Mark just in case, both phones rang one after another in the living room.

Vince once again drew his weapon and pressed it hard against Summer's head.

"Normally in such a situation I'd have your brains redecorating this room. However, it's your lucky day, I love cats! I have three of my own, that's what's saving you. You also impressed me with your ragdoll story. However, that being said, you mention anything, anything at all to your friends, your parents, the police or anyone else and your mother will lose the use of her legs."

"She's in a wheelchair," said Summer, "has been for the last three years."

Vince laughed.

"Ok, bad example, I'll shoot her through the heart then, you get the idea?"

"Totally!" said Summer.

*

Outside in the car Vince took the hotel brochure out of his inside pocket.

"What's that you've got there?" asked Dave.

"I found it in the flat. Looks like our two friends have been scoping out some country hotels, all pretty expensive ones too, all in smaller out of the way places."

"Can I have a look?" asked Dave.

"Knock yourself out" said Vince handing the brochure to Dave.

After five minutes Dave looked up.

"There's only eight circled, all around the central belt, if we split up and took four each, we could probably cover them all in a few hours."

"Good idea, we'll get a map and start early tomorrow. I have a feeling they've holed themselves up in one of those out of the way hotels until the auction's over, so I don't think they'll be going anywhere anytime soon."

Chapter Fourteen

Buchanan parked his car in Morrison Street and took the keys out of his pocket. Terry had given him the address of the safe house Vince had hidden him in; just to make doubly sure he got his protection. The guy was really spooked, thought Buchanan.

He let himself into the flat.

It was tastefully decorated and dominated by a huge stone fireplace and a wine coloured chesterfield suite. The walls were panelled in wood, it looked like oak, they matched the thick wooden doors and they contained a vast amount of art prints highlighted by sunken lights. He recognised a couple. He had the same ones at home, Irises and La Nuit Etoille (Starry night) both by Van Gogh, another Vince. Michelle had bought them. He never really appreciated art but he admired the starry night, he liked the way the stars reflected off the water.

The rest of the furniture was all antique and on the wooden floor sat a thick Persian rug. It looked like it cost a bob or two. He walked over to the window and spotted a small round table in the corner where he found a crystal decanter and four glasses. He opened the top and gave it a sniff, definitely Malt he thought. He poured himself a measure into one of the whisky glasses, sat down and surveyed the room. Off to his left he heard a ticking noise; it came from an ornate clock above the fire place. He watched the pendulum swinging back and fore hypnotically. When he'd finished his drink he decided to take a good look around the flat. He found nothing; he looked in the wardrobe, no clothes; the fridge, no food; and the phone, no messages. He was just about to check the bathroom when the toilet flushed and out of the bathroom came what could only be described as a monster. The guy was huge and must have weighed about three hundred pounds. If he'd been wearing a loincloth Buchanan would have sworn he was a sumo wrestler. He had a spiderweb tattoo on the left side of his face and half a dozen earrings in each ear, not the sort of person you would mistake in a line up. Not the kind of person you wanted to see coming towards you with his fists raised and practically foaming at the mouth.

"Who the fuck are you?" he said as he waddled across the room.

"DI Buchanan, don't come any closer." The guy kept coming forward.

"You're obviously deaf as well as ugly, so I'll tell you again - DON'T come any closer."

The man kept coming, and threw a left hook. Buchanan dodged it, he threw a right. Buchanan blocked it and followed it up with a vicious head butt. Mr Ugly's nose exploded. Just as he let out a scream, Buchanan stepped forward, put his right leg behind the man's ankles and threw his weight forward, the guy went down. As he flopped about the floor like a beached whale, Buchanan put his size ten boot across his throat and put some pressure on his windpipe.

"Do I have your attention now?" he asked. "Why are you here?"

"Fuck off, Pig!" he squealed.

Buchanan increased the pressure.

"Vince, I'm looking for Vince!"

"Snap!" said Buchanan. "Who sent you?"

The guy stayed silent.

More pressure.

"Was it Harry Black?"

"Yes, yes, you're fucking choking me."

"You're doing great fat boy, now answer one more question and I'll let you go and get that nose fixed. Why is Harry Black searching for Vince?"

"He's gone AWOL, won't even answer his phone, so he sent me

and another two guys through to see what the hell's going on."

"Right, get yourself up son, and go and get that nose fixed, here take this handkerchief."

The big guy got up wiped what was left of his nose and left the flat.

Buchanan phoned Max.

"Any joy with the CCTV footage?" he asked.

"Yes sir, we have Lucy on camera, the stupid cow left her car unlocked, and we have footage of the two guys who rummaged through the car."

"Is the footage good enough for an ID?"

"Hard to tell who they are sir, but the lab reckons the footage can be cleaned up. They're getting on to it now, hopefully we should get the cleaned up copy tonight."

"Great" said Buchanan, "soon as you get it, e-mail Dundee and see if we can get their names and addresses."

As soon as he disconnected the call, another one came through.

"Ronnie, it's John; where in the hell are you?"

"I've just been checking out the flat in Morrison Street."

"Come up with anything?"

"Nothing much, but one of Harry Black's goons was here, seems they want a hold of Vince as much as us. He's gone AWOL, hasn't checked in with them all day and he's not answering his phone."

"Just happened to volunteer that information did he?"

"He attacked me first; I got the better of him and simply took advantage of the situation."

The DCI laughed.

"What I'm phoning for Ronnie, is to tell you that the rumoured coke auction is real. Strathclyde Police sent us a link to the website, thing is it's untraceable and you need a password to bid, so we can watch the bids going up and watch the countdown going down, but we've no idea whose running it, or where it's being run from."

"How long's it got to go?"

"Till one p.m. the day after tomorrow."

Chapter Fifteen

Vince sat in the dark in his hotel room and helped himself to another whisky from the mini bar, half an hour and he'd get going, he had work to do.

This drug run was always going to be his last; he'd told Harry that. Harry wasn't pleased. But tough, he wanted out.

All the money he'd made for the last few years, which was quite a tidy sum, had been piled into his legitimate businesses abroad ready for him to retire to with a new identity. It was all set up, but no one just walks away from Harry Black. He knew Harry would have already sent some of his heavies through to find him, just in case Vince had decided to retrieve the coke and keep it for himself, and he must admit the thought had already crossed his mind. It would be a nice going away present to himself and with his contacts, no trouble at all to off load.

The only problem that stood in his way was Harry and his goons, but Vince had a plan for them. Vince checked his gun. Fuck it why not!

Scotland's second city was the murder capital of Europe, an average of about seventy deaths a year mostly down to gangs vying for control of the city's drug trade.

A few more won't make much difference, thought Vince.

He grabbed his car keys and set off to drive the eighty miles to Glasgow.

*

Harry Black had a rival, another gang worked out of the Southside of Glasgow headed by Billy Ringo. Vince always thought Billy was a funny guy. He never went anywhere without his bodyguard come driver, Willard, and he could always be seen driving around Glasgow in his big black Limo with the private registration R1NG01.

He loved to gamble, and every night from about midnight until roughly two in the morning, he frequented the Riverboat Casino in the Broomielaw Quay, which had been Glasgow's Harbour since the late Seventeenth Century.

Why someone with a rival like Harry, and involved in such a dangerous game, should keep such a routine every night and announce himself to everyone with such a distinctive car, defied logic. Vince always thought he'd be as well wearing a target on his back.

*

Just as every other night, Willard walked to the car park to get the car ready to drive round to the casino to pick up his boss.

He unlocked the door, started the engine, turned up the heater and prepared to drive to the casino. Checking his rear view mirror he saw Vince in the back seat a split second before he felt the gun equipped with the silencer at the back of his neck.

"Drive!"

He drove around to the quayside where they sat outside the casino waiting for their passenger.

The building was clearly based on the design of the great passenger liners of the early 1900's. It reminded Vince of the Titanic, and its spectacular neon signs lit up the area around it, adding a warm glow to the cold dark Glasgow night.

Vince had been there only once. Some big business associate of Harry was playing in a poker tournament. The guy had received some threats and since the tournament had been well advertised, everyone knew he'd be there, so Vince was sent along with him for protection. He was an odious little man with few redeeming features, who talked with a pronounced lisp. It hadn't been the easiest of jobs, the Casino was mobbed and lots of spectators hung around the card table. The tournament had gone on until four a.m., and the guy had treated Vince as his own personal lackey, so he was glad when the job had ended.

He slunk back into his seat behind the tinted safety glass as Billy Ringo got into the back seat of the Limo.

"I've had a lucky night tonight, Willard."

"Not that lucky!" said Vince thrusting his second gun into Billy's ribs.

Both guns were untraceable; they had to be for Vince's plan to work.

"You," he said to the driver, "drive a hundred yards and pull over." Willard did as he was told.

"Ringo, get out!"

"This is Harry's doing, isn't it?"

Vince never answered.

"I'll double what he's paying you, to let us go."

Ignoring him, Vince told Willard to put down the driver's side window and release the boot mechanism.

Covering the driver, he told Ringo to get in the boot. Once he was in, he jumped in the passenger seat and told Willard to drive to Old Bearsden.

"So you are working for Harry, that's where he stays isn't it?"

"Just drive!" said Vince.

"What's this got to do with me, man?" asked Willard. "I'm only the driver. If Harry has a beef with Ringo fair enough, I've often thought of shooting the bastard myself. He treats me like a piece of shit at times." Willard reached down to the shelf below the dashboard, but his gun wasn't there.

"Nice try, asshole" said Vince. "If you're going to hide a gun, don't hide it in plain sight, I spotted it the minute I got in the car. I also found the knife below the driver's seat, so don't bother even looking."

"Shit!" muttered Willard.

"Look, how does this sound? Ringo has a safe built into the floor of the car, I know the combination and I reckon it contains at least 20 grand. Let me go and I'll open the safe, give you the keys to the motor and you can drive off with Ringo in the boot. No one will ever hear anything about this whole incident from me. I'll give you my word."

"This isn't about money and it isn't personal," said Vince. "You two just happen to find yourselves in a position that's going to help me out of a sticky situation, so stop trying to make deals and just drive."

About a hundred yards from Harry's luxurious mansion, Vince told Willard to pull over.

The car pulled to a stop.

"Listen very carefully, get out the car, walk ten paces and turn round and come back. Try and run and I shoot."

"What the fuck's this all about?" asked Willard.

"Just do it!" said Vince.

Willard did as he was told, just as he turned round Vince shot him through the heart, not an instant kill, he could live up to a minute, he lasted about ten seconds. Vince picked up the body by its feet and dragged it off the pavement to the grass verge where he placed it behind a large shrub. After checking that it couldn't be seen from the road by any passing cars, he continued with his plan.

Leaving the car with his holdall, Vince walked round to Harry's where he pounded his fists on the gate. As he expected Harry's two bodyguards Chas and Dave, who patrolled the grounds every night, came running towards the gates, guns drawn.

"Hey guys, put the guns away. It's me, Vince."

"Hey, Vince! Where the hell have you been buddy? We thought you'd gone AWOL."

As the two men put their guns away, Vince took them both out with a head shot, making sure to wing one in the arm first.

He climbed over the wall and pressed the automatic gate release, then dusted himself down and walked towards the front door. He put on his gloves and rang the bell.

A minute later it was opened by Harry himself who was still up as usual. Another gangster with routines thought Vince.

"Vince, where the fuck have you been?"

Vince raised the holdall.

"Getting your fucking coke back!"

"Excellent work Vince, I didn't doubt you for a minute, come through to the office. By the way, what was that racket out there?"

"That was me, Harry; I had to bang on the gate to get Chas and Dave's attention. I would have phoned but my mobile's knackered."

"Take a seat Vince, help yourself to a drink."

Vince poured himself a large whisky.

"I'll have to get this straight to Aberdeen to keep our clients happy," said Vince.

"The thing is I could do with a bit of cash. I haven't had time to go to the bank."

"A couple of grand do you?"

"That'll be fine."

Harry put in his code and opened the wall safe just as Vince expected.

Vince paced the room to get the distance just right, crouched down behind the leather armchair drew out gun number three and shot Harry right between the eyes as he turned round. He put another round in his left arm as he went down. Vince cleaned out the safe, emptying the contents into the holdall and picked up Harry's gun from the ornate holster at the back, then began to put phase two of his plan into action.

Vince marched Billy Ringo at gunpoint through the gates, past Chas and Dave's bodies, through the door and into Harry's office.

"Get behind the leather seat!"

"What the fuck for?"

"Just do it!" said Vince.

Billy crouched as Vince stood directly over Harry's body.

"Now slowly stand-up."

"You'll fucking shoot me!" said Ringo.

"I'll shoot you through the chair if you don't. This gun is a .44 Magnum, from this short distance the bullet is more than capable of going through the chair, your body and probably the wall behind you as well, so it's your choice. You're a gambling man, stand up and you might live."

Billy Ringo stood up as far as he could until the two bullets entered his body, one through the neck and one between the eyes; the huge exit wounds splattered the life sized portrait of Harry behind him on the wall.

Vince took a few seconds to admire the gun in his hand before wiping it free of his prints.

He sat down took a deep breath and had another whisky.

So far so good, he thought to himself.

Forensics had come on in leaps and bounds in the last few years. The thing was, thanks to the Discovery Channel and things like the CSI franchise, everyone knew how it worked, what it entailed and you could basically learn what not to do if you were a criminal and didn't want to get caught. It all had to do with possible scenarios and how the evidence backed these scenarios up.

Take ballistics, they'd look for who fired what gun and from what distance and angle the shots were fired.

In fact the scenario Vince was about to set up would seem totally plausible. Two well-known drug bosses with a long history of violence and shootings, with the help of their henchmen had taken each other out.

And now, Vince thought to himself, time to set up the evidence.

First he placed the magnum from Harry's safe into Harry's hand and fired a shot off in Billy's direction; this would leave a trace of gunshot residue, telling forensics Harry had shot the weapon, then he walked behind the leather chair and put the gun he'd shot Harry with in Billy Ringo's hand and fired back in Harry's direction, the distance and angle would match up perfectly just as he'd ensured. An obvious shoot out!

Out in the garden he approached Chas and Dave's bodies, swapped Dave's gun with the one he'd used to shoot Willard, removed Willard's body from behind the shrub and placed it on the spot where he himself had originally shot from.

He'd set the second scenario.

Willard had approached the gate, forced Chas at gunpoint to open it then shot him.

Dave heard the shot and came running, Willard winged him and Dave shot him through the heart, just before dying Willard shot Dave dead.

All he had left to do now was to move Ringo's limo nearer to the gate and he was done.

He checked his watch, the whole thing had taken him less than an hour.

Chapter Sixteen

'"Five men were found shot to death in an affluent area of Glasgow last night. Two of the men were believed to be well known rival gang bosses, according to police sources.
Harry Black and Billy Ringo had come under police suspicion on numerous occasions, for illegal importation of drugs. Both are believed, along with known associates, to have been involved in a turf war for some time, which seems to have culminated in last night's shootings in Old Bearsden."'

"Jesus," said Buchanan, "that's a bit of a coincidence, isn't it?"

He and Max were sitting in their hotel having breakfast and watching the regional news.

"What do you mean by that?" asked Max.

"Well let's see, old Harry's drugs go missing. He sends some of his goons through to check on this guy Vince, who remember, works for Harry. Then a few hours later, he's wiped out in a gangland shooting. Why now? It seems that anyone with any connection to Vince at all, no matter how tenuous, ends up fucking dead."

"Could be a coincidence, sir, I mean we are talking about Glasgow, there's always drug gangs shooting the shit out of each other."

"You know me by now Max, I don't believe in coincidences. Now hurry up, finish your coffee. We have to get going; besides I'm going to be lucky today, I'm also going to take up painting and create a masterpiece, and then I'm going to piss off Michelle by forgetting to phone her yet again."

Max choked on his cup of tea.

"What!"

"It says so here," said Buchanan pointing to the daily horoscope in the paper.

"You will have an extremely lucky day today. Your imagination, intuition, and creativity are all high, and inspiration for new artistic works will be filling your heart and head. You'll be happy to discuss your plans with anyone who shows even the slightest interest. The one blot on the day might be that a close friend, or lover becomes rather upset with you because he or she feels forgotten about."

"What a load of horse shit!"

"What does mine say?" asked Max.

"What's your star sign?"

"Pisces."

Buchanan looked at the paper once again.

"Someone in authority will get really peeved today Pisces, by being asked to check on your horoscope. This could result in a swift kick to the nuts. You may also find yourself being financially out of pocket sometime this morning."

Buchanan winked. "Go and buy us a couple of coffees to go, son."

*

"Hello!"

Dave knocked on Vince's door at the Dundee motel.

"Hello Davy boy, how'd you sleep?"

Dave seemed perplexed at Vince's good mood.

"Eh? Pretty good Vince, yourself?"

"Absolutely fucking magnificent, I woke up feeling like all my troubles had been blown away. Here have a bonus."

Vince handed Dave a grand.

"Look at it as an incentive. Let me get dressed and we'll grab a coffee, and remember to take that map with you, its lying on the bed."

A large hard covered book lay open on the bed next to the map.

"What are you reading Vince?" asked Dave.

"Take a look," replied Vince as he put on his tie. Dave looked at the cover.

'The Art of War by Sun Tzu'

On the first page there was a quotation – *"to know your enemy, you must become your enemy."*

"What's it about?" asked Dave, flicking through the pages.

"It's a book on military strategy, written 2500 years ago, some of the strategies are still used by the military today," replied Vince.

"It can't be of much use to civilians though?"

"On the contrary Dave, I've used his teachings on many occasions. It's helped me get out of a few dodgy situations, and his strategies are top notch."

"How so?"

"Think about it, we're villains, villains doing battle with the establishment, you have the police on one side and us on the other, what's that if it's not a war? And you saw the quote on the front of the book, if you put yourself in your enemy's shoes, think like him, pre-empt his moves, it keeps you ahead of the game."

"I've never thought about it like that before."

*

Downstairs in the cafe they unfolded the map of the central belt and circled the various destinations.

They split the list of circled hotels into two loads of four. Vince decided he'd take the ones in Perth, Stirling, Falkirk and Peebles, that left Dave to check Oban, Dunoon and a couple near Largs.

"Before we set off Dave, you'll need a passport photo, there's a machine in the lobby."

"What do I need a photo for?" asked Dave.

"For this!" Vince gave Dave a blank police warrant card, "just fill in your name and stick in your own photo, when you get to the various hotels, just flash the ID, show the desk clerk or whoever, the photos of the guys from Dundee and ask if they're booked in. You could try asking for them by name, but I'm pretty sure they'll have given false ones just in case someone like us comes looking for them. The main thing to remember is to act officious, you have to come across as a cop for this to work."

"What about transport?"

Vince pointed to the window.

"There's a whole car park full out there, take your pick."

*

"Never again," said Liam, as the three Dundonians shuffled through for breakfast looking like extras out of a zombie movie.

"Is tequila supposed to make you blind?" asked Jimmy rubbing his bloodshot eyes.

"Hair of the dog anyone?" said Mark as he produced a bottle of whisky seemingly from thin air.

"I'll have some," said Liam, as he reached for the bottle.

"Where does that expression come from anyway?" asked Jimmy.

"The hair of the dog that bit you, comes from medieval times, when someone was bitten by a rabid dog, they believed a cure could be made by applying the same dog's hair to the infected wound," said Mark.

"So!" said Liam. "You're telling me that back then if you got bitten by a big mad bastard dog, you had to go and find the bloody thing and pull its hair out?"

"That's right," said Mark.

"But the dog wouldn't just sit there, and let you rip out its fur would it, it would fucking bite you again, or eat you!"

"Where do you find out all this shit, Mark?" asked Jimmy.

"The Discovery Channel," answered Mark. "Watch it a lot, all day sometimes."

"How much cash are we looking at now, Jimmy?" asked Liam.

"A hundred and twenty eight grand, at least it was first thing this morning."

"I wish it was all over," said Mark.

"It soon will be. Now come on let's eat, then we can get to the outdoor shop and get some gear organised for our walk. It'll take our mind off things for a while."

116

In the incident room everyone was gathered around the television watching the replay of the report of the Glasgow shootings that Buchanan had watched at the hotel earlier.

"Bit of a coincidence Ronnie, what you think?"

"Exactly what I said to Max, in fact it wouldn't surprise me if Vince was behind it."

"Don't take this the wrong way Ronnie, but are you not getting a bit obsessed with this guy. According to the latest report the forensics all stand up, there's no sign of any one else being involved," said the DCI.

"Hear me out, John. We know Vince is trying to track down this missing coke, I'm sure he'll know about the auction and I've no doubt he'll make sure he wins it. When he gets it back, which I'm sure he will, I reckon he's going to keep it for himself. Think about it, with Harry Black dead, who's going to stop him? Remember, this coke is uncut, by the time he cuts it and splits it up into smaller amounts you're talking about a helluva lot of money."

"But don't forget Ronnie, it's going to cost him to get it back," said Brannigan.

"Are you kidding me? You think someone like him has any intention whatsoever of handing over any money?"

"He'll turn up to the drop, take his coke and blow the fuckers away, period!"

"So our job now is to find these guys before he does, I don't know how but we have to try."

"Sir, you have to see this," said DI McLean as he handed Brannigan the e-mail he'd received from Dundee.

"Shit!" said Brannigan.

"What is it, John?" asked Buchanan.

"They have given us an ID on the two guys from the Road Chef, but when the officer in Dundee looked up their records they noticed someone else had accessed it yesterday, and get this, whoever did it used the login details of a guy who retired months ago."

"Looks like someone at Tayside Division is taking a backhander," said Buchanan.

DCI Brannigan handed the e-mail back to McLean. "Make sure their names and photographs go in the papers as soon as possible. If you hurry up, it might make this afternoon's locals."

"Right away sir," said the DI.

"Do you still want us on the case, John?" asked Buchanan.

"What do you mean, Ronnie?"

"Well, we have Terry for the two girls' murders. I know he says it was down to the other guy, but all the evidence points to him. We have more than enough for a conviction."

"I want you here till this is sewn up, as far as I'm concerned that's not until we have Terry's partner and this Vince guy in custody."

"That's fine by me, John."

"There's not much for you to do at the moment though, not until the names and photos of those two toe-rags go out. But there is another matter you could help me with, totally unrelated to the case."

"Anything you want."

"There's a fancy restaurant up the High Street and the owner has got it into his head that someone in his kitchen staff has stolen a family heirloom off him."

"What sort of heirloom?"

"His grandfather's watch, he says he took it off this morning to wash his hands, turned his back to dry them, and when he looked back it was gone."

"Surely a Constable could see to that?" said Buchanan.

"Normally yes, but this just so happens to be a favourite eatery of the Superintendent. He's very friendly with the owner."

"Enough said, I'll get right on to it, I'll take Max."

*

Driving up the High Street, Max carefully dodged the pedestrians milling about everywhere and pulled over next to the restaurant where a man was anxiously waiting for them at the door. They both got out the car and Buchanan approached the man.

"I take it you're the owner, Mr...?"

"Abercrombie, Brian Abercrombie."

Buchanan shook his hand.

"I'm DI Buchanan and this is DS Maxwell."

"Well Brian, any chance of a couple of coffees?"

"Sure, come right in."

They sat down in the empty restaurant at a huge table with their coffee.

"Was anyone else in the building this morning apart from yourself and the kitchen staff?" asked Max.

"No one, we don't open until twelve, so there were no customers."

"Is it worth a lot, this watch of yours?"

"It's an antique, belonged to my grandfather, worth about twelve grand."

Buchanan whistled.

"How many staff do you have in the kitchen?"

"Twelve. Seven full time and five part-time."

"Any of them happen to be women?" asked Buchanan.

"Two."

"Get them to send over a female PC will you, Max?"

Max picked up his mobile.

"Right away, sir!"

"Has anyone left the building since the watch disappeared?" asked Buchanan.

"No one, it only happened about an hour ago. I thought it had maybe fallen down the back of the sink so I moved everything out and had a thorough look and that's when I phoned Henry."

"That would be Superintendent Henry Wilson?" said Buchanan.

"Yes, he's an old friend of mine, has been for years."

"Could you show us the kitchen, please?"

The kitchen was a hive of activity and felt like a sauna, the heat and steam coming from the various pots and pans bubbling away on the three huge stainless steel hobs. Someone opened an oven door as Buchanan passed by, the hot air singeing his eyebrows. "Jesus, be careful with that you almost roasted me alive."

"Sorry pal," said the guy in the white overalls slamming the door shut with a bit too much force.

The noise in the kitchen was deafening, food sizzled, kitchen utensils clattered as they were discarded into the sink, and everyone seemed to be shouting to be heard above the din. He watched as an angry man he presumed was the Chef, gave a younger guy a bollocking for not adding enough garlic to some sauce or other. He had an accent Buchanan couldn't quite place. In fact they all seemed so engrossed in their activities that no one seemed to realise he was there. He felt invisible.

He needed to grab their attention.

"Excuse me!" He bellowed as he bashed a metal meat tenderiser against a wooden chopping board like some demented judge with a gavel.

Max covered both ears and laughed just as the WPC arrived wondering what the hell was going on.

They all stopped what they were doing and looked his way, all except the Chef. He threw a strop. He flung a huge ladle against the wall, put his hands on his hips dramatically and headed towards Buchanan.

"Who are you to interrupt things in my kitchen?"

Buchanan held up his ID.

"Police! Can I please have everyone's attention?"

They all gathered round the three officers.

"Morning, folks, my name's DI Buchanan and this is DS Maxwell and WPC…?"

"Mirth," replied the woman.

Funny name, thought Buchanan as he laughed inwardly.

"We have reason to believe a crime has been committed on the premises and we'd like you to participate in a voluntary search. I say voluntary but anyone who refuses will be taken from here and searched at the station."

There were a few mumbles and grunts but everyone agreed.

They were asked to empty their pockets, and one by one they were searched.

There was no sign of the watch.

"You were obviously mistaken, sir" said Buchanan. "No one here seems to have your watch." He lowered his voice and whispered to the owner. "Could I have a word with you next door?"

Buchanan and the owner moved through to the office.

"I want you to do something for me, sir. Five minutes after we leave, I want you to set off the fire alarm then go into the kitchen and tell them the building's ablaze."

"Whatever for?"

"Just humour me; it might get you your watch back."

"Very well then," said Brian. "I'll do it."

Buchanan and the other two officers left the restaurant.

"C'mon you two, cross the street."

"What for?" asked Max.

"Watch and learn!" said Buchanan.

They watched from across the street as the alarm went off, the staff were piling out the restaurant.

"Follow me!" said Buchanan as he returned to the restaurant.

He walked straight up to the member of staff who came out last.

"Search his pockets, Max."

Max did as he was asked and removed the watch.

Buchanan turned to the owner. "Do you want to press charges sir? Or are you just going to sack the thieving bastard?"

"You have five minutes to get your stuff out my restaurant, you're fired," said the owner to the thief.

"How can I ever repay you, Inspector?" asked Brian.

Buchanan rubbed his chin. "You could stand me a free meal, me and a few other officers?"

"Anytime at all, just let me know."

Back in the car Max looked at Buchanan.

"What the hell just happened there, sir?"

"Simple," said Buchanan, "whoever stole the watch wasn't going to just leave it wherever he'd hidden it, when he thought the building was on fire, now was he son."

"But how did you know who had it?"

"Obviously the last person out had it. Whoever stole the watch had to stash it somewhere, right?"

"With you so far," said Max.

"Well they couldn't risk being seen by anyone else in the kitchen when they went to retrieve it, so they had to hang back till the kitchen was empty. Hence, they were last out."

"Brilliant!" said Max as he swerved to avoid the approaching fire engines.

"Shit!" said Buchanan, "Maybe I should have told him to take his monitoring off line before I got him to set off the alarm."

Chapter Seventeen

Jimmy parked the car at the west end of Peebles High Street, next to an old church. They got out one by one and checked they had everything they needed.

"We got enough beer?" asked Liam.

"Plenty!" replied Jimmy. "It's all in Mark's backpack."

"Aye and it weighs a fucking ton!" said Mark. "I'll be knackered in half an hour, anyway how come I've got all the heavy stuff?"

"Don't worry about it. We'll all take a turn carrying it" said Liam, "in fact I'll lighten the load now, give us a can."

"I'll have one too," said Jimmy.

Mark took off his backpack, set it down on the grass and took out three cans of lager, handing two of them to his friends.

"I hope the coke and the cash is safe in your backpack, Jimmy?" said Liam.

"Perfectly safe, that's why I bought the one with the built in padlock; no way is anything falling out of this baby."

Cans in hand, they turned right onto the path and started their long walk uphill.

A few miles further along, the path split into three.

"Where do we go now Mark?" asked Liam.

Mark studied the map.

"Depends how steep you want to go?"

"Steeper the better, what do you think Jimmy?"

"I'm cool with that."

"We go right then, towards that hill," said Mark pointing off to a fog covered mass in the distance.

An hour later, halfway up the hill they stopped for a rest.

"Skin up Jimmy," said Liam.

Jimmy opened the side pocket of his backpack and took out the best part of an ounce of grass and a packet of king-size cigarette papers.

"What are we going to do for weed when we get to Spain?" asked Mark.

"Not a problem, Uncle Frank gets a few ounces sent over from Morocco every month, I'm sure he can spare some."

"Is he really your uncle?" asked Liam.

"I'm not sure to be honest," said Jimmy. "He's been there at family gatherings for years and everyone just seems to call him Uncle Frank."

Mark passed on the joint and then removed three walking poles that had been hanging from the side of his backpack.

"What the fuck did you buy them for?" asked Liam.

"Protection, check this out."

He removed the plastic covers from the bottom of the poles revealing the blunt spikes.

"Think about it," he said. "Three guys walking about in the middle of nowhere with a shit load of coke on them. What are we supposed to do if we have to protect ourselves?"

"It's not the Wild West," said Jimmy. "We're not likely to get attacked by bandits now are we?"

Liam laughed, almost choking on the smoke.

"Well I like to be prepared for whatever sort of shit fate throws at us."

"Let me see one of them poles?" said Liam.

"They're not exactly sharp, though, are they?"

"Ah! But check this out!"

Mark removed an object from his pocket.

"What's that now?" asked Liam.

"A knife sharpener, I got it from the same shop, watch!"

Liam and Jimmy watched as Mark beavered away sharpening the spike at the end of the pole.

A couple of minutes later he had a spear.

"Feel the point now," he said handing it to Liam.

"Jesus, that's sharp right enough."

An apple suddenly appeared in Mark's hand.

"Put this on your head Liam, see if I can spear it off."

"Fuck that!" replied Liam.

He turned to Jimmy. "How about you?"

"No danger! I'm quite attached to my head."

"Oh well, I suppose a rock will have to do then."

Mark wandered over to a waist high rock and put the apple on top.
He walked back ten paces and threw the walking pole at the apple.
It hit its target dead centre, a shot William Tell would have been proud of.

The other two clapped in unison.

"Nice throw Mark!" said Jimmy. "If we run out of food perhaps you could go hunt us some rabbits."

"Chuck me over the sharpener thing," said Liam. "I'm going to spear up my walking pole as well."

After sharing another joint and drinking another beer, they picked up their backpacks and headed further up the hill.

*

Dave pulled into the car park of the Lumsden Hotel in Dunoon, the second hotel on his list.

He walked through the foyer and approached the desk; he flashed his ID and gave the same spiel as he had in the last hotel.

"I wonder if you could help me, sir, I'm DI Duncan from Lothian and Borders Police could you tell me if you recognise these two men?"

"They don't ring any bells" he said from behind the front desk, "but you could always ask Mike the Barman, he never forgets a face."

"Where is the bar?"

"Just go along the corridor, it's the first on your left."

Dave headed for the bar, where he found Mike wiping down the tables. He showed him the photos, again to no avail.

"You staying for a drink?" asked Mike.

"Why not" said Dave. "I'll have a pint of Lager."

Dave helped himself to the day's newspaper from the rack on the wall and settled down to his pint at a table in the corner.

He unfolded the paper and looked at the front page headline, *'GLASGOW GANGLAND SHOOTOUT!'* He recognised the name Harry Black as soon as he read it.

Vince wasn't aware that Dave knew he worked for Harry, Terry had mentioned the name one day and Dave had done a bit of digging. It wasn't exactly hard work, a quick search online and he'd found numerous mentions of his suspected links to drug trafficking. By all accounts he'd been quite a scary guy, but now he was a dead scary guy, meaning that if Vince got the drugs back he was now answerable to no one. He could even sell them on himself if he wanted to, with no repercussions whatsoever.

Dave chuckled to himself.

No wonder he was in a good mood this morning, he must have seen the paper earlier.

Looking at his watch, Dave realised he was making good time.

Fuck it: he thought, I'll have another pint, but first I'd better contact Vince.

He took out his mobile and sent a text.

"-Hotel no2 no luck-"

*

"-I'm not doing any better hope you have more luck with no 3-"
Vince sent the message, put his phone away and got out of the car. He'd had no luck himself in Perth or Stirling, but before the next hotel on his list he'd decided to take a detour to Dunfermline to look up an old friend, who could possibly help give him an edge with winning the auction.

*

"Hi Vince, long time no see."

Vince sat down in the centre of a room that he always thought would be more at home in NASA than a small semi in Dunfermline.

It was filled wall to wall with computers, external hard drives, laptops and other IT equipment that he couldn't even hazard a guess as to what they were used for.

"I have a job for you Nico, something that needs your particular talents."

Vince told him about the auction and how he had to win it.

"A coke auction eh! That's a new one, but winning shouldn't be a problem, I'll just modify a sniping programme."

"What the hell is sniping?" asked Vince.

"What is sniping? It's bidding in an online auction at the last moment before the auction ends, usually you set a maximum bid but with a few adaptations, I can overwrite that thus making sure your bid kicks in at the last millisecond just slightly higher than the one before."

"Sounds like just what I need, I'll give you the web address and the password and leave it in your capable hands. That ok?"

"Fine, I'll get right on it."

"Here, this is for you." Vince left a bundle of cash on the chair on the way out.

"I'll be in touch."

Vince returned to his car and set off for Falkirk.

*

"I'm knackered," said Liam. "How much further have we got to go?"

Mark looked at the map.

"It's fucking miles. It does say here though that the walk can be split into two halves, the first part ending at Stobo."

"Stobo, what sort of a name's that for a place?" said Liam.

"Does it have a pub?"

"One or two, why?" asked Mark.

"Because it looks like it's going to rain and I'm fucking starving.

What do you think, Jimmy?"

"Sounds good to me."

"Right, pub lunch it is then," said Liam as they carried on towards Stobo under the grey cloud covered sky.

*

Vince approached the last place on his list, the Castle Hotel in Peebles. He drove up the driveway and parked his car in the tree covered court yard.

He walked through the entrance hall and approached the check-in desk.

As on the last three occasions, he produced Liam and Mark's photos and asked if they were staying there.

This time he struck gold.

They had arrived the day before with another guy, and they were posing as three young business men who, according to the desk clerk, "were dressed in expensive suits and spending money like water."

"Do you know if they're in the hotel at the moment?" asked Vince.

"I'm afraid not Inspector, they said they'd be out sightseeing all day, they did ask me to book them a table at the restaurant for later this evening though, so they are intending on coming back before seven thirty."

"Could you let me into their room?"

"I shouldn't really, but if you could show me some ID, I'll give you the key."

"Certainly!" said Vince, "here you go."

The clerk took a good long look back and forth between the ID and Vince and then handed him the key.

"Here you are, second floor, suite 2B."

"Thanks!" said Vince.

The suite was huge; he stepped into a large lounge area with two bedrooms off to either side, one with a huge four poster bed, the other with two singles.

They must have enjoyed themselves the night before judging by

128

the empty beer cans and the three quarter finished bottle of tequila.

He decided to check the smaller of the two bedrooms first.

In the closet he found a strange mixture of clothes, a couple of pairs of cheap jeans, some grubby t-shirts and a couple of very expensive designer suits.

 That's strange, thought Vince.

In the larger of the two bedrooms he found something far more interesting. Next to the four- poster bed on a cabinet sat a laptop, Vince fired it up.

And there it was, the confirmation he'd been looking for, in the surfing history he found a link to the auction site.

"Bingo!" Vince said aloud.

He phoned Dave.

"Where are you?"

"Just approaching the third hotel at Largs, no luck so far I'm afraid."

"Don't bother, I've found them, at least I've found where they're staying. Meet me at the Castle Hotel in Peebles. If you put your foot down you could make it in just over an hour. I'll be in the restaurant."

"Nice one Vince, I'll see you there, in under an hour."

After asking the clerk to inform him when the three guys came back Vince headed for the restaurant, he picked a table where he had a good view of the door.

"Can I take your order, sir?"

"Do you mind if I just order a bottle off your wine list, I'm expecting company and they've been delayed."

"Not at all, sir, I'll go get you the list."

About an hour later, true to his word Dave appeared.

"Grab a seat," said Vince.

Dave sat down. "Any sign of them yet?"

"Not so far, no, but it's definitely them without a doubt. I found a link to the auction on their laptop."

"No sign of the coke I take it?"

"That would be too easy; they've either stashed it, or taken it with them."

"Did you hear about the Glasgow shootings?" asked Dave.

"Yes I did, I heard it on the news."

"You knew Harry Black didn't you?"

"Now why would you want to know that?"

"I'm just making conversation, Vince."

The waitress came over and took their orders, two steaks medium rare with all the works.

Vince ordered another bottle of wine and filled both their glasses.

"I more than knew Harry Black, Dave. For the last few years I've been a major part of his operations. In fact Harry owns the coke, or at least he did."

"How much is the four kilos worth?" asked Dave.

"Fucking loads, it's uncut so maybe two hundred grand as it stands. Once its cut however, and remembering your average purity on the street is about ten to twelve per cent, although I usually leave it about twelve, well, you can work it out for yourself."

"Jesus, you're talking about over a million quid!"

"Yep, a cool million, and once I sell it, I'm off."

"What do you mean off?" asked Dave.

"Off abroad, I have various interests set up in Spain, all legitimate. I'm giving all this playing outside the law shit a break. I've been lucky over the years Dave, but luck doesn't last forever, so I'm getting out."

"Well I for one will miss you Vince although, if I'm being honest, I'll miss the work, the pay's good."

"It'll be even better this time, you make sure we get the stuff back and I'll pay you an extra hundred grand."

"A hundred grand huh, I might think about going straight myself!"

"You should, you're relatively young, you could start your own business somewhere, put the money to good use."

*

In a quiet pub in Stobo, the three guys from Dundee sat down to their steak pie and chips.

"Another pint?" asked Jimmy.

The other two nodded.

"Not a bad pub this," said Jimmy. "Nice atmosphere."

"Nice food," said Liam. "It's true what they say eh, fresh air and exercise make you hungry."

"Aye, especially after half a dozen cans and a couple of joints!"

"Too true" said Mark. "I've got a proper case of the munchies."

"What we doing next, Jimmy?" asked Liam downing the last of his pint.

"A couple more pints then a taxi back to the hotel, I think."

"Suits me," replied Liam. "What do you think Mark?"

"I quite fancied this!" He showed them a page from the brochure he'd picked up at the hotel.

"There's a health spa not far from here."

Liam and Jimmy looked at the brochure.

"Full body Swedish massage, to ease tension and sooth tired muscles."

Liam rubbed his hands together.

"Now you're talking. I could go for a busty Swedish bird oiling and massaging me all over!"

"Hold on a minute" said Jimmy, "what makes you think she'll be Swedish? Come to think of it what makes you think it'll even be a woman?"

"It says it right there, Swedish massage, look!"

"That doesn't mean the person doing the massage is a Swede, you twat. It means it's a particular type of massage that evolved in Sweden and nowhere in the brochure does it mention the person doing the massaging being female, it could be some big buff guy called Nigel."

Liam made a strange face.

"I'll phone and check first then, just to make sure."

Jimmy laughed.

"How's that going to go then?"

"Hello I'd like to book a massage please, but only if it's done by a Swedish bird and only if her bust size is 36DD."

Jimmy carried Mark and Liam's drinks back to the table and went back for his own, stopping to pick up the discarded local paper lying on the bar.

He sat down and casually flicked through it and froze.

"Holy shit!"

"What's wrong man, you look like you're having a stroke?"

"Listen very carefully, both of you put up your hoods, leave the drinks, and follow me pronto!"

"What the fuck is this all about?" asked Liam.

"Just fucking follow me will you, I'll show you outside."

Outside the pub they both looked over Jimmy's shoulder to see their own faces staring back at them from the paper with the caption,

'POLICE SEEK MEN FOR QUESTIONING RELATING TO STUDENTS' MURDERS!'

"Murder!" said Liam. "What the fuck are they talking about?"

"It says here you were caught on camera at the Road Chef, the same time as one of the victims."

"Shit, look at the photo below" said Mark. "It's her, don't you see, the lassie whose car we got the coke from."

Chapter Eighteen

"What you planning on doing with your cash, Larry?" asked the man in the driver's seat of the Ford Focus.

"I'm not sure Tam, I'm going to pay off the rest of my mortgage with some of it, but as for the rest of it, God knows. How about you, any plans?"

"It depends how much we get, but hopefully it'll be enough to buy a boat."

"What sort of boat?"

Tam removed a crumpled up page from a magazine from his pocket and showed it to Larry.

"This boat, it's the Quicksilver 580 Pilothouse. Standard equipment includes engine instruments, hydraulic steering, bilge pump, electric anchor windlass, navigation lights, boarding ladder, rod holders, picnic table, cooker, and it even has a chemical toilet. I'm right into my fishing and that's the perfect boat for me."

"How much would that set you back then?"

"It costs just under twenty five grand!"

"By my calculations we should be getting about ten times that amount, now put the picture down and let's go to work."

The two men pulled on their balaclavas as they watched the cash delivery van pull to a stop outside the bank in St Andrews Square. The delivery man entered the bank while the driver, totally against company protocol opened the door slightly to have a cigarette.

This was what the two robbers were waiting for, they'd observed him doing this on several occasions and that was what had given them the idea for the heist.

Creeping around to the driver's side door, robber number one pushed the double barrelled shotgun through the gap in the door and held up the sheet of cardboard to the windscreen.

The shocked driver, dropping the half-finished cigarette at his feet, read the words crudely written in black marker pen. '*You have two seconds to open all the doors or you're dead!*'

Panicking, the stunned driver complied and the second robber, also equipped with a weapon, grabbed the strongboxes from the back of the van.

They jumped in their vehicle and took off at high speed watched by the many shocked pedestrians going about their daily business. The whole incident took two minutes from start to finish and even though the silent alarm had been triggered, the robbers were well away from the city centre before the first of the police vehicles arrived at the scene.

Half an hour later they'd arrived at the secluded derelict farmhouse, blown open the security boxes, and split the money between them. Their ill-gotten gains amounted to just over two hundred grand each, not bad for two minutes work. Putting their cut into their holdalls, they bid each other farewell, jumped in their cars and drove off in opposite directions.

*

Dreaming of what he was going to do with his newly acquired wealth Tam took his eyes off the road for two seconds to change a CD and looked up just in time to see the deer, which had appeared out of nowhere, directly in front of him on the road. "Jesus!" he said aloud as he tried to avoid it. He could have swerved either right or left. Unfortunately he chose left, a very bad choice, which he would regret for the rest of his life. All ten seconds of it! He veered down the steep embankment at high speed cutting through the two foot high weeds interspersed with foxgloves and crashed into a huge oak tree, killing himself and a bemused looking squirrel stone dead.

Buchanan was in the incident room when the call came in. The two men from Dundee had been spotted at a hotel in Peebles. The caller, who had himself been a resident there, had seen them the night before in the restaurant.

He left the room to be met by what could only be described as pandemonium, people were running in all directions and raised voices could be heard throughout the building.

He stopped a young Constable mid run.

"What's all the commotion about, son?"

"There's been a robbery, a security van in St Andrews Square. It's all hands on deck!"

Then he saw a red faced DCI Brannigan coming towards him.

"I heard we got a sighting of the two Dundee guys," he said, in between heavy breaths.

"Yes, it's what I was coming to see you about," said Buchanan.

"You and Max will have to take care of it Ronnie, we're up to our necks in it here."

"No problem, you seem to have your hands full here, so we'll get on to it and leave you to your robbery investigation. Good luck!"

*

"I'm soaked to the bone," said Liam.

After a rain drenched discussion outside the pub Jimmy, Liam and Mark had decided it wouldn't be safe to return to the hotel, so they'd looked under accommodation in the newspaper and found a small out of the way B&B. The plan was to rent a couple of rooms with Jimmy doing all the talking, while Liam and Mark kept themselves hidden under their hoods. They all stood outside shivering as Jimmy knocked at the heavy wooden door of the old whitewashed farm house. The rain fell like mini waterfalls through the cracks in the guttering above their heads, soaking them even more. He turned to his friends.

"Remember keep your faces hidden, you two, and don't make eye contact."

They heard a slow shuffling from the other side followed by the sound of the huge door being unlocked.

"Can I help you?" said the old woman, wiping her flour covered hands on a flour covered apron.

"Do you have any rooms free?" asked Jimmy.

"I only have two rooms but I don't usually let them out this time of year."

"How much do you normally charge?"

"Twenty five for the single, forty for the double, per night."

"We'll pay you double if you put us up, it'll only be for two nights?"

The old woman pondered on this for a moment.

Could she trust these guys, her son was off working and she was on her own, but she desperately needed the money.

"It's a deal, but only if you pay upfront. Come away in and dry yourselves off; I'll just go and get you some towels. I will give you the tour later."

After wiping the mud from their boots, on the worn welcome mat, they entered the old farmhouse, appreciative of somewhere warm and dry.

The lounge of the farmhouse was massive, the walls panelled in wood with a blazing coal fire against the far wall. The ceiling had a large wooden cross beam and the furniture consisted of four solid wood bookcases full of leather bound books, a large coffee table, a few old but comfy looking armchairs and a huge settee.

They all removed their backpacks and jackets and gathered round the fire to dry themselves off. The smell of home baking hung in the air giving the place a real homely feel. Holding his hands near the flames Jimmy turned his head towards the old woman.

"Do you run this place yourself Mrs…?"

"Anderson, call me Elsie, and yes just me on my own mostly, my son helps out now and again. Would you like a coffee and some homemade bread? I've just made a batch."

"Yes, we'd love some!" said Jimmy.

"One of you give me a hand then. I've misplaced my glasses you see, I've been looking for them all day."

"You mean you can't see anything?" asked Liam.

"Oh I can see all right just certain things are a bit of a blur like reading, watching the telly and suchlike."

"Mark, go and give her a hand," said Jimmy.

Mark followed Elsie in to the Kitchen, drying his hair with the towel as he went.

"This is fucking perfect!" said Jimmy. "The old bat can't possibly identify you and Mark. She can't see properly, help me find her glasses, we'll keep them hidden for the next couple of days."

Frantically searching the room they eventually found them down the side of a beaten up old armchair, Jimmy stuck them in the side pocket of his backpack just as Mark and Elsie arrived with the coffees and the still warm buttered bread.

"That smells gorgeous," said Liam, "you got any cheese spread?"

Elsie came back from the kitchen with a large tub of cheese spread and three knives.

"It makes a nice change to have a bit of company this time of year," said Elsie. "What are you boys doing up this way anyway, if you don't mind me asking?"

"A bit of hill walking, maybe some sightseeing" said Liam. "I see you have Satellite TV. Do you mind if we put the telly on?"

"Go ahead," said Elsie. "Now what would you like for your tea, I do a nice steak pie?"

"That sounds great," said Jimmy. "Eh guys?"

"Perfect!" they both replied.

"It'll take a wee while to cook but there's some beer in the fridge while you're waiting, help yourself."

"Are you having one, Elsie?" asked Liam who had decided to forego his coffee and went to get the beers.

"Oh go on then, just the one, I'll show you where they are."

In the kitchen Liam went to open the fridge.

"No! Not there, here!" Elsie opened a walk-in fridge; it was lined wall to wall with every beer imaginable.

"Jesus, where'd you get all the beer?"

"My son Gerald, he loves his beer, pity you couldn't have met him.

He left yesterday for Aberdeen, he works off shore you see. Now you go through and watch the telly with your friends, and I'll get the steak pie started."

"Fucking steak pie again!" said Liam.

"You can't have too much steak pie," replied Jimmy, "besides she obviously likes making them, so just let her get on with it."

"This coal fire's great though," said Mark. "They're a bastard to light in the morning though, I mind we used to have one at home. My dad used to get up early and screw up the pages from an old newspaper to get it started."

"What's that smell coming from it?" asked Jimmy. Mark picked up the poker and pointed to a smouldering lump on the fire. "That's peat, we used to burn it at home, it burns for ages. I love the smell, some folk don't, it's a bit like marmite I suppose."

"What do you guys fancy watching?" said Liam. "She's got the whole package here, sports, movies and everything!"

"Have a flick through the movie channels, see what you can find," said Jimmy.

"Would you fucking believe it" said Liam. "Look what's on in ten minutes."

They all looked at the TV.

"The Thirty Nine Steps!"

Chapter Nineteen

From his vantage point in the restaurant Vince sipped his glass of red wine and watched as the two men entered the hotel. He saw the older one in the crumpled suit flash some kind of ID. After conversing with the desk clerk, he looked through the glass panel in the restaurant door and then made a call on his mobile phone.

When the desk clerk told Buchanan that there were already two cops on the premises, he had an idea it could be them. How they had found out the guys from Dundee were staying here though, that dumbfounded him. A quick glance through and he saw them, they looked slightly different but going on the information supplied by Terry, he knew there was a good chance that this could be Vince and Dave albeit in disguise. Anyway the one whom he assumed to be Vince was the right height. Even though he was sitting down Buchanan could tell he was over six feet tall.

He took out his mobile.

"This is DI Buchanan, we need back up. Two suspects wanted in connection with the Edinburgh murders are at the Castle Hotel in Peebles, at least one of them I believe to be armed."

"What do we do now, sir?" asked Max.

"Well, I don't know about you Max, but I could do with a pint?"

"Sir, shouldn't we wait for the backup to arrive first?"

"Don't panic son, we'll just go in and keep them occupied until the other officers arrive."

Buchanan strolled through to the restaurant bar and ordered a Guinness.

"Do you want a lager, Max?"

Max nodded nervously. Buchanan paid for the drinks and walked over to Vince's table.

"Mind if we join you?" asked Buchanan.

"Make yourself at home," said Vince, "but first, you could do me a big favour?"

"And what would that be?"

"Call off the backup!"

"I have no idea what you're talking about."

"Let's see, you arrived here looking for two guys from Dundee, the desk clerk told you there were already two detectives here, after the same thing, obviously bogus ones you thought to yourself, so you had a quick look and couldn't believe your luck when you realised we could be the two guys that Terry told you about. But they look so different you thought, but then again, thanks to Terry you know about my penchant for disguises, so you called for backup and came through here to await the cavalry."

"How the fuck do you know that?" asked Max.

"I had my suspicions which you have just confirmed, Bright Boy!"

Max was about to rise off his seat but Buchanan held him down.

"Ok smart arse," said Buchanan, "say that's true, why would I call them off?"

"Mm, let's see, maybe because of the silenced firearm I have under the table pointed at your groin."

"You're bluffing!" said Buchanan.

As he bent down to look under the table he saw the hand gun, sat up and stared at Vince and grudgingly, he took out his mobile to make the call.

"On speakerphone if you don't mind!" said Vince.

Buchanan hit the speaker button on his phone.

"This is DI Buchanan, call off the troops, it's not the two men were looking for, my mistake."

"Now turn off the phone and give it to me," said Vince.

"You too, Bright Boy!"

"Sergeant Maxwell to you, shit head."

"You can get these back when we leave," said Vince.

"What now?" asked Buchanan.

"A round of drinks I think, get them in Dave."

Dave went to the bar.

"So how did you know the two guys were staying here, Vince?"

"I don't see any problem with telling you that. They left a holiday brochure behind, with a few hotels circled, eight actually, so we just checked them all until bingo, and we found ourselves here. By the way it's three guys, they have someone with them. How about you, what led you here?"

"CCTV footage from the Road Chef, we put their faces in the press and got a tip off."

Dave came back with the drinks.

"So Vince, how does it feel to order the deaths of two young women?" asked Buchanan.

"No one asked Terry to do that, he did it off his own back."

Buchanan turned towards Dave.

"What about you? We know you were there at the flat in Edinburgh when one of them was tortured and killed, and I'd put money on you being the driver that drove Terry from the murder scene up in Aberdeen. That makes you an accessory to two counts of murder."

"I never knew he was going to kill them, you can't pin anything on me."

"Let's change the subject eh?" said Vince. "All this talk of killing is giving me indigestion and I don't have any antacids on me. Besides you have Terry and if you checked his room, which I'm sure you did, you have all the evidence you need for a conviction. In fact the only witness to Dave even being there is Terry. Who's going to believe him?"

"Aye your right enough, I suppose, but, we have the prints of course."

"What fucking prints?" asked Dave.

Buchanan leaned over the table.

"The partials you left at both crime scenes, in fact make that three crime scenes, I'm including the murder in Summerhill last year!"

"Shit!" said Dave. "You're bluffing, you can't place me at any of those, and anyway, even if I was there I make it a rule to always wear my gloves."

"Well maybe you ought to buy a new pair because either they have a split seam or a hole in the index finger of the left one."

"Give me your gloves!" said Vince.

He examined the left one.

"He's right you know, Dave. Very impressive Inspector, you remind me of a dog I once owned, a terrier, he'd never give up on anything once he got his teeth into it. I'm not sure I like having someone like you on my case."

Vince unzipped the holdall at his side of the table and took out two bundles of what used to be Harry Black's cash.

"I take it a bribe's out of the question? There's a hundred grand there, it's yours if you take yourself off the case. What do you say? Just blame it on personal reasons and get yourself and Bright Boy here out my face."

"Tempting as that is, I think I'll pass if you don't mind," said Buchanan.

"Well, you can't blame a guy for trying!"

"You better hang on to it anyway," said Buchanan. "You'll need it to buy back your coke. I hear it's your coke that's up for auction. How are you going to ensure you win the bidding war anyway?"

"So, you know about the coke too, you got that piece of information from Terry I've no doubt."

"Terry's a mine of information. He wanted protection you know, protection from Harry Black, he named him as your boss, said he overheard you two talking on the phone, but that doesn't matter much now does it, not since you took care of him."

"Now your fishing, Inspector, I was in Dundee when that went down, ask Dave here."

"Barking up the wrong tree there, asshole," said Dave.

"Anyway," said Vince, "the police aren't looking for anyone; it was the outcome of a turf war, pure and simple."

"You benefit from it more than most though, don't you?" said Buchanan. "After all if you do get the coke back, it's as good as yours, dead man's coke."

Vince laughed.

"You have a way with words, dead man's coke, I like that!"

"Well as much as I've enjoyed our little conversation, it's time for us to go, Inspector. Give us a couple of minutes or else I might change my mind and shoot you on the way out."

Vince and Dave left the restaurant.

A couple of minutes later Buchanan was in the car park just in time to see the black car leaving. He took a mental note of the registration, got in his own car with Max and began to follow the car in front.

"Not too close Max, this Vince is a clever bastard; he'll be looking for us."

*

They had followed Vince's car through the High Street in Peebles and were now heading on to the Edinburgh Road.

"Do you think he knows we're following him, sir?" asked Max.

"I doubt it. He doesn't know what car we're driving and besides anyone using this road is more than likely heading for Edinburgh, the same place he's heading probably so there's no reason for him to get suspicious."

"Not much scenery around here though," said Max. "Fields, sheep, and the odd tree and that's it."

"It is pretty desolate right enough," replied Buchanan. "Mind you my dog would have a field day, pardon the pun."

"How do you mean?" asked Max.

"He's a sheep dog Max. In fact he was born not too far from here. He's a proper Border Collie. He came from a long line of champion working dogs. Michelle got him from her Uncle's Farm.

"What's he called?" asked Max.

"Sam," replied Buchanan. "I toyed with the idea of calling him Guinness, on account of him being black and white but Michelle would have none of it."

Max laughed.

"They're very intelligent as well, the world's smartest dogs, they say they can learn and fully understand over a thousand words. If

I mention the word 'out' while I'm talking to Michelle, his ears prick up and he runs for his lead and I usually end up running for my coat and taking him out for a walk. We tried spelling it, O, U, T but he still understood.

"That's amazing, a dog that can spell, wow," said Max, slowly losing the will to live.

As they headed onto the motorway Buchanan was still awaiting the arrival of the Armed Response Vehicle. He'd phoned in their pursuit earlier and given them his position but there was still no sign of backup.

An Armed Response Vehicle, or ARV, is a type of police car used by the UK police which is crewed by Authorised Firearms Officers to respond to incidents involving firearms or other high risk situations, and Vince was a high risk situation. The car ahead suddenly started picking up speed.

"Shit, looks like we've been spotted; put your foot down, Max."

Max weaved in and out the traffic at high speed trying to keep up with Vince, but his car was too powerful and he started pulling ahead.

"Don't let him get away, Max."

"I'm almost at top speed, sir."

"Almost isn't good enough, boot her up man!"

The engine roared as Max squeezed every bit of power out of the car as he could.

"Watch out!" screamed Buchanan.

"Oops!" said Max as he knocked off the wing mirror of an expensive looking sports car, the driver expressing his fury by continually flashing his headlights.

"I wonder how much a Ferrari's wing mirror costs?" asked Buchanan.

"Quite a bit, I would think," replied Max. "But fuck him, he should have pulled over."

The car engine roared as Max once again found a bit of clear road. Vince's car headed for the hard shoulder, overtaking the cars on the inside lane, narrowly missing an HGV that had pulled over.

"He can handle his cars, can our Vince," said Max following suit.

Back on the motorway the traffic was getting heavier.
"Careful, Max!" shouted Buchanan.

The driver of the car pulling the caravan in front of them was weaving from lane to lane.

"What sort of fucking driving is that?" screamed Buchanan. Max expertly dropped down a couple of gears, pressed the accelerator to the floor and timed it just right. He sped past the caravan mid weave and once again hit clear road.

"Nice driving Max, we're back on his tail."

"A lot of good that will do us if we can't get passed this tanker, the outside lane's jammed with traffic."

"Use the rest stop!" cried Buchanan.

"Good call, sir."

Max drove into the lay-by and increased his speed, then shot out of the end, just ahead of the bemused looking tanker driver who was forced to hit his brakes hard.

"Jesus, that was close!" said Max as he once more entered the outside lane. Vince's car was only a few hundred yards ahead. They watched as he narrowly avoided hitting the central barrier but he recovered well, once more increasing the distance between the two cars.

"We can't keep this speed up much longer, sir, the engine's overheating."

Then they heard the sirens.

He looked in the rear-view mirror.

"Here comes the cavalry!"

The cavalry consisted of five police cars, one of which was the ARV.

Three went shooting past Buchanan and Max while two blocked off the traffic behind.

Once the three managed to get well ahead of Vince's car one of them slowed to a stop, the officer getting out and deploying the stinger device in a bid to puncture the vehicle's tyres.

The stinger did its job and the officer pulled it back off the road allowing Buchanan and Max to keep up with the pursuit.

"Now we've got the bastard!" shouted Buchanan.

The four by four started to slow down eventually coming to a stop at the side of the road.

Max braked sharply and pulled to a stop next to the speed cops and the ARV.

Quick as a flash Buchanan was out the car and ran over to where the armed police were waiting.

"I take it you're the one who called us in?" said the guy with the gun.

"Yeah, DI Buchanan, the bastard pulled a gun on me."

"I don't suppose you noticed what kind?"

"Couldn't say, he had it pointed at my groin at the time, son. I was more interested in leaving the place with both nuts intact."

The officer laughed.

"Well, the vehicle's stolen, nicked from Saint Andrews yesterday."

Just then a loud voice boomed out from one of the other cars.

"Get out the car and lay on the ground with your hands behind your back."

The door of the car slowly opened and the driver, a small skinny teenager got out.

"Don't fucking shoot me!" he shouted.

Buchanan and Max looked at each other incredulously.

"Is this your guy?" asked the officer with the gun.

"Is it fuck!" said Buchanan as he walked towards the driver.

"Who the fuck are you, son?" asked Buchanan.

"Jamie, Jamie Fisher."

"I know this isn't your car, Jamie."

"No man! This guy came up to me at the Castle Hotel, offered me two hundred bucks to drive the car to Edinburgh, said I could make even more if I put my foot down and made it in an hour. I wasn't going to knock that back considering the shitty wages I'm on, was I?"

"Vince, you bastard!" Buchanan thought aloud.

*

Vince sat in the vehicle outside the coffee shop in Peebles

contemplating his next move; he'd given the barman a few quid and his phone number so he would inform him when the guys from Dundee returned. He didn't hold out much hope though, since their photos were now in the papers, they were probably hiding out elsewhere, somewhere low key.

That was the trouble with the police going to the press. Granted the photos might provide them with a sighting, but it also gave a warning to the very people they were looking for.

The hotel workers were a bonus though; a few quid and you could practically get anybody to do anything. Vince had watched as the two cops had come running out assuming the car that was leaving contained himself and Dave, just as he'd planned. He'd given them five minutes to pursue the vehicle and then he and Dave had driven away in the complete opposite direction. He wished he could have been there to see Buchanan's face, though. It must have been a picture when he got hold of the driver.

After opening the passenger door Dave came in with two coffees handing one over to Vince.

"What's next?"

"Back to square one Dave, we win the auction and get the coke back."

"That's assuming the cops don't pick the Dundee guys up first."

"I think we'll be all right there, they only have to keep their heads down until tomorrow and then as far as they think, they'll disappear into the sunset with about two hundred grand. Out of interest Dave, what are you planning on doing with your share of the cash?"

"Buy a new set of gloves for one!"

Vince laughed.

"Bit of a bummer, right enough, that whole prints thing."

"I'm not too worried," said Dave. "They may have my prints but I've got no record so what are they going to match them up to?"

*

Buchanan and Max walked into police headquarters.

"Shit! I almost forgot. Max, go back to the car and get the two wine glasses I picked up from the restaurant, and pop them along to Forensics, would you?"

"When did you pick them up, sir?" asked Max.

"First thing I did when Vince left us in the hotel."

"Let's see what the prints tell us shall we?" Max looked at him in amazement.

Chapter Twenty

The rain had finally stopped and a slightly less wet Jimmy got out of the taxi in the centre of Peebles, paid the driver and headed towards where he'd left the car. He'd had visions of the motor being surrounded by cops, tipped off as to what car they'd been driving.

After watching from across the road from a shop doorway and assuring himself everything was okay, he went to the nearest bar to get something proper to eat. Elsie was a nice old woman but her cooking left a lot to be desired, so they'd all agreed that they would phone in pizzas, Chinese food and the like for the duration of their stay.

He ordered himself a pint, picked up the beer stained menu from the nearest table and stood at the bar trying to decide what to order just as the uniformed Police Officer arrived.

Shit! thought Jimmy. He knew he'd taken a chance heading back into town. He knew it wouldn't be too long before the police got a description of the third guy seen with Liam and Mark, for all he knew they could have it already. They probably did, considering they'd left a trail all over town, at the tailor's, the barber's, the hire car place and God knows where else. He started to panic but there was no way out for him without causing suspicion, so he decided to ride things out. He pulled up the hood on his sweatshirt, not much of a disguise he thought, but wait. Elsie's glasses, he'd decided to keep them safe for her, he'd taken them from Liam earlier and they were in his pocket. He put them on and things became a blur. Jesus, real bottle bottoms he thought. He did his best to blend into the background. It didn't work the policeman headed straight towards him. Now was the moment of truth.

"Excuse me, gentlemen?" said the police officer focusing on the guy with the huge eyes.

"I wonder if I can have a moment of your time, we're looking for these two young men." He gave a copy of Liam and Mark's photos to Jimmy and everyone else in the pub.

"If anyone sees them, could they please phone the number at the foot of the page?"

"You fuckers again," said the man to Jimmy's left. "Can't a man enjoy a pint in peace? I've already talked to your lot at the hotel this afternoon."

"Thanks for your time," said the officer, completely ignoring the obnoxious man's rant as he left the bar.

"Would you like another," asked Jimmy removing the glasses and nodding towards the man's almost empty glass.

"Aye, son! A pint of lager."

Jimmy bought the man's drink and placed it in front of him next to the near empty glass.

"What's happening up at the hotel?" asked Jimmy.

"Well son, the cops have been up there all afternoon," he pointed to the photos of Liam and Mark. "These two guys booked in last night along with another guy but they haven't returned so the police are camped out in the car park, bugging the shit out everyone with their questions."

"Do you work there?" asked Jimmy.

The man scratched his chin and gave Jimmy a funny stare.

"You're asking an awful lot of questions yourself, son."

"Sorry I should have introduced myself," Jimmy shook the guy's hand.

"Jimmy Fallon, I'm a journalist."

"Like in the papers?" he asked.

"Exactly!" said Jimmy.

"Would I have read any of your stuff?"

Jimmy racked his brains.

"Possibly," he replied. "Did you read about that politician up north, the one caught with two hookers in the boot of his car?"

"Oh aye, that dirty bastard, pissed out his skull at the wheel of his motor, wasn't he?"

"Too right he was, anyway that was my story, sold it to all the major papers. I had to follow the bastard for days till I got the photos, made a few bob out of them though."

The man raised his glass.

"Well done son. I like to see these crooked politicians get their comeuppance. You want to serve the public, keep yourself clean I always say. Well, tell you what, you buy me a shot of whisky to go with this pint and I'll give you an exclusive," said the man as he gave Jimmy a wink.

Jimmy caught the barman's eye.

"Could I have a whisky for my friend here please?"

The man looked from side to side and drew himself closer to Jimmy.

"I have it on very good authority that there are more than just the police looking for these guys."

"How do you mean?"

"Earlier on today two guys come in to the hotel, said they were CID and showed the guy at the desk these photos right, but they were impostors."

"Who told you that?"

"Pat, the desk clerk. The thing is you see, half an hour later the real CID appear, go in to the restaurant, talk to them for a while and then after the bogus cops leave the real guys go tearing off in pursuit like their arses are on fire."

"That's very interesting, Mr…?"

"Geddes, Paul Geddes. Two D's in Geddes. Make sure you get my name right when it goes in the paper."

"Excuse me a minute Paul; I just have to nip to the loo."

Jimmy walked into the men's toilets, checked that the cubicle was empty and phoned Liam.

No answer!

He phoned Mark, same again.

"Shit!"

Next he phoned Elsie at the guest house.

"Hello, its Jimmy here, are Liam and Mark still there?"

Liam came to the phone.

"Why the hell have you two assholes not been answering your phones? The police and heaven only knows who else are searching for you two door to door."

"Yeah I know! They've already been here."

"What!"

"Elsie said she's never seen us."

"Why would she do that?"

"She had reason to. She's been hiding her own wee secret."

"What secret?"

"Oh, that you'll have to see for yourself!"

*

Jimmy parked the car at the side of the farmhouse behind a large shrub, hiding it from prying eyes and walked round to the front where Liam was waiting for him.

"What's this secret you were on about then?"

"Follow me!"

Liam walked round the back of the house, heading towards an old derelict barn.

"Earlier on today while you were up town I went for a wander and found myself here."

He opened the old creaky barn door.

"Smell anything?"

Jimmy took a sniff.

"Too right I can, you can't mistake that smell."

"Exactly what I thought," said Liam, "and then I noticed the smell was stronger right at the end here."

Liam walked to the far end of the barn and the smell got stronger.

"This must be a false wall," said Jimmy.

"It is, and here's how you get in."

Liam bent down and scraped back some of the hay covering the floor revealing a small trap door.

"Follow me!"

He lifted the trap door, removed a small torch from his pocket and turned it on.

Jimmy followed Liam down a dozen steps, along a small damp corridor and then up some more steps to a similar sized trapdoor to the first.

They came out into a room about twenty foot squared where each wall was covered with tinfoil. Each corner contained a huge electric fan and the roof contained a wall to wall skylight edged with some sort of industrial heaters.

The room must have contained about forty, five foot high cannabis plants.

"Jesus!" said Jimmy, "there's a few quid's worth here. No way is this just for personal use. Look at this," Jimmy pointed to the rubber hose that snaked its way round each row of plants.

"It's attached to a timer that controls the water intake of the plants."

"Elsie's son set it up; he harvests it and sells it to his workmates offshore. She says she turns a blind eye to it since it helps pay the second mortgage on the farmhouse."

"I take it she caught you in here?" said Jimmy.

"Yeah, I felt sorry for the poor old bat; down on her knees she was pleading with me not to turn her in."

"I get it now," said Jimmy. "You came to an arrangement."

"Exactly, we keep quiet about the weed and in return, if anyone comes looking for us, she's never seen us."

"Perfect because it's not only the cops that are looking for you two, someone else is sniffing about, and my money's on the owner of the coke."

"Bloody hell!" said Liam. "That's all we need."

He looked towards the plants and yawned.

"How easy are they to grow anyway?"

"Well!" replied Jimmy. "First you need to supply the plants with light. Fluorescent lights are the best just like these ones. See how they're on pulleys, that's so the lights can stay within two inches of the soil before germination. Then after the plants appear above the ground, you can hoist them up a bit and continue to keep the lights within two inches of the plants. I tell you this is some set up. I was planning on putting together a similar thing myself at one point but on a smaller scale."

"What are the heaters and fans for?"

"The heaters regulate the temperature you want; hot through the day and cooler at night. They probably have some sort of thermostat hooked up somewhere. As for the fans they create some movement of air. They'll also stimulate the plants into growing a healthier and sturdier stalk just like the wind would naturally if they were grown outside."

Jimmy walked to the side of the room and examined the various dials on a small metal box. "This is a humidifier, it controls the moisture in the room."

"What for?" asked Liam.

"Since the resin in the cannabis plant serves the purpose of keeping the leaves from drying out," said Jimmy, "there is far more chance a lot of resin will be produced in a dry room rather than in a humid one. And that's what you're after, lots of lovely resin," said Jimmy as he closed his eyes and inhaled the smell of the plants.

"What are all these barrels of water doing all over the shop?" asked Liam, "don't tell me they wash the bloody things."

"De-chlorination probably. You don't want to contaminate the plants with that chlorine shit, so all you have to do is leave the tap water lying for over twenty four hours and the chlorine evaporates."

"What are you, some sort of stoned Alan Titchmarsh?"

"I'm not an expert I just looked it all up online not too long ago. Anyway, I couldn't see him growing these plants can you? It would be funny though."

Jimmy put on his best English accent.

"Today on Gardener's World we're going to be planting seed potatoes, on second thoughts scratch that. I'm off to the corner of the allotment to get shit faced on my home grown weed." They both burst into hysterics.

*

Back in the farmhouse, Mark came running up to them.

"Check this out, guys."

He put two fingers in his mouth and let out a shrill whistle.

A weird snorting sound came from the direction of the kitchen and it was getting closer by the minute. Then suddenly the lounge door barged open and the ugliest creature Jimmy and Liam had ever seen came tearing into the lounge.

"What the fuck is that?" asked Liam.

"That's Cyril; he's a Vietnamese pot-bellied pig."

"He's an ugly bastard."

"Stop it! You'll hurt his feelings," said Mark.

"Hurt his feelings? He's a fucking pig."

"A very clever, very well trained pig, watch this."

"Sit. Roll over. Beg."

Cyril went through an obedience routine on a par with any well trained dog.

"Ok, I must admit that's quite impressive," said Liam.

"I've been reading up on them online, you can put a lead on them and take them for walks and everything, I'm going to buy one when we get to Spain, think they'd have them there?"

"So!" said Liam, "when we get to Spain and we're trying to keep a low profile, you plan on walking about the place with a fucking pig on a lead?"

"What's wrong with that?"

Liam and Jimmy just laughed and shook their heads.

Elsie looked at the pig and she also shook her head.

"Never known him to climb before though," she said.

"How do you mean?" asked Jimmy.

"Well, I was going to give you some more of my steak pie; it was up on the worktop in the kitchen, but Cyril's scoffed it."

Mark winked at the other two.

"That will be pizza's all round then lads, what do you think?"

"Great idea," said Liam, "and make sure you order one for Cyril here, I'm beginning to like this ugly little guy."

Chapter Twenty One

"Thousands of pounds worth of protection, reinforced with steel and the prick opens the door so he can have a smoke. Unbelievable!"

Buchanan let the DCI finish his rant.

"Any leads, John?"

"Not really, we found the getaway car and the stolen strong boxes behind a disused farmhouse near Bilston, but judging by the tracks left behind, the two men have split up and driven off in opposite directions."

"You sound as if you've had as bad a day as me, let me take you out for a meal tonight. How does Chez Leonard sound?"

"That's a bit pricy on a cop's salary, isn't it?"

"It won't cost a thing, the owner offered to give me, and a few well-chosen friends a free meal. I'll phone him now and set it up."

"I was always going to take my wife there, I never seem to get round to it," said Brannigan.

"Take Lesley along, it'll be nice to see her, I'll pick you up at seven."

"It's a date then, I'll see you at seven."

*

"What tie do you think, sir?" asked Max.

"Do I look like your wife, Sergeant?"

"I just want to look smart, sir. This is a top notch restaurant we're going to, I looked it up. You wouldn't believe the amount of celebrities that go there to eat when they're in town."

"Like who for instance?"

"Sean Conroy was in there last week."

"Who the hell is he when he's at home?"

"He starred in this summer's blockbuster, Reaper Man."

"Big and muscley with cropped hair?" said Buchanan.

"That's him, sir."

Buchanan picked up his cigarettes.

"You can finish tarting yourself up Max. I'm going downstairs for a pint. I'll see you down there."

The lounge was quite empty, there was an old couple sat in the corner and a young woman standing at the end of the bar sipping her drink and having an animated conversation with someone on the other end of her mobile phone. Buchanan walked to the bar and ordered his usual. The barman shaped a shamrock on the creamy head of his pint as he poured it.

"Nice touch," said Buchanan.

"The black stuff should be treated with the respect it deserves," answered the bar man in a thick Irish accent.

"What part of Ireland are you from?"

"Dublin, the same place as your pint there, I haven't been back for a few years mind."

They were interrupted by a female voice.

"DI Buchanan?"

He eyed the woman suspiciously.

"Who wants to know?"

"Gemma Barclay," said the woman extending her hand.

"A reporter, I take it?"

"Is it that obvious?" she replied as she flashed him a smile. "The laptop bag gave it away. That and the word deadline, you mentioned it three times in the phone conversation you had a couple of minutes ago."

"Wow! You're good."

"Flattery will get you nowhere," replied Buchanan as he turned back to his pint.

"I just want to ask you a few questions; I won't take up much of your time."

"Correction, you won't take up any of my time. Anyway, how do you even know who I am, let alone where I'm staying?"

"It wasn't hard to find out where you were staying. I simply phoned round a few hotels, B&B's and suchlike to find out where you'd booked yourself into, and asked for you."

The woman reached into her oversized hand bag and pulled out a copy of The Evening Express, Aberdeen's local evening paper, and showed him the front page. The headline stated *'ABERDEEN DETECTIVES PART OF JOINT MURDER TASK FORCE.'* He looked below the bold lettering and found himself staring at a picture of the Aberdeen crime scene. It had been taken with a telephoto lens and Max and he could be seen clearly.

"I did a bit of digging and found out who you were. There couldn't be that many fit looking grizzled detectives in Aberdeen."

"What did I tell you about flattery?" said Buchanan downing his pint.

The woman laughed just as Max walked in.

"You about ready to leave, sir?"

"Sure Max, just as soon as I can get rid of my stalker here."

"At least let me give you my card," said the woman. "I'd be grateful for anything you could give me."

Buchanan thought for a moment and then pointed to the reporter. "No promises mind." He accepted her card, sticking it in his inside pocket as he and Max left the bar.

"Attractive woman," said Max. "She's got a nice smile."

"Indeed she has, and she knows how to use it."

*

They left their hotel and drove to DCI Brannigan's house, where Lesley was waiting for them at the door.

"Ronnie it's great to see you, and you must be Max, come right in."

"You look incredible Lesley," said Buchanan.

"Don't look too bad yourself Ronnie, how's Michelle?"

"Still teaching cheeky little bastards," said Buchanan.

"I take it you haven't any cheeky little bastards of your own yet then?"

Buchanan laughed.

"None yet, but I'm still enjoying trying."

Brannigan appeared from the kitchen, red faced and fighting to uncork a bottle of wine. As far as Buchanan could see, the cork was winning.

"Let me do that, John," said Lesley.

"Glass of wine anyone?"

They all sat down with their drinks in the lounge.

"I have some news Ronnie, we caught one of the robbers. It was a pure fluke too."

"What happened, like?"

"The traffic cops tried to pull him over for speeding and he panicked and took off at a rate of knots, hit a crash barrier and the car ended up on its roof. They found half the morning's robbery on his backseat in a holdall."

"Did he tell you where the second guy was heading for?"

"He doesn't have a clue."

"I hope you two aren't going to talk shop all night?" said Lesley.

"Sorry love!" said Brannigan. "Car or taxi, Ronnie?"

"There's no point in forking out for a taxi John, Max can drive us, and he can just stick to cokes."

Max tried not to look disappointed,

"I'm sure he's only joking Max, I'll go and phone the taxi," said Lesley. "You sit down and enjoy your drink; you deserve it working with those two buggers all day."

"No need for a taxi, I've arranged the transport," said Buchanan. "It should be here any minute now."

*

The chauffeur driven White Mercedes Benz pulled into the side of the road outside Brannigan's house. The immaculately dressed chauffeur got out and approached the door; he removed his hat,

159

tucked it under his right arm and pressed the bell.

"Your chariot awaits, madam," said Buchanan holding out his hand.

Lesley linked arms with him and proceeded to walk down the path towards the car as Max and Brannigan walked behind. The chauffeur opened the doors for them and they stepped inside the stretch limousine.

"Wow, this is amazing!" said Max as he took in his surroundings. The decor was more suited to a plush lounge than the inside of a car.

The seats were made of fine soft leather and the lighting was subdued. The windows were very darkly tinted keeping the streetlights outside at bay, and the far end was dominated by a huge plasma screen and DVD player.

A voice came from the centre speaker.

"Just to the left of the television you'll find a fully stocked bar. You'll find some crystal glasses to the right. Please feel free to help yourself."

"I could get used to this," said Lesley.

"No chance of that on my bloody salary," said Brannigan. "But we might as well enjoy it while we can."

He approached the bar.

"Whiskies all round, okay?"

They all nodded in unison.

Drinks in hand they all relaxed into their journey as some classical music played on the expensive looking surround sound system.

"Wagner, nice choice," said Brannigan.

The limo pulled up to the restaurant at the Royal Mile. The smartly dressed driver got out and opened the passenger door. The four passengers were then escorted upstairs to their table which sat next to a huge window with a picturesque view of Edinburgh Castle.

"Wow! Now I know how a rockstar must feel," said Lesley.

A waiter approached their table and set down a huge bottle of Champagne in front of Buchanan.

"Compliments of the owner, sir. Would you like to eat now or enjoy your Champagne first?"

"Give us about half an hour and we'll order then, if that's ok."

"Perfectly okay, sir."

"I've got to hand it to you Ronnie, you've planned this to perfection."

"None of my doing John, the owner keeps a limo to chauffeur celebrities and the like to the restaurant. He was so pleased with getting his watch back that he said he'd pull out all the stops to make sure we enjoyed ourselves, he also said we could order anything we like, free gratis."

"I went there when I was a kid," said Max, pointing out the window.

"Went where?" asked Lesley.

"Edinburgh Castle, I have a photo of me sitting astride a huge cannon."

"Mons Meg" said the DCI, "that's what it's called; it used to be one of a pair. In 1457, King James II was presented with two massive siege guns by his uncle by marriage, Philip the Good, Duke of Burgundy. The surviving gun is Mons Meg."

"What was the other one called?" asked Max.

"No idea, but you ought to see the size of the cannon balls they weigh over three hundred pounds, they're bloody huge."

"Right, enough of you talking balls John, time to change the conversation," said Buchanan.

"History, it's all he bloody talks about," said Lesley. "What's that crap we were watching last night?"

"Time Squad, that's a bloody good programme, in fact they're supposed to be coming here soon to dig up part of Arthurs Seat."

"Christ, Time Squad! Michelle watches that," said Buchanan.

"You've got to laugh when they come away with shit like, day two and we're very excited, we've just found the remains of Exxon Castle, and what have they found? Two fucking bricks!"

Lesley laughed.

"Or, how about the guy who holds up a one inch wide piece of pottery, the sort of shit you find in your own garden and then says we reckon this could be, see there's the key, could be, an ancient Roman burial urn. Cue the artist's impression of the jar with the one inch piece of pottery super imposed over the top. It could be fucking anything."

"I've seen that a couple of times I think," said Max, "it's not a bad show." He turned to Brannigan. "When did you say they were coming here?"

"Pretty soon, I'm sure of it, why?"

"Sooner than you think I'd say, they're sitting three tables along to the left."

The DCI looked round.

"You're right enough Max, that's definitely them; I'd recognise that scruffy bastard of an archaeologist anywhere. I'm going over to have a word."

With that Brannigan left his seat, heading towards their table.

"Surprising how fast he can move if he wants to," said Lesley.

"So how's the twins, Lesley?" asked Buchanan.

"Both of them are doing great, not long started secondary school, Jim's already talking of joining the force like his dad."

"I'd like to bring up my kids here, if I ever have any," said Max.

"Why particularly here?" asked Lesley.

"Don't know, I just feel comfortable here, it's a beautiful city."

"So Ronnie, John's been telling me that you are off on one of your fixations again, with this guy Vince. Tell me it's not going to be another Ally Reynolds job!"

"Who is Ally Reynolds?" asked Max.

"I think Ronnie should tell you that story," said Lesley.

They both looked at Buchanan.

*

"A few years ago when I worked for Strathclyde there was a spate of vicious attacks on women. They weren't sexually assaulted, just viciously slashed again and again across the face and body with a craft knife. The one thing they had in common was that each victim was due to be married within the next two or three days of their attack. We figured the attacker whoever he was, must have been checking wedding announcements, when the bans went up and picking his victims from there. We were wrong. We found out from their fiancés that while they'd been planning their wedding, each victim had initially gone to a wedding photographer called Ally Reynolds who had his own photography business in Sauchiehall Street. I was still a Sergeant at the time, so I was sent to his shop to take a statement. The guy acted strange from the start, very nervy and agitated. He said he couldn't remember either of the women, yet his records confirmed that they had all at some time or another approached him to take their wedding photos."

"What made them change their minds and go with a different photographer?" asked Max.

"It was in April, a popular time to get hitched and a new guy on the scene, a young photographer called Tommy, I forget his second name, was trying to drum up some trade for himself by offering spring wedding specials at way better prices than Reynolds. So a few of his clients jumped ship and went with the cheaper option. We figured he attacked the women and disfigured them as some sort of punishment for dumping him. His motive, as he confirmed himself later, was to make sure that regardless of where they went, their photos were never going to come out too good, not with their faces in pieces."

"Sick bastard!" said Max. "I take it you eventually caught him?"

"Eventually but the thing was we had no evidence and a line up was out of the question as he'd worn a mask during the attacks. He had however, kept each woman's engagement ring. So against my better judgement, I waited outside his flat one night and when he left I did an illegal search, thinking if I found something I could get a warrant and then go back and obtain it legally."

"That was a bit dodgy wasn't it, sir?"

"You're right Max it was, but I just had a gut feeling he was the guy. Anyway in the flat in a cupboard under the stairs, I found this eerie shrine sort of thing, the walls were covered with press cuttings of the three women which he'd covered in slashes from a red felt tipped pen. The weirdest thing though, was below that sat three mannequin hands, each one with a ring on it."

"That's fucking creepy!" said Max.

"Anyway I'd found the rings so now I needed a warrant which wasn't easy but after arguing my point, the judge gave into my request. When I got back to his flat however, the cupboard had been cleaned out, no freaky voodoo mannequin hands or bugger all else, and what's more, Reynolds' solicitor hit me for harassment."

"On what grounds?" asked Max.

"He must have spotted me watching him earlier on and waited for me to make my move, because he'd photographed me entering his flat, the bastard had set me up, Max."

"So what happened?"

"I was taken off the case and given a week's suspension which left me in an impossible situation. I knew it was him but could do bugger all about it. He'd got the better of me just like Vince, so I couldn't leave it at that. I started following him, camping out in the car and watching him all night."

"You were obsessed Ronnie, Michelle never saw you for three days, she eventually moved out and you didn't even notice," said Lesley.

"It was all I could think about but then, finally I got a break."

"It was a Friday night, I'd followed Reynolds to a pub in the West End, and he was doing a bit of bar hopping following some women on a hen night. The women ended up in a night club in the West End and that's where he struck. One had gone to phone a taxi and I watched as he put a knife to her back and forced her outside.

I acted immediately before he had as much as got a look at me. I rammed him against the wall, head first, he was knocked unconscious so I cuffed him and waited until the backup arrived. I couldn't just phone anyone though as I was supposed to be keeping away from the guy so I phoned John, he took care of everything. Reynolds was so cocksure of himself that when his house was searched, he'd recreated his shrine. We finally had plenty of evidence to put the bastard away."

Just then the DCI returned to the table.

"They're digging up Crow Hill near the top of Arthur's Seat starting tomorrow. There's an ancient fort up there, well at least the remnants of one."

"Let me guess," said Buchanan. "Two bricks worth!"

Looking bemused, the DCI wondered why his friends around the table simultaneously burst into laughter.

Chapter Twenty Two

After putting on the dark wig and securing it with the spirit gum, Vince checked himself out in the mirror. Happy with his new look he double checked his bags to make sure he had everything he'd possibly need for the next day. Nico had the programme running, as good as guaranteeing him a win on the auction. He was prepared, but he still had one last thing to do before leaving. Time to sacrifice his pawn!

He didn't like giving Dave up to the cops but he'd become a liability. The recent incident with the gloves was unacceptable, and how the hell did he find out about the connection to Harry Black. Hopefully once the police had him in custody, they'd stop looking for Vince quite so hard, he hoped it would get them off his back, especially DI Buchanan, he was far too tenacious. Fuck it, thought Vince as he picked up his phone and adopted an English accent.

"I've seen the guy you cops are looking for in connection with the recent girls' murders."

"Let me take some details, sir."

"Fuck the details, he's in room 122 of the Far Point Hotel, just get your ass down here."

"Could I at least have your name, sir?" said the woman.

"No, you cannot."

Vince ended the call and put his mobile back in his pocket.

He picked up his bags, had a last quick look around to make sure he hadn't left anything incriminating and left the hotel room pausing outside Dave's door.

"Nice knowing you, Davy boy!"

He left the hotel heading for the car park; he put his stuff in the boot just as the three police cars flew past him, sirens blaring. He watched as the officers went running into the hotel then took off in his own recently rented car, leaving Dave and the police far behind him.

Approaching the centre of Edinburgh, he decided to push the boat out. He parked the car and booked himself into a suite at the Galaxy, a luxury hotel in Edinburgh's West End.

He booked in using a stolen credit card, dropped his stuff off in his room, had a shower and headed for the bar. After ordering himself a drink, he fired up his laptop and checked the auction. The bidding had eased off; it was stuck at just over two hundred grand with no new bids made in the last four hours. He didn't expect it to go much higher. Pure coke needed a lot of cutting to make a profit and only a certain amount of people had the connections and the wherewithal to sell on such a vast quantity. He remembered a few years ago in Aberdeen some asshole was selling pure coke on the street, ripped it off from a drug lab somewhere, almost a dozen people had died over one weekend, all overdoses, junkies expecting their normal purity. People buying coke on the street were lucky if their score contained ten per cent coke and ninety per cent cut.

The cut contained anything from milk powder, starch or sometimes stuff far more sinister like a local anaesthetic. The anaesthetic emphasised the numb feeling, made people think the crap they were buying actually contained a higher percentage of coke than it really did. It could of course also be turned into crack, a mix of cocaine and baking powder which came in small lumps or 'rocks'. When smoked, the cocaine vapours reach the brain much quicker than snorting, producing an intense but short lived euphoric rush and a compelling desire for more. Very addictive stuff, but then again, very profitable!

"Do you mind if I join you, honey?"

His thoughts interrupted, Vince closed his laptop and looked up at the petite blonde woman hovering over the table; her smile was as sweet as her perfume. Dressed in a summer dress in winter, she had to be a visitor from a far warmer climate. The American accent was a further clue.

"Please do."

Vince looked at the woman.

"You're American, West Coast, maybe San Francisco?"

"Exactly right, now how on earth would you know such a thing as that?"

"Just a gift I have," Vince pointed to her drink.

"Would you like another?"

"I wouldn't say no, bourbon, plenty of ice."

Vince returned with the drinks.

"So, what's a San Franciscan doing in Edinburgh at this God awful time of the year?"

"I'm giving a lecture at Edinburgh University, just for a couple of days."

"What on?"

"Cognitive Thoughts of the Mentally Impaired!"

"So you're a shrink?"

"Well sort of, but I promise not to analyse you if you join me for an evening meal. I absolutely hate dining alone. My name's Meg by the way, Meg Carter."

Vince extended his right hand.

"Vince Jones, and yes I'd love to join you for a meal, we can go to the restaurant once we finish these drinks."

"Well Vince, what do you do?"

"Have a guess!"

Meg looked him up and down.

"You're a hit man?"

"Nope!"

"That's a pity because my ex-husband is being a real pain in the ass."

Vince laughed.

"Actually I'm in import and export."

"So, you're a drug smuggler then?"

"If you can call antiques drugs and importing smuggling. I search out particular items for clients abroad, and then import them and sell them, usually at a decent profit."

"Is there much money in that?"

"Loads, last year I found a Chinese vase in Portugal, paid two grand for it, sold at auction for a hundred and sixty eight."

"Wow, I'm in the wrong game."

"Are you ready to hit the restaurant? I'm starving, I haven't eaten all day."

Vince stood up, helped Meg put on her jacket and they both walked through to the restaurant, he opened the door for Meg.

"After you," said Vince.

"You Brits and your courtesy, you don't get that in Frisco."

*

Liam gave out a loud belch.

"Beg your pardon!"

"That's disgusting," said Mark. "There's a lady present, mind your manners."

"Sorry Elsie. But like my Mum always says, better out than in."

"I'm absolutely stuffed," said Jimmy. "How many pizzas have we eaten?"

"Six," said Liam. "Mind you Cyril had two."

Cyril gave a snort as if in answer.

"Where did you get the pig, Elsie?" asked Liam.

"Hoi! Stop calling him the pig, give him his proper name," said Mark. "I've told you before, he has feelings."

Liam shook his head.

"You've grown attached to that ugly porker, haven't you?"

"So what if I have, he's cute."

Liam turned towards Elsie.

"Where did you get Cyril, Elsie?"

"We got him from a farm not far from here. The farmer bought him as a pet for his grandkids but it didn't work out. Cyril here kept chasing the kids and trying to hump his Labrador."

Mark laughed, almost choking on the last of his pizza crust.

"I wouldn't be without him now though. At first we kept him outside but he kept trying to barge his way through the back door so nowadays he stays indoors most of the time."

"How do you stop him crapping all over the house?" asked Jimmy.

"Easy, he just scratches at the door like a dog would, when he needs out to do his business. He's quite clever really, aren't you darling?"

Cyril gave another snort and rubbed himself against Elsie's leg as she stood up.

"Cup of tea, or another beer?" asked Elsie.

They all went to the kitchen for beer.

"I'm having another one of those Bavarian ones, they're fucking excellent," said Liam.

"Get us all one!" said Mark.

Jimmy turned to Elsie. "Do you mind if we smoke some weed? We have our own; I thought you wouldn't mind, with your son smoking it and all."

"Go ahead; you could try some of mine if you like."

"Yours! I thought it belonged to your son?"

"It does really, I mean he grows it, but he keeps some for me, it helps with my arthritis you see."

"She's right you know," said Mark, "it helps with the pain. I saw a programme about it on the box the other night."

Elsie wandered over to a sideboard on the left side of the room, opened one of the drawers and took out an ornately carved wooden box.

"I keep my stuff in here."

"Nice looking box," said Jimmy. "It looks quite old."

"It is," replied Elsie. "My late husband brought it back from Singapore."

She wandered back to her seat, and then expertly proceeded to roll a joint as the three guys from Dundee watched in amazement.

"Man, that just looks plain weird," said Liam.

"A woman, old enough to be our grandma, rolling a doob."

After one of Elsie's joints the three guys from Dundee were flying.

"Jesus Elsie, that stuff's wicked!" said Jimmy.

"What kind of beer is next, lads?"

"Surprise us!" said Liam.

Mark went through to the kitchen and returned with three huge dark coloured bottles. "This one's made with Peruvian mountain water drawn from a two thousand foot deep well."

"How the fuck do you know that?" asked Liam.

"It says so here on the label."

Jimmy looked at his phone.

"Guys we've got our two hundred grand, anymore between now and midday tomorrow's just icing on the cake."

"Woo-hoo!" shouted Liam and Mark in unison.

"Spain here we come!"

"When I get to Spain I'm going to become a script writer," said Mark.

"You couldn't write a script if your life depended on it," said Liam.

"Yes I could, I've already got the idea for one in my head."

"Come on then, tell us the plot."

"Right, it's a crime series about this serial killer who goes about Dundee cutting people's heads off. He's called Cheesy. Want to know why?"

"Go on then humour me."

"Because he cuts their head off with a cheese wire, get it? Cheese wire, Cheesy…!"

"What a pile of shit," said Liam.

"No it's not, it's a sure fire hit, my mum says so."

"Well she would, she's your mum. I mean she's not going to say Mark that TV series idea of yours is the biggest piece of shit I've ever heard of, is she?"

"Guys stop the arguing for once in your fucking life, would you? We have a big day tomorrow, we're supposed to be relaxing," said Jimmy.

"Aye you're right enough Jimmy. Sorry Mark, your script idea's not shit."

"No it's not" said Mark, "it's utter bollocks!"

They all laughed.

"Anyone for another joint?" asked Elsie.

Liam looked at her.

"Yes my good woman, and another round of Peruvian mountain water."

*

"That was a delightful meal Ronnie, thanks," said Lesley as she kissed Buchanan on the cheek.

"My pleasure," said Buchanan.

They were all standing outside the restaurant about to enter a taxi when the DCI's phone rang.

"You're joking; right we're on our way."

The DCI turned to Buchanan.

"Dave's in custody, we got an anonymous tip off."

"On you go guys, I'll see myself home," said Lesley.

"Are you sure we shouldn't leave this till the morning, sir?" asked Max. "I mean we've all had quite a bit to drink."

"Nonsense Max, the longer we give Dave to get a story worked out, the more we lose, besides a few mints and a couple of cups of John's famous rocket fuel before the interview, no one will be any the wiser."

"Rocket fuel?" said Max.

"It's a unique experience," said Brannigan. "It's a coffee made so strong you could practically stand a spoon in it."

"You two are leading me astray," replied Max.

"We're of a different generation to you, Max," said Buchanan putting his arm over Max's shoulder. "Me and John here, we both come from an era where you got the job done at all costs. When a case came up you knocked your pan in until it was resolved simple as that, no red tape, no filling in half a dozen forms simply because you gave a guy a caution. I suppose, nowadays, some would call us dinosaurs but the point is we got things done. We still do, and our arrest record is second to none. So what if we've had a few drinks, the case comes first."

Brannigan applauded.

"Nice speech Ronnie, it brought a tear to my eye."

Buchanan winked in his direction.

"So Max what's it to be? You coming with us or are you heading back to the hotel? I'll think no less of you either way."

Max rubbed his chin.

"Bugger it! I'm in."

Chapter Twenty Three

Buchanan yawned loudly, gave his tired eyes a rub with the palms of his hand and wearily put his pen back into the inside pocket of his jacket. Finishing the dregs of his second cup of John's extra strong black coffee, he folded up the sheet of paper he had just ripped out of his notebook and approached the young PC who was standing ram rod straight outside the door to the interview room.
"Do me a favour, son, in about two minutes I'll call you in, when I ask you what the guy said when he phoned in the tip off, just you read this out." Buchanan handed him the folded sheet of paper, took a deep breath and entered the interview room.
"Well, well, well Davy boy, I told you I'd see you here soon enough, how's tricks?"
"Fuck off, where's my solicitor?"
"He's been held up," said Max.
"So, Vince ratted you out," said Buchanan.
"You're making that shit up."
"How come you find yourself here then?"
"Someone recognised the photo fit in the paper."
"Sergeant Maxwell, who took the phone call?"
Max looked through his note book.
"PC Stanton."
Buchanan picked up the phone.
"Could you send PC Stanton in please?"
Two minutes later Stanton entered the room.
"I believe you took the phone call that lead to Dave here's arrest?" said Buchanan.

"Yes, sir!"

"What exactly was said?"

The PC looked at his notebook where he'd copied Buchanan's note earlier.

"First he asked for you, sir. I told him you were unavailable, then he told us where to find Dave, then added make sure you tell Buchanan Vince did him a favour."

"That two faced bastard!" said Dave slamming his fist down on the table.

"Right Dave, you have two options open to you, one you deny everything, not a good choice, or two you give us everything you have on Terry and Vince. Option two will get you a reduced charge at the very least. You help us catch Vince and you're maybe even looking at a suspended sentence, hell I'll even put in a good word for you myself. There's no need to make your decision now, have a think about it, talk to your solicitor and get back to me."

Buchanan turned to Max.

"C'mon son, let's grab some more of that coffee."

*

Max and Buchanan carried their coffees over to a corner table in the police canteen, the harsh strip-lights emphasising the tiredness in their eyes.

"Think he'll go for it, sir?"

"I'm pretty sure he will now he thinks Vince grassed him up. I'm sure his solicitor will tell him to play ball."

"Do you think it really was Vince?"

"I've no doubt whatsoever, you saw the look on his face, when he found out Dave had left prints all over the shop, he had become a liability. He probably thinks that now we have the two people involved in the girls' murders, it'll take some of the heat off him, but make no mistake, he was running the show. He gave the orders that led to the girls' deaths, and I for one won't rest till we've got the bastard."

The young police officer that Buchanan had handed the note to

175

earlier approached the table.

"Seems your plan worked, sir. He wants to talk."

*

After confirming he was there when the two girls were killed, Dave insisted that as far as he was concerned he never knew that was going to be part of the plan. He said as far as he knew, Terry was just going to interrogate the girls and rough them up a bit.

"So, now tell us about Vince," said Buchanan.

"What do you want to know?"

"Start with the incident at the Castle Hotel. How did Vince know where they were staying?"

"Like I said earlier, we searched their flat in Dundee where Vince found a Scottish Hotel Guide with eight hotels circled in it. We took four each, made out we were police officers and showed the staff at the various hotels the photos, which led to us eventually finding them in Peebles."

"How did you find out the guys came from Dundee?"

"A process of elimination, the flatmate didn't have the coke; neither did that outdoor guy, so it must have been ripped off in Dundee. Vince knows a guy on the force there, he got him to look up people known for stealing stuff out of cars, that's what those two do, and they're well known for it."

"So there's a good chance they're behind the auction?"

"We know they are. Vince found a laptop in their room at the hotel with a link to the website."

"We never found a laptop," said Max.

"That's because Vince took it with him."

"Do you know the name of the cop who gave him the information?"

"No idea."

"So what's he up to now?" asked Buchanan.

"He aims to win the auction and get his drugs back."

"So he's just going to turn up, wipe them out and take the coke."

"He might do but that's not really Vince's style, he likes to catch

176

you unaware. I know he intends to hand over the cash with some sort of tracking device attached, so if things don't go in his favour, he can take the drugs as if it was just a normal drug deal and then go after his money."

"How's he so sure he'll win the auction?" asked Max.

"I'm not sure of the technicalities involved but some guy he knows, I don't know his name, has come up with a programme that will make sure his winning bid goes in at the last second."

"Who is this guy?" asked Buchanan.

"No idea but Vince uses him quite often. It's down to his expertise with computers that Vince can track down exactly where you are through your mobile phone."

"How do you mean?"

"He gave him some sort of hacking code to use in a legitimate site that helps you track down mobile phones. If Vince has your phone number, he knows where you are. How do you think he found out Terry had been nicked? He simply typed his mobile number into the web site and it gave us his location."

"So!" said Buchanan stifling another yawn. "Vince wins the auction, he gets back the coke and then gets back his money, what next?"

"Soon as he gets back the coke, cuts it, splits it into smaller quantities then sells it on, he's off abroad with no intention of coming back. Says he has legitimate interests over there. Remember, the money he makes off the stuff is his, now that Harry Black's out of the equation."

"Tell me what you know about his legit stuff."

"I don't know much but I've overheard a few phone calls. He keeps a special phone, you see, just for his business stuff."

"What sort of phone calls?"

"Some are in Spanish, Vince speaks it fluently. I can't make head or tail of them. The other ones, they're mostly to do with some sort of property development, something big is going on at the moment, a hotel I think."

"Whereabouts?"

"On the coast somewhere, I know it's overseas but I don't know whereabouts exactly. It could be anywhere, but anyway it's not going to help you much. Knowing Vince, there's no way the company will be in his name. All I know for certain is he's had his legit stuff going for a while now. As I said earlier, he's set everything up so he can disappear. If you don't catch him in the next couple of days you're fucked. He'll have a new identity already set up and you'll never see him on these shores again."

Buchanan yawned.

"Are you positive that Vince was nowhere near Glasgow the night of the shootings?"

"Positive," said Dave. "He went to his hotel room early that night and he was still there next morning."

"What time did he retire for the night?" asked Buchanan.

"About ten and I saw him the next morning at seven."

"So that gave him a window of nine hours, how do you know he never left, then drove back to Dundee before you saw him again?"

"It's possible I suppose," replied Dave.

Buchanan stopped the recording.

*

"The legit stuff," said Max as they walked down the stairs, "it could be in Spain, after all Dave says that Vince was taking a lot of the calls in Spanish."

"Could be I suppose," replied Buchanan, "but there's a hell of a lot of Spanish speaking countries, Max. It could be anywhere from Argentina to Venezuela, besides he hasn't given us that much to go on to dig into that side of things. We'll put that on the backburner for now. Anyway I plan on collaring this bastard before he gets the chance to flee."

"Do you think we will, sir, catch him I mean?"

Buchanan stayed silent.

*

Just as Buchanan and Max approached their car, ready to drive to their hotel for some well-earned rest, DCI Brannigan came running out towards them red faced and out of breath

"Ronnie, we have a hit off the prints from the wine glasses."

"So much had happened that day it took a few seconds for a tired eyed Buchanan to register what he was talking about.

"Oh aye that'll be Dave's, we have his partials on record."

"Not Dave's you asshole, Vince! We have a hit on Vince."

*

Buchanan read the file for the third time he couldn't believe what he was seeing.

Charles Vincent Mackie aged thirty eight, born in Edinburgh. Mother, Jane Mackie (deceased) and Father, Bob Mackie, aged sixty five still resides at the family home in Edinburgh. Buchanan read on; Vince had been charged ten years ago with armed robbery. He'd been the mastermind behind an audacious heist of eighty high powered weapons from a Ministry of Defence armoury down south. Only eight of the weapons were ever recovered.

He'd have probably got away with it if one of the gang hadn't been caught on a fairly minor offence, made a deal with the cops and given the gang up. Vince was sentenced to twelve years but he'd only done eight weeks when he escaped from the prison workshop in Wandsworth.

Max entered the office.

"I've got the details on his escape, sir."

"Spit it out then!"

"Once a week, the workshop got a delivery of materials, wood, metal sheeting, etc. The driver was tall, overweight and bearded and always wore the same get up, a red boiler suit and a scruffy baseball hat.

He had a habit of using the workshop toilet before he left each week, seems the prisoners were always complaining about the smell he left behind.

Anyway this one week, he went to the loo as usual, waved

goodbye to the guards, waddled into his truck and drove off, straight through the check point at the gate, cool as you like, the thing was it wasn't him. It was Vince. He'd followed the driver into the loo, knocked him unconscious and then dressed in his dungarees and hat and put on his glasses, he'd even applied a false beard made from his own hair and used his own prison clothes to pad himself out. The guards all said he even had the fat guy's walk down to a T. Anyway the driver wasn't discovered for half an hour as Vince had put an out of order sign on the cubicle."

"Did they find the truck?"

"They found it abandoned about ten miles from the prison, and get this, next day a local business man at the airport car park was unceremoniously shoved in to the boot of his car and had his suitcase stolen, he never had a chance to see the guy, he was struck from behind as he was getting his luggage out the boot."

"I take it that was Vince?" said Buchanan.

"They can't be certain but the business man was six foot three, roughly the same height as Vince, looks like he purposely picked out a specific size of person, maybe so the clothes would fit."

"Well," said Buchanan. "He could have left the country I suppose, till the heat was off and then sneaked back in with a new identity. He must be an arrogant bastard though."

"How do you mean?" asked Max.

"Well if you were going to do such a thing, would you use your middle name?"

"Right enough, I see what you mean."

"He never popped up on the drug squad's radar until about what? Three or four years ago, what was he doing until then I wonder?" Buchanan looked at his mug shot.

"You can see how he's never been spotted though, he looks fuck all like that nowadays, check out his poodle perm. He looks like the front man for a Swedish rock band."

"Or an American wrestler!" said Max.

"No wait a minute, I've got it," said Buchanan. "A nineteen seventies porn star!"

They both laughed.

Buchanan entered the DCI's office. "I have an idea John, bit of a long shot but it could work."

"I'm all ears, Ronnie."

"Say you're about to leave the country, possibly for good, what would you do?"

"Say my goodbyes to any friends and family I was leaving behind I suppose, why?"

"I'll tell you why. Dave told us Vince was planning on leaving these shores once he had sold the coke, right?"

"Right!"

"Well, what I suggest is we post an unmarked car outside his father's house. There's a good chance Vince will turn up there in the next couple of days, what do you think?"

"Good idea Ronnie, I'll get right on it and then I'm going home to sleep. I'm dead on my feet and that meal we had earlier has given me terrible bloody heartburn."

"Good idea, I could do with some shut eye, I'm a bit knackered myself."

*

Vince crept out the bed, leaving quietly so as not to wake Meg. It didn't work.

"Where are you off to?"

"I've a busy day tomorrow, I have to get some stuff organised."

"Sneaking off in the middle of the night, eh, and I thought you were a gentleman."

"I'm sorry. I wouldn't go if I didn't have to."

"No worries, here I have something for you."

Meg gave Vince her card.

"If you ever find yourself in San Francisco, look me up."

"I might just do that. Bye Meg!"

Vince kissed her on the forehead and headed for his own suite.

*

"Well, I suppose we better call it a night," said Jimmy.

"Must we?" said Liam.

"I'm afraid so, we have an early start tomorrow and there are a few things I need if we want this drug deal to go down smoothly."

"Such as?" enquired Liam.

"You'll find out tomorrow, no need to worry about it tonight, give Mark a shake will you."

"Look at him," said Liam.

"How the fuck can he sleep upside down on the sofa?"

"I'm not sleeping shit head, I'm thinking."

"Thinking about what exactly?"

"About whether we'll still be alive this time tomorrow or not."

"Not only will we be alive, we'll be rich," said Jimmy. "Now let's hit the sack."

Chapter Twenty Four

As the sun rose over the small farmhouse in Peebles, the three Dundonians sat down in Elsie's kitchen awaiting their breakfast.

"Surely she can't ruin bacon and eggs?" said Liam.

"Surely not," said Mark.

Elsie dished up the three perfectly cooked breakfasts.

"So, what's first on the agenda in this master plan of yours?" Liam asked Jimmy.

"There are a few things we need to get, which I think we'll be safer going to Edinburgh for."

"What sort of things?" asked Liam.

"Here," he handed Liam a list.

Extra thick tie wraps, powerful torch, two black sets of overalls, two balaclavas, three replica hand guns, one motorbike and two helmets.

"Where the fuck are we going to get replica hand guns?" asked Liam.

"That's easy enough, there's a model shop in Lothian Road that sells them, all different kinds."

"Can I see that list?" asked Mark.

"I'll take care of the motorbike, how powerful you want it?"

"At least five hundred cc," said Jimmy.

"No problem! When we go to Edinburgh for the stuff, buy me a helmet and drop me off. I'll find a bike and meet you back here. I could do with a leather biker's jacket as well; apart from the safety issue it would be better if I looked the part. I mean I don't want to steal the bike and get stopped by the cops halfway back here just because I look like a prat, driving a big ass bike dressed in that outdoor jacket."

"Good point," said Jimmy. "Make it two jackets though, Liam will need one."

"Liam you'd better put these on, I got myself the same." Jimmy threw a baseball hat and sunglasses across the table. "Just to make sure no one recognises us. Mark's all right, he'll be hiding behind the bike helmet. The first thing we have to do is find a location to hand over the coke, somewhere not too close to here, but it has to be pretty isolated."

"What sort of place?" asked Liam.

"Somewhere with a deserted barn or a disused cottage, anything of that sort. The main thing is the seclusion; it has to be off the main road, away from prying eyes."

"Why not just use Elsie's place?" asked Liam.

"Are you fucking nuts man? You want to lead some psycho here? I told you before we're dealing with villains, they're not just going to turn up, hand over the cash and bid us farewell. We're going to have to work for this money. The whole plan depends on the image we project to them. We have got to come across as bad asses. You got that?"

"Loud and clear! No need to get bent out of shape."

"We should take the back roads to Edinburgh, and then we can have a look for a place on the way there," said Mark trying his best to calm the other two down.

"I agree, let's eat our breakfast and we can get going."

"You lads decided if you're staying another night yet?" asked Elsie.

"More than likely," said Jimmy. "We'll let you know for definite tonight."

*

Vince was already on his third cup of coffee. He checked the GPS tracking device which once turned on, could be monitored at any time from his phone. Next he emptied the cash out of his holdall, removed the false bottom and placed the device in the bag. Placing his gun in his shoulder holster he picked up the morning paper.

-'GANG WARFARE'- There had been four more shootings in Glasgow, one of which was Ricky Francis, another one in the top echelon of Harry Black's crew. Perfect, Vince thought to himself, these two rival drug gangs will be fighting for weeks. Harry's mob will be far too busy to wonder what's happening to the coke I'm supposed to be retrieving. There's just one more thing to do, check on Tony and his cutting crew.

"Tony! It's Vince."

"Vince, when the hell's that coke arriving? I know you said it was held up but we've got the premises set up, the crew's all here and we've fuck all to cut."

"You'll have the coke tomorrow, are the usual buyers in place?"

"They're all waiting, what's the cut?"

"Like I said, make it fifteen per cent. I'm feeling generous, but put the word round I want them all ready with the cash by noon tomorrow, I'll be up there first thing in the morning, have your crew ready. I want it cut as soon as I arrive. Get that sorted for me Tony and I'll put a little extra in your pocket."

"Cheers man, I'll go get things organised."

Vince ended the call.

Now he had four hours to kill until the auction closed, time to focus his thoughts.

He picked up his I-Pod. What to play? He thought to himself as he tapped his bottom lip. He looked through the list of artists and hit L as he knew he would. Led Zeppelin Four it was the obvious choice. As the opening bars of Black Dog kicked in, he lay back and relaxed, going over his plan once again in his head.

*

Stuck in traffic Buchanan was on his way to Morningside, an affluent area in the south west of Edinburgh, to see how the surveillance was going at Vince's father's house.

He'd dropped Max off earlier at headquarters to see if he could dig up anything else on Vince.

The traffic was terrible even at that time of the morning, and he found himself stuck under a huge old fashioned metal clock for what seemed like hours. He finally reached his destination and parked across from the terraced villa in Morningside Grove and went looking for the surveillance vehicle.

He saw the signs before he saw the officers. Outside the car were a few squashed cardboard coffee cups, and a pile of cigarette butts. Caffeine and nicotine, thought Buchanan, the staple diet of a stake out. He entered the car with the two coffees he'd bought from a local shop and sat in the back seat and introduced himself.

"DI Buchanan, here, these are for you."

"Buchanan, you're the bastard that's had us sitting out here all night freezing our bollocks off."

"Sorry lads, but needs must. Is there much happening?"

"Not really, he's just left; he's away to the local community centre for a game of carpet bowls."

"He'll be gone a while then?"

"About three hours the coach driver says."

"Perfect, I'm off for a sneaky look round the house."

"What! Without a warrant?"

Buchannan gave them a wink.

"You never saw me, lads."

He approached the house and instantly noticed the alarm box on the wall, and spotted some door sensors. He shoulder charged the door, which split the door jamb, then flew open as the alarm went off with a high pitched wail.

Next he took out his mobile and phoned the police to report the break in before walking back to the surveillance vehicle.

"Wait for it, lads."

Two minutes later, the two policemen received the call.

"Yes, we're still in the area along with DI Buchanan, we'll check it out right away," said one of the officers.

"I'll see to it lads," said Buchanan as the incredulous officers looked on.

He entered the front door, located the alarm panel and silenced the alarm, then made his way through to the lounge to begin his search.

The room was musty smelling with not much in it at all, a television, two grubby couches, a well-worn carpet and masses of photos on the wall. One of the corners had an ancient looking desk top computer on it, which was turned on.

Buchanan clicked on the documents folder; it contained a few letters but nothing pertinent to the case. He clicked on the Hotmail icon to see if he could find anything more interesting in his emails. The familiar box popped up, *enter password*. Shit, thought Buchanan. The photos on the wall gave him an idea; he took a couple off the wall and looked at the back. He was in luck. Vince's father was one of those people who labelled and dated the back of the frames, so he took out his notebook and wrote down anything he could find.

There were family members including his late wife; his brother and sister with Vince; there were pets Bubbles and Shep; and even a holiday home in a place called Ben Law. He methodically entered all the names into the password box, nothing. Next he entered the kitchen, nothing out of the ordinary in the cupboards or drawers. Looking out the window to the back of the house he saw a black Labrador; he turned the key in the back door and went out. It was a friendly dog, but obviously not much of a deterrent for burglars. Strange he thought, he couldn't remember seeing this pet's photo on the wall with the others.

"Here boy, what's your name then?"

The collar said Rudy.

Back in the living room, he typed Rudy into the computer.

He was in, just as he was about to check the e-mails when his phone rang.

"Buchanan, you'd better get your arse out of there, sir, he's back."

"Shit!"

He quickly logged off and headed for the front door.

"Mr Mackie? I'm DI Buchanan just checking your house over. We had a report of an alarm going off."

"Aye so I heard, a neighbour phoned me at the centre."

"If you could just take a look around and tell me if anything's missing, I'll be on my way."

The man was tall and stocky. He looked like he could have taken care of himself in his younger days. His hair was grey and practically cut to the bone.

"Bugger all worth stealing in here," he said, "but I'll take a look around just in case."

Buchanan followed him upstairs.

"Do you live here alone, sir?"

"I have for the last five years since the wife died."

"No kids?" asked Buchanan.

"I have a son but he lives abroad, I only hear from him occasionally. Why do you ask?" said Mr Mackie eyeing Buchanan suspiciously.

"I just wanted to know in case we could have contacted him for you sir, some folk find it quite harrowing having their place broken into."

He wandered into one of the bedrooms.

"At least my bowling trophies are all here, took me a bloody age to win these."

"If you could just have a quick look downstairs sir, then I'll be on my way," said Buchanan.

They wandered from room to room, Vince's father checking drawers and cupboards as they went.

"There doesn't seem to be anything missing Inspector, it looks like it was only an attempted break in, they must have kicked the door in and legged it when the alarm went off."

"That's what it looks like right enough," said Buchanan guiltily.

"I'll find you a local joiner if you'd like? Get that door fixed."

"No need for that, I've got a workshop round the back, I've always been handy at the old DIY."

Buchanan looked at his shoes, he felt sorry for the old guy.

"Well if you're sure everything is fine, I'll leave you in peace."

He shook Mr Mackie's hand and walked down the path heading for his car.

Chapter Twenty Five

A few miles outside Rosslyn they spotted a derelict barn.

"Let's check that one out," said Liam.

"It's isolated enough," said Mark. "It might just do the job."

Jimmy hit the brakes, performed a U turn and pulled off the main road. He drove slowly up the narrow pothole covered track for a few hundred yards, so they could give it a look over. Getting out the car, they walked up to the barn. It was made of corrugated iron and wood, and only about three quarters of the roof was left on it. Inside, the floor was covered in straw and the walls were lined with troughs, the only other thing inside was a pile of old hay bales strewn across the floor.

"It's an old byre," said Jimmy.

"What's a byre?" asked Liam.

"A barn for housing animals, this is perfect, help me pile these hay bales up in the far corner."

Taking a side each Liam and Mark moved the heavy bales.

"What the fuck is that smell?" asked Liam.

"Just pigeons," said Jimmy. He pointed to the roof. "They're getting in up there, look."

Liam looked up at the corner of the barn where six pigeons were sitting on the rafters staring down at him with what he saw as a look of disdain.

"I fucking hate pigeons, they give me the creeps. I hate the way they stare at you, and I hate that weird bobbing head shit they do, they're nothing more than rats with wings."

"Never heard of anyone being scared of pigeons," said Mark.

Jimmy walked towards the farthest away wall and checked that the food troughs were well attached to the floor.

"This is the place guys, no doubt about it."

*

Ignoring the red light and the car horns from the other road users, Buchanan put his foot down all the way to the station. He rushed up the stairs taking them two at a time, narrowly avoiding the cleaner and her hoover on the way up. He barged into the office, sat down and turned on the first computer he found.

"Hurry the fuck up," he said aloud as the computer was going through its start-up sequence.

Once he heard the familiar start up sound he clicked on the browser icon, logged into Vince's father's Hotmail Account and checked the inbox where he found twenty three messages. Most were of no interest, a mixture of spam and information telling him what was on at the local community centre. Three however were obviously from Vince, simply signed V, they all concerned the same subject, all sent in the last week. Buchanan opened the sent folder and matched up the replies to Vince's e-mails, printed them off and sat down to read them.

': I'm up in Aberdeen for a couple of days I will try to pop by on the way back. Have you given any thought to what I asked?-V:'

':Be nice to see you. I don't know if I could stand living in all that heat. I think I'll give it a miss:'

':I have been held up, can't see you until I've dealt with something, but I've made my mind up I'm definitely going back abroad for good this time.
Please reconsider-V:'

': I'm thinking about it but what about Rudy? I can't leave the poor thing here on her own, besides I'd miss her:'

': All you need is the proper documents and vaccinations and then after about thirty days you and Rudy can travel to Spain. I'll take care of all that- set it all up for you and you can join me there. And REMEMBER delete these emails, they can't be left on your computer.'

Below the text were half a dozen photos of a large villa, one which had a grinning Vince in front of a swimming pool. Vince had been his usual careful self though. Not one of the photos gave what could be considered a complete view of the villa. They were more parts of a villa. Two huge French doors opened up to a large patio in one. Another showed a large driveway containing half a dozen fancy motors the plates had been blurred out by some sort of fancy photo editing software. Even the one with Vince by the pool showed nothing in the background that could be used for identification purposes.

"Canny bastard!" said Buchanan.

Buchanan took the printed e-mails through to the DCI's office.

"So Ronnie, your hunch paid off, they are in contact with each other. Convenient you being there when the alarm went off or we wouldn't have found out any of this."

"I think we should put a tap on Mr Mackie's phone, in case Vince calls rather than e-mails him."

"What if Vince phones his mobile?"

"He won't, he's lost it"

"How do you know that?"

Buchanan produced the mobile from his pocket.

"Because, I have it here!"

"I didn't see that!" shouted the DCI as Ronnie left the office.

Out in the corridor, he bumped into Max.

"I have a job for you, I found out Vince's father's e-mail address and the password, they've been in constant contact with each other so I want you to monitor it, see what else comes through, I'm off to see Dave before they move him."

"You'd better hurry up then," said Max. "The van's already here to pick him up."

Dave was sitting in the corner of the holding cell, looking rather sorry for himself.

"What do you want now, Buchanan?"

"If things had gone to plan and Lucy had turned up with the coke, what would have happened next?"

"It would have all been cut, split into smaller amounts, and sold off to a network of small dealers, why?"

"Who saw to that?"

"A guy called Tony, a fat slimy bastard he is, stinks of B.O."

"Where do these cuts take place?"

"Usually in small warehouses in out of the way industrial estates."

"Like the one in Whitemyres?"

"Exactly, although I doubt Vince will use that one again. Vince is a careful guy, he'll have figured out you know about that one."

"How does he get a hold of these warehouses?"

"I have absolutely no idea."

Soon as he left the cell, Buchanan phoned his Divisional Headquarters in Aberdeen and asked to speak to Rob Bennie from the drug squad.

"Rob, its DI Buchanan. I've got a tip off for you."

"Go on," said Rob.

I have it on good authority that a rather large quantity of coke is heading your way."

"How much?"

"Four kilos! The thing is I believe it's going to be cut and split by a guy called Tony, don't know his second name but he's seemingly quite fat."

"Let me think, a fat guy with drug connections called Tony, could be Fat Tony."

"Are you taking the piss?"

"No, I know exactly who you're talking about, stays up in Northfield. He's more a distributor than a dealer, cuts large quantities into smaller ones, delivers it to local dealers and collects the money."

"That sounds like the guy," said Buchanan.

"Tell you what Ronnie, we'll put a tail on him for the next couple of days, see where it leads us. By the way thanks for this, I could do with a good collar."

"It's all yours Rob, just keep me up to date with what you find out."

*

Mark walked in to his second bike shop of the day, he'd bought the jackets and helmets from a separate shop as he thought it might look suspicious buying the stuff from a shop he was going to rip off a bike from. He'd got Jimmy to stop earlier when he'd seen a bike, so he could steal the plates which he now had zipped inside his leather jacket. He'd also stashed a full petrol can a couple of miles away from the shop, as he knew these places usually kept a minimum of gas in the tanks. He also knew no one was going to let him test drive a bike in case he did exactly what he was planning to do, these places often had test days but he didn't have the time to wait around for that, so he'd have to be clever.

He entered the shop and approached the counter, lifting the visor off his helmet.

"Is there any chance of test-driving the second hand Suzuki out there?"

"The 750cc?"

"That's the one."

"Sorry sir, we have a strict policy, test drives are only at the weekend and you'd have to hand over your license together with some other ID."

"That's cool, you can't be too careful nowadays, is it ok to look it over? Maybe start it up and get a feel for the thing, you know what I mean?"

"I don't see a problem with that. You go outside and have a look at it. I will be out with the keys in a couple of minutes."

After having a quick look, the guy arrived with the keys and went through his spiel.

"With a fuel injected 750cc liquid-cooled engine and reliable six-speed gearbox, this is one bad ass motorbike."

The guy turned on the engine as Mark sat astride the machine.

"Rev it up," said the salesman.

Mark did as he was told, feeling the power vibrating through his body.

"You know what? said Mark. "I think I'll take it!"

With that he put down his visor, kicked the bike into gear, spun through a hundred and eighty degrees and took off from the bike shop forecourt, watching the salesman get smaller and smaller in his mirror.

*

At about the same time Mark was on his way back to Peebles, Liam and Jimmy entered Greg's Model Shop on Lothian Road.

The model shop was huge. The ground floor had everything from model kits to huge expensive remote control cars and aeroplanes.

"Jesus! Check out the size of this thing," said Liam.

He was staring at a model of a huge German bi-plane.

"I fancy one of those babies."

"Aye, it's smart right enough," replied Jimmy. "But it's not exactly what we're here for, is it. What we're looking for is down in the basement."

They went downstairs walked past a collection of samurai swords and medieval weapons and approached one of the assistants.

"Can I help you gentlemen?"

"We'd like to look at your replica fire arms."

"Follow me."

The guy led them to a display cabinet near the back of the shop.

"Here we are, gentlemen."

"Jesus!" said Liam. "You've got a whole fucking armoury here."

"How much for the replica shotguns?" asked Jimmy.

"Depends what kind, a hundred and seventy five for the pump actions."

"I'll take two, and one of those small hand guns."

"If you don't mind me asking," said the assistant. "What do you need the replicas for?"

"Well we're not going to hold up a bank if that's what you're thinking," said Liam.

The assistant laughed.

"Actually," said Jimmy. "They're props for a movie we're helping out on."

Jimmy extended his hand.

"Jimmy Fallon and this is my assistant Charlie. Part of our work involves acquiring replica weapons and suchlike for the film industry. We get sent a list of items and it's our job to go find them."

"Wow, what's the movie called?"

"Auction, it's some kind of British gangster thing."

"Would you like them wrapped up?" asked the assistant. "I should think so," replied Jimmy. "We wouldn't last five minutes out there before being stopped by the cops, if we walked about with them in our hand now, would we."

The assistant laughed once again and wrapped up their purchases. "How the fuck can you do that?" asked Liam when they left the shop.

"Do what?" asked Jimmy.

"When someone puts you on the spot, like that guy just did, you always seem to come out with any shit that enters your head and make it sound believable."

"It's just a gift," replied Jimmy.

They took their purchases back to the car.

"Fancy a quick pint?" asked Liam. "There's a pub just across the road."

"Alright, just a quick one then, but you will have to keep that hat and shades on. I don't want anyone recognising you this late in the game."

They entered the pub, ordered their drinks and sat down at a table near the back.

"What time is it?" asked Liam.

"Twelve forty-five. Why?"

"That means the auction's about to finish. I'll have a quick check; see what it's up to."

Liam logged on with his phone.

"Two hundred and twenty-five, that'll do for me," said Liam.

*

The call came through at two minutes past one, just as Jimmy and Liam got back to their car.

"Jimmy, its Uncle Frank. You have two hundred and thirty, do you have a pen and paper there?"

Jimmy searched the glove compartment.

"Got them Frank!"

"Write this down."

Frank gave him a mobile number and a code word, '*Avocet*'.

"It's up to you now, give them a phone, check the password and set up the drop."

Jimmy ended the call.

"It's on," said Jimmy.

He looked for the nearest public phone box to call the auction winner.

"Why can't you just use your mobile?" asked Liam.

"I don't trust them, they can be traced."

*

Vince answered the phone on the first ring.

"Password…?"

"Avocet…!"

"The drop will be tonight, near Edinburgh," said Jimmy. "You will be given directions. You come alone. We will be watching you, deviate from these rules and the deal's off."

"I'd rather it was sooner rather than later."

"Tough, it's tonight or not at all."

Jimmy ended the call.

Vince didn't like waiting but he had no choice.

To kill some time he opened his laptop to check his emails and saw one from his father.

':Some Bastard broke into the house, seems to be nothing missing except for my mobile, the detective who responded to it took a good look round but said everything was safe enough. It made me miss my bowling match:'

Shit, that had to be Buchanan, thought Vince. How the fuck did he find out my true identity?
He replied to the e-mail.

': Is this the guy who responded? :'
He attached the photo of Buchanan he'd taken with his phone earlier at the restaurant.

*

Liam and Jimmy arrived back at Elsie's to see Mark proudly sitting on the motor bike.
"Any problems?" asked Jimmy.
"It went like a charm; you ought to have seen the guy's face when I took off. Did you get everything we need?"
"We did," said Liam as he pulled out the shotgun from behind his back and pointed it at Mark.
'That's a scary looking fucking thing, looks damn real as well."
"It's a pump action shotgun, well a replica, but good enough to do the job we need it for," said Jimmy. "Now let's get inside, we have things to discuss."

*

"Tommy! its Vince. You still up in Aberdeen?"
"Aye, I'm still working the clubs, what can I do for you?"
"I want someone worked on."
"Hold on till I get my notepad. Do you want them hurt?"

Vince thought for a moment.

"No, I just want them scared, left a message, but give it one of your dramatic touches. You know what I mean."

"When do you want this done?"

"Right now, if possible."

"No problem, give me the details."

Chapter Twenty Six

Buchanan, Max, McLean and DCI Brannigan were all staring at the computer screen, reading Mr Mackie's reply to the email.

': Aye that's him, the one on the left, the ugly, scruffy bastard:'

"He's on to us, Ronnie," said the DCI.

"The sneaky bastard, I never even saw him take the photo," said Max.

"One thing we do know, the auction's finished, so that means the handover will be happening pretty soon. I've been on to Aberdeen, they've put a tail on the guy Dave says is most likely to cut the coke, so hopefully that should lead to picking up on Vince at their end," said Buchanan.

The DCI turned to McLean.

"Any sign of the guys from Dundee yet?"

"No sign at the hotel, they never returned last night and we've done door to door around Peebles and came up with sod all. I think they've done a bunk. They probably saw our boys handing out their photos and scarpered."

"How about you, Max, did you dig up anything else on Vince?"

"Quite a bit, actually!"

Max referred to his notes.

"I got on to the M.O.D, he's ex-Army, worked his way up in the Marines and did his sniper training, one of the hardest things to get into seemingly. It says here each Royal Marine sniper must master seven basic sniper skills: Knowledge, Navigation,

Concealment, Observation, Stalking, Judging Distance and Shooting. Trainees have to calculate wind and range solutions. Navigation standards are passed by trainees making their own map from an aerial photograph and then being dropped off to use their own skills in finding their way out."

"Jesus, no wonder we can't catch the bastard," said Buchanan.

*

The man in the car adjusted his rear view mirror and watched as the woman came out the door of her house and locked up. He had been waiting for over an hour but that was okay, it was worth it. This side of things paid far more than his legitimate work. He watched her leave the house with her dog and cross the street. Once he was convinced she was well out of sight, he got out the car and walked round to the boot. When he was absolutely sure no one was watching he removed the long strip of towel and the petrol can. He soaked the towel with the can, prised open the petrol cap from the woman's car and threaded the strip of towel down into the tank, leaving about eighteen inches hanging out. He walked to the door of the house and pinned the note to the heavy wooden door with the switch blade knife.

On the way back to his vehicle he paused briefly, took out his lighter and set fire to the tail end of the towel. He watched the flames crawl slowly up the side of the car before getting in his own vehicle and driving away.

*

Buchanan answered his phone.

"Ronnie, its Vince, how's it going?"

Buchanan mouthed, "Vince" to his colleagues and pointed to his phone. They all gathered round as Buchanan put the call on speaker.

"What do you want Vince, or should I say Charles?"

"Very good Inspector, how did you find out?"

"I got your prints off the wine glass from the restaurant."

"How foolish of me!" replied Vince. "That's not like me at all, I must have things praying on my mind, speaking of which, I believe you met my father. That takes our little cat and mouse game to a whole new level; you should never have involved him."

"Did you phone me to tell me anything in particular Vince, or just to bore the shit out me?"

Brannigan tried to stifle a laugh, he was unsuccessful.

"There was something" replied Vince, "let me think; how's Michelle by the way?"

"What!" Buchanan froze.

"I hope she's got good car insurance."

The line went dead as a blanket of silence enveloped the room.

*

"I'm terrified Ronnie, I came back with the dog and the car was in flames but that's not the worst of it, there was a note stuck to the door with a knife."

"What did it say?"

"Next time we'll make sure you're in."

"Bastards!" said Buchanan.

Michelle broke down crying then took a few deep breaths and managed to gain control of herself.

"I've arranged for protection for you, just until I get this bastard Vince. I'll make sure you're safe, trust me Michelle."

Buchanan ended the call and threw his mobile straight through the PC monitor.

"Calm down, Ronnie!" said the DCI.

"Calm fucking down! This bastard's really beginning to get on my nerves. If we're going to catch him it's not going to be here, it's going to be up in Aberdeen and that's where I'm heading."

"Are you fuck, you're staying right here till this case is finished. That's an order!"

Buchanan looked at the DCI for a minute.

"I have to get out of here," said Buchanan. "I'm off outside for a cigarette."

He slammed the office door and went downstairs.

Buchanan lit up the cigarette and thought things out for a while. He had a dilemma on his hands, stay in Edinburgh or go with his instincts and head up to Aberdeen.

After the nicotine had worked its magic, he stamped out his cigarette and paused with his hand on the door handle.

"Bugger it! I know I'm right," he said to himself.

He walked round the back to the car park and got in his car, started it up and took off.

"I thought you might try something like this," said the familiar voice from the back seat.

"Max! What the fuck are you doing here?"

"I'm coming with you."

Buchanan stopped the car.

"You can drive then, but I need some coffee. Stop off at the first service station you see on the way up."

Just past the Forth Road Bridge, they exited the motorway, pulled into the rest stop and headed for the cafe.

They took their coffees over to the nearest table.

"Right Max, what do we know so far?"

"Vince has probably won the auction and is awaiting instructions to buy back his coke," said Max.

"Which, due to the fact that now we know who he really is he'll want to get rid of it as quickly as possible, more than likely with the help of this guy in Aberdeen," said Buchanan.

"Something bugs me about that, sir."

"What do you mean, Max?"

"Well this guy Vince, he plans everything down to the last detail, right?"

"Right!" replied Buchanan.

"Well, why would he give us Dave on a plate knowing he's likely to tell us about his contacts in Aberdeen and then turn up to use those people?"

"That's a very good point, Max."

"Would you like a top up?" asked the waitress.

"Yes please," replied both men.

"How about this Max, he expects us to find out, expects us to put this guy Tony under surveillance and while everyone's watching him he changes the venue to somewhere else."

"That sounds more like him. I still think it will be in Aberdeen though. There will be a lot of folk up there itching for that coke. It'll be a few days late mind, so he's got a long list of desperate clients."

"Good point, Max."

Buchanan let out a long sigh.

"It's a gamble Max; no doubt about it but it's better than sitting back in Edinburgh with our thumb up our ass. Now let's finish these coffees and get going, but first turn off your phone."

"Why, sir?"

"He phoned me remember, so he must have taken a note of our numbers when he took our phones off us at the restaurant. If he has our numbers he can trace us and know exactly where we are. We'll get ourselves some cheap temporary ones in Dundee with new sim cards."

"Good thinking," said Max as he drained the last of his coffee.

*

Dressed in his Sunday best, Mr Mackie locked his newly installed front door. He wheeled his tartan shopping cart with the squeaky wheels down the path, bumped it down the concrete stairs and crossed the road. He headed towards the bus stop and slowly walked past the car with the two men inside, two men who were trying hard to look in every direction but his. He allowed himself a smile then caught the first bus that arrived; he sat down at the back and headed towards the centre of Edinburgh.

He closed his eyes and thought about his son. He'd named him Charles after a favourite uncle of his, but he'd never liked it, preferring to use his middle name. He was well educated, taught in a fee paying school, one of the best, by the best teachers available, and then straight into the army where he'd excelled himself, rising up the ranks rapidly.

Why he'd decided to use his skills for more nefarious purposes was hard to pinpoint. It was simply a case of getting in with a bad crowd according to Vince. He'd left all that behind him now of course, since his escape he'd became legit, reinvented himself. Let's face it everybody is entitled to a second chance. It took him a while to convince Vince's mother about that but she eventually came round to his way of thinking. He found it hard getting used to his various looks mind you. Every time he appeared he looked different. It was quite understandable of course; he didn't want to end up back in jail. Not long after the escape the cops were always round asking questions about this and that but that eventually petered off, no one had been round for years, at least not until the recent visit by that scruffy detective. Who ever heard of a break in where nothing was stolen, it must have been a ruse, an excuse to poke around a bit. There was nothing to find of course he'd made sure of that, even his computer was password protected. It hadn't half got Vince agitated though. He seemed to know the cop who was sniffing around. There must be some history there.

He laughed to himself and thought back to a particular day many years ago, it's funny how some days appear so clearly in your mind. He could remember it like it was yesterday.

It was a warm spring day with a slight breeze and he'd taken Vince for a hike up Arthur's Seat. He'd promised the boy he'd take him for ages and he had a day's holiday. It was one of Vince's favourite places, the boy loved the fact that he was climbing up an extinct volcano smack bang in the centre of Holyrood Park.

They started the day by feeding the swans and ducks at St Margaret's Loch. He'd impressed the lad by reeling off the names of the various birds like an expert. He wasn't to know that his father had sat up half the previous night reading a Guide to British Bird Life. He'd planned on reading up on rock formations as well, but had given up by page five. Next they climbed the steep path up to St Anthony's Chapel, the only building to be found anywhere in the park apart from the Palace itself. What was left of the structure looked more like the medieval ruin of an old fortified castle than any kind of religious building. It stands on a rugged cliff dominating the surrounding landscape above the Loch, reminding people of a time long past. No one knew much about it, he'd looked it up in the local library. Some said the Chapel could possibly have served as some sort of religious beacon, giving direction to sea-borne pilgrims journeying to the nearby Holyrood Abbey, itself, now a desolate ruin lying in the grounds of the nearby Palace.

He remembered how a young American couple spending their honeymoon in Edinburgh had asked to take Vince's photo probably due to the fact he'd been wearing his tartan trousers, his favourites, he'd worn the damn things everywhere that year. To them he must have looked like a typical Scottish laddie.

After being rewarded a couple of quid by the couple, they'd continued on their journey towards the summit. As the path got steeper they had stopped for their lunch. They sat down on a nearby boulder and ate their corned beef sandwiches and drank their cans of Irn Bru, trying their best to ward off the swarms of midges that had been their constant companions all the way up. Vince fed his crusts to the crows, he told his father that he thought it unfair that everyone fed the ducks and swans but no one fed the crows.

He could remember the conversation verbatim.

"It's probably because most people see crows as a bad omen," he told him. "They have this sort of creepiness attached to them."

"How come?" the young Vince asked.

"In some Celtic cultures, the crow was a sign of death, especially after a battle. They often circled battlefields waiting to feed on the dead."

"Creepy!"

"Do you know what they call a load of crows gathered together?"

"No idea!"

"A murder of crows."

"Your freaking me out Dad, stop it."

"Just make sure you don't lie on your back too long, they might make a meal out of you."

"Dad!"

The crows took off en masse, cawing as if in thanks for their meal. After their lunch they decided to stay off the tourist path, and walked along the top of a steep craggy cliff looking down on Hunters Bog far below them. They squeezed themselves through the sharp yellow flowered gorse bushes scaring a few rabbits from the undergrowth, and then scrambled up the rocky path until they finally reached the top. The view was magnificent, a 360 degree panorama. He pointed out the various landmarks to Vince, the Bass Rock, the Pentland Hills, and the Firth of Forth among others. His son followed his directions with his new set of binoculars, given to him only that morning.

The bus jerked to a stop its brakes screeching. The noise pulled him out of his day dream. He rubbed his eyes, stretched his arms and drew himself back into the real world. The young Vince once again becoming a distant memory, lost to the annals of time.

*

He got off at the shopping centre on Princes Street, dumped the shopping cart and headed towards the upmarket hotel at the other side of the road. He walked through the door held open by the concierge.

"Good afternoon," he said with a smile on his face.

"Hello sir," said the immaculately dressed man, "not a bad day for this late in the year."

"Aye, no bad just now, but I think it might rain," said Mr Mackie. Heading to the bar, he paused to take in the luxurious surroundings then bought himself a beer and headed towards the man sitting in the corner with the open laptop.

"Hello son."

"Dad, you came!"

"Aye son, I got your note, you were right enough about the cops though, there's two of them sitting in the car across the road."

"You weren't followed then?"

"No chance, I made sure I sat at the back of the bus beside the rear window so I could make sure, the shopping cart idea of yours worked a treat, they obviously thought I was just nipping out to the shops."

"Anything else out of the ordinary been happening?"

"Not really, the phone company phoned, said there was a problem with the line. First I knew! They're sending someone round to fix it this afternoon. I left the key with the neighbours."

"Something wrong with the line my ass," said Vince, "they'll be away to bug your phone."

"So what's all the sudden interest in you again? Cops turning up at my door with daft excuses and people trying to bug my phone."

"It's that Buchanan guy, he's behind it all. A couple of guys I hired to do a job for me once ended up murdering someone, and he seems to think that I'm behind it."

"Murder!"

"Calm down dad, I had nothing to do with it, and besides as I told you, I'm leaving the UK for good, just as soon as I tidy up a few things and get my finances in order. The police will be chasing shadows."

"How did this cop manage to find out who you are? You're always so careful about hiding your identity."

"He got lucky, Dad, and I got careless, simple as that."

Vince's father shook his head.

"That's not like you at all, son. I worry about you sometimes. Anyway regardless of what they want you for I'm still here for you. I'm your dad and I don't want to see you back in jail, so the sooner you get your stuff in order and get the hell out of here the better. Then, and only then mind you, I'll maybe give some thought to moving over there with you."

"Thanks dad. That means a lot to me."

Vince put his hand on his father's shoulder.

"Anyway like I said earlier, I've booked a suite in here, it's paid up till the end of the week so you can stay here for a few days."

"Suits me son, I've got Mrs Taylor next door watching the dog so I'm looking forward to it, I've never been here before. It looks a classy place."

"Enjoy yourself, you deserve it, I have to go up to Aberdeen tonight but I should be back by tomorrow afternoon if things go to plan."

"You do what you have to do. I'll be alright here on my own. Now let me buy you a drink."

"Cheers, Dad, I'll have a whisky."

Chapter Twenty Seven

Liam, Jimmy and Mark entered the barn behind Elsie's farmhouse. Jimmy took out his phone and studied the photos he'd taken of the byre earlier on in the day. Elsie's barn was practically the same size and a similar shape, which was a good thing for what Jimmy had in mind. They put a few empty boxes in one corner to represent the hay bales and an old tree trunk at the far end became the troughs.

"Right guys, put on your boiler suits and balaclavas and get behind the hay bales."

"You mean the boxes?" said Liam.

"Stop being an asshole Liam, we're trying to recreate the byre, so they're fucking hay bales, ok?"

"You're the boss!"

Jimmy closed the barn door.

"Before you start Liam, I'm closing the door because the drop is taking place tonight, so it will be dark, you got that?"

"Affirmative!" replied Liam.

Mark and Liam got behind the boxes in their new attire.

"Right!" said Jimmy, "Later on tonight when I arrive at the byre with the guy with the money, we'll both park up and walk towards the entrance, you two are going to jump up, turn on the torch to dazzle us and point the shotguns at us, try to look menacing. Let's try it, one, two, and three."

Liam jumped up.

"Get your hands in the air, mother fucker!"

"Stop!" shouted Jimmy.

"Liam what the fuck was that? We're not in fucking LA and the last time I looked you weren't a 'Gangsta' and where were you, Mark?"

"Sorry, I slipped," said Mark. "The legs on this boiler suit are too long."

"Listen lads, our life may depend on this. We want to create the impression that you two are hijacking me and the other guy so let's try it again, and this time remember the torch, and Mark, roll up your trouser legs."

After running through the scenario a few times, they had a break. After a quick beer and a sandwich, it was on to stage two.

Jimmy pulled out two sizes of thick cable ties.

"You all know what these are?"

They both nodded.

"We're going to use them as makeshift handcuffs." Jimmy took two of the larger ones tied them loosely to create two wide hoops then joined the two hoops together with a smaller one.

"Mark come over here and put your hands behind your back."

Mark did as he was instructed.

Jimmy put on the makeshift cuffs and pulled them tight.

"Try and get out of them."

Mark tried, to no avail.

"Ouch! Get them off, they're hurting my wrists."

Jimmy took out his knife and cut them off.

"You'll have to practice a few times under torchlight, and then work on tying them to the trough; I've put some bolts into the tree trunk, that will have to do for the moment."

*

Buchanan was leaning against the car outside the shopping centre in Dundee High Street. He was smoking his second cigarette in a row watching the clouds ominously growing darker and darker above. I hope that's not an omen, he thought to himself as he waited for Max to arrive with their new phones.

He opened the passenger door and got in when he saw him

arriving.

"I just got cheap ones sir, but they're on the same network."

"These will do fine Max. Before I transfer my numbers I'm going to take a risk and turn on my old one, just for a minute," said Buchanan.

"Might as well do the same" said Max.

"Fuck!" said Buchanan looking at the screen, "Eight missed calls, three voicemails and four texts."

"I've almost got as much," said Max.

Buchanan scanned the text list, one from Michelle and three from Brannigan, one of which informed him that Mr Mackie had gone shopping and never returned.

Max leaned over to look at the DI's phone.

"I got that one as well, sir."

"I'd better phone Michelle and give her the new number."

"Hi love, it's Ronnie."

"Where the hell have you been? I've been phoning you all afternoon."

"I've had a bit of phone trouble, had to buy a new one, that's why I'm calling you to give you the new number."

"So! You're not phoning to see how I am then, that's just great."

"Sorry love," said Buchanan. "How are you?"

"Still a bit shaken up but they've put me up in the Queens Hotel till you find this guy, so it could be worse. I phoned Linda so she's over here with me. Where are you anyway? Still in Edinburgh?"

"Dundee actually, I'm on my way back to Aberdeen but if anyone asks, you haven't heard from me ok."

"What's that supposed to mean?"

"Well, let's just say John and I had a difference of opinion, he thinks we're more likely to catch the guy back in Edinburgh whereas I think Aberdeen's a better shot."

"Linda's back from the bar, I'll have to go. Keep in touch Ronnie."

"Will do love, bye, and say hello to your sister for me."

Next he phoned DCI Brannigan.

"John, it's Ronnie!"

"I've been trying to phone you for the last two hours, where the fuck are you?"

"I'm just leaving Dundee."

"Is Max with you?" asked the DCI.

"Yes, but he's just following my orders, if anyone gets reprimanded it should be me."

"No one's getting reprimanded, the Superintendent paid us a visit he thinks it's a great idea for you to follow the leads in Aberdeen. You're a jammy bastard, Ronnie."

"He's right enough though, it is a good idea. It keeps both bases covered."

"I suppose you're right," said the DCI. "It's a high profile case now, especially since we found out Vince is not only a drug dealer but also an escaped felon. Even the drug squad in Glasgow are sticking their oar in," said Brannigan.

"No wonder, they've been trying to get a lead on Vince for years, we've found out who he was in three days."

"Don't get too cocky Ronnie. By the way I've called off the surveillance at his father's house since he disappeared, there doesn't seem much point to it now."

"How do you know he's not just off on a big shopping trip?"

"We checked with the neighbours, he asked the woman next door to watch his dog for a few days, so he's obviously off somewhere."

Buchanan reached behind him to the back seat and picked up the box from his new phone. "I'll give you my new mobile number, me and Max thought it would be better to change our phones, you never know when Vince is checking up on where we are."

"Good idea Ronnie. Well, keep in touch, if we have any news this end I'll keep you informed. Oh, and by the way, you'd better phone Michelle, she's phoned me four times. I couldn't tell her much mind, mainly because I didn't have a clue where the fuck you were."

"I've just phoned her, she's fine. Cheers John."

*

212

Vince picked up his phone.

"Where are you?" asked Jimmy.

"That depends on who's asking."

"Don't be a smart arse or we'll take the coke elsewhere."

"I doubt that very much!"

"What do you mean?"

"Well let's see, if you had access to anyone who would buy the coke you wouldn't have had to put it up for auction now would you."

The other end of the phone was silent.

"So why don't we end this right now, you meet me in Edinburgh, I give you the cash, you give me the coke, job done, what do you say?"

"No! Stick to the plan; make your way to Loanhead. We will phone you at ten with further instructions."

"So what the fuck am I supposed to do in Loanhead for the next five hours?"

"I'm sure you'll find something to do."

The line went dead.

"That was intense," said Jimmy.

"How do you mean?" asked Liam.

"This guy sounds a bit of a scary dude, and he's close by, he's in Edinburgh already."

"We'll be alright man; we have the plan down to a 'T'. What could go wrong?"

"Yeah, you're probably right but go and give Mark a shout. We'll run through it one more time but this time at the byre, I'll go and get the car and you two follow on the bike."

"Will do, but give us five minutes to get the equipment together."

*

Vince couldn't believe his luck, he couldn't have picked a better place for the drop if he'd set it up himself. He was planning on heading out in that direction anyway, he was off to meet an old friend and hopefully talk him in to helping out. He needed a

213

professional and no one was more able for the job than Barney.

Barney was an old army buddy of Vince's. They'd served in the same unit and then applied the skills they'd learned in the military to more mercenary activities.

While traditionally people think of mercenaries as soldiers hired to fight in armed conflicts or sometimes used to overthrow governments. Vince and Barney were mostly hired for private security; they became experts at it and ended up eventually forming their own private security firm. Listing some high profile clients, they had begun to make a real name for themselves and the money was good while it lasted. They had to eventually disband the company when the police took an interest in their activities. He didn't want them digging too deep into his background so he'd had no choice. He'd enjoyed the work involved though, much of it carried out overseas. The services and expertise offered by Armco was similar to those the military or police forces offered, but being a private firm they could afford to bend a few rules to meet the needs of their clients. Most of the work revolved around providing bodyguards for high profile staff or the protection of the company premises themselves, especially in hostile territories. They were basically there just in case anything should happen. Most of the time it didn't, so quite often they more or less got paid mega bucks for a free holiday in some sun drenched country. Nowadays such firms were common place. He laughed as he remembered watching a report on the BBC News channel a couple of weeks ago telling him that due to cost-cutting measures, the West Midlands and Surrey forces had invited bids for contracts from private security firms, on behalf of all forces.

Jesus, he hoped the firms doing the bidding were a bit more law abiding than his.

He thought back to Barney. He could be a bit high maintenance what with his chirpy character, his habit of talking at a million miles an hour, and that annoying catchphrase of his, but if you wanted someone to get you out of a sticky situation or come up with an escape plan, he was the man you wanted in your corner.

Vince once again reached for his I-Pod, poured himself a drink

and hit shuffle.
"Cocaine by J.J. Cale"
"Would you fucking believe it?"

Chapter Twenty Eight

With his windscreen wipers on full, and his car de-mister working overtime, Vince made his way through the driving rain. He approached Loanhead, a small town in Midlothian, situated just south of Edinburgh with a population of just under seven thousand. It was a town built on coal and shale mining, a lost industry nowadays, thought Vince, once providing a livelihood for thousands. In recent times however, British coal mining had been relegated to museum shelves and old miners' memories. Vince's uncle had been a miner around here, at the Bilston Glen Colliery. He worked right up until the mine closed in 1988. The colliery was an industrial estate now and, out of interest, exactly where Vince was heading.

He drove into the car park of Barney's Pistol and Rifle Club and walked to the main entrance.

"I'm here to see Barney."

"Who shall I say wants to see him?" asked the huge guy with the stern face standing at the door.

"Tell him it's Vince."

The man turned round and picked up the phone.

"A guy here to see you says his name's Vince."

The man replaced the phone.

"He says to go right up."

*

"Hey Vinnie-Mac long time no see. Fuck man, you look different every time we meet, take a seat. Would you like a drink?"

"Cheers Barney, I'll have a whisky. Did you manage to get what I asked?"

"Here you go!"

Barney handed Vince a long wooden box and a smaller box of ammo.

Vince opened the box and checked out the rifle. It was an L85-A2, an improved version of the original 5.56mm SA80, a rifle that Vince was at one time very familiar with. The magazine has a capacity of 30 rounds, which can be fired as single shots or burst. He knew if he found himself in a dodgy situation, this was the weapon to get him out of it.

"Any chance of you telling me what you've gotten yourself into? Because it must be some heavy shit, if you need that sort of weapon to get yourself out of it."

"I'm not sure I'll need this, but it will be handy to have, just in case."

"In case of what?"

"Something of mine was stolen and I aim to get it back. I think the guys who stole it are in way over their heads but I can't be sure they don't have some heavy backup, so when I turn up to retrieve this item, I might need a bit more firepower than my hand gun."

"Better to be well prepared I always say," said Barney. "By the way what is this 'Item' ?"

"Four kilos of pure Colombian!"

"I take it we're not talking coffee here?"

"Nope!" said Vince, "Definitely not coffee."

"How's business with you anyway, Barney? Still dealing with mercenaries?"

"Not so much, Vince. I make enough off the legit stuff now. The firing range makes a fortune, over two hundred grand a year. I don't know if it's this recession we're in but something's happening at the moment that seems to make folk just want to shoot shit up. Do you have time to stick around for a bit? I'll give you the tour; we could grab something to eat in the bar."

"You have a bar in here?"

"Oh yes, The Parabellum is strictly members only."

"Nice name."

"I thought you'd like it."

*

The lounge was dark with some bright red neon lights hanging from the roof. There were small lamps that seemed to be made out of hand grenades at tables on the side of the white leather seats. "Very seventies," said Vince.

"That's what I was aiming for," replied Barney from behind the bar.

The walls were covered in a camouflage material and there were ammo boxes, old weapons and various other military items lying haphazardly around. The centre piece was a full size replica Sherman tank.

"Jesus Barney, how the hell did you manage to get this?"

"I got it on e-bay, believe it or not. It always amazes me some of the shit you can get on there, it was a movie prop, they used it on Saving Private Ryan."

Behind Barney a brass plaque hung above the bar. 'Si vis pacem, para bellum'. If you wish for peace, prepare for war. Very apt, Vince thought to himself.

He wandered over to an old fashioned jukebox.

"This is cool Barney, makes a change from all the modern ones you see nowadays."

"It's a Rock-olla circa 1955. I shipped it over from the States last year."

"I see you have our old army song on there."

"Yep, 'Keep a Knockin'!"

Barney put a coin in the slot and hit play.

They carried their drinks over to a table as Little Richard sung in the back ground.

Vince was wondering how to approach Barney about helping him out. Hopefully, knowing Barney, he'd volunteer.

"Do you remember that Saudi job, Vince?" Barney laughed.

"I was just thinking about that the other day."

Barney was talking about one of their security jobs.

They had both been hired as protection for a rich Arab's daughter. Someone had tried to drag the girl into the back of a car on her way home from her work in his jewellery store one day. Her father saw it as a kidnap attempt so he and Barney were hired as her personal body guards.

"She didn't half have the hots for you. She followed you around like a dog on heat."

"I remember," replied Vince. "She always wandered around the house in that skimpy see through bikini but she never actually seemed to go swimming in the pool, funny that."

Barney laughed once more and slapped his leg.

"Good money though," said Vince. "Twenty five grand for two weeks work."

"It could have been more than two weeks though if it weren't for your little faux pas."

Vince raised his hands.

"Not my fault Barney. Like I've told you before, I got up in the morning, went into the en-suite bathroom, had a shower and a shave and when I came back she was in my bed completely starkers. I didn't go near her."

"That's not what her father thought though, was it?"

"That was just bad luck, he walked in put two and two together and made five."

"What a look he had on his face, I thought he was having a stroke. I could see the veins in his neck pulsing from the doorway."

Barney put down his drink and rubbed his beard.

"What the hell was her name again?"

"Sarana, I won't forget that in a hurry."

"Nice looker though," said Barney finishing his drink.

"She looked like Madonna."

He slapped his hand on the table.

"Enough small talk, I'll get us another couple of drinks and when I get back you can tell me the full story Vince. By the way, check out the photo behind you."

Vince turned around and saw a younger vision of himself, with his left arm around Barney's shoulder.

They were both dressed in their army fatigues against a half destroyed wall under a deep blue sky. There were no landmarks, it could have been anywhere but they both looked happy, both grinning from ear to ear. Much simpler times, thought Vince as Barney arrived back at the table.

"It's in Bosnia if you're wondering," said Barney putting down the two glasses and nodding at the photo, "1995 I think. Now spill the beans."

*

Vince told Barney everything, from the drugs disappearing, about the auction, right up to Buchanan finding out his true identity.

"So how are you going to handle this Vince?"

"I'll pick up the drugs tonight. If I get a chance I'll leave with my money as well. If not I have a backup plan, I've put a tracer in the money bag, so if I have to it should be easy enough to track down."

"Then what?" asked Barney.

"Then straight back up to Aberdeen, get the coke cut and collect the drug money. Then my friend, I'm off back abroad with a shit load of cash, never to grace these shores again."

"How's the property development going in Spain?"

"Going great and that's what I'm going to concentrate on from now on, and it's all strictly legit."

"Do you remember what you always told me about chance, Vince?" asked Barney.

"Chance favours the prepared mind," said Vince.

"Exactly!" said Barney. "So you need to be prepared for every eventuality. You know what you need, Vince?"

"What's that?"

"You need a partner, someone to ride shotgun, pardon the pun, and I'm the very man."

"I couldn't ask you to do that, Barney."

"You're not asking. I'm volunteering, big difference. You've helped me out enough in the past, let me pay you back."

Vince thought for a minute, and then stuck out his hand to shake Barney's.

"It's a deal, Barney."

"So tell me all about this cop!"

"Ronnie Buchanan, he's from Aberdeen, he's just up here working on this case."

"So he's drug squad?"

"Not at all! You know how I always hire locally for these distribution jobs of mine?"

"Yeah, you always have."

"Well, one of the hired hands was a bit shall we say enthusiastic, he bumped off the courier and her flatmate."

"I saw that in the press, two girls, one in Aberdeen and one in Edinburgh."

"That's them; the police now have both him and his partner in custody. I thought that would be the end of it, but this bastard Buchanan he just won't let it go until he gets a hold of me as well."

"Don't worry about it Vince, if things go to plan you should hopefully be sitting on a plane come this time tomorrow. Fuck this Buchanan."

Vince raised his glass.

"I'll drink to that."

*

Buchanan was on the A90 approaching Aberdeen when he got the phone call.

"Ronnie, its Rob! We're on this guy Tony's case; he's definitely up to something."

"What do you mean?"

"We followed him to a cash and carry where he bought a shitload of baby milk and talcum powder, all things commonly used to cut coke."

"Where did he drop the stuff off?"

"He hasn't, at least not yet, the thing is he's driving about in a big-ass mobile home type vehicle and get this, while he was shopping we had a quick look through the window and it's been customised to shit."

"Customised for what?"

"The whole inside's been stripped out, replaced with long wall to wall counters and bar stools."

"Go on," said Buchanan.

"Well, we think he might be going mobile, rather than using a warehouse or a flat or whatever to cut the drugs, we think he might be planning to use the vehicle. Think about it, he could drive anywhere and park up. Christ he could even make the cut while he's on the move."

"Good work Rob, where is he now?"

"He's parked outside his mother's house. We have a car here ready to follow him, and we also have the use of an empty council house across the road. It has a perfect view of the whole street, that's where I'm phoning you from."

"Right Rob, I'm about twenty minutes away, I'll see you there."

Buchanan turned to Max.

"I think you could be right Max. Vince and this Tony guy, looks like they could be creating a decoy."

"Why, what's happening?"

"Well, it's almost like he's following a script. He's managed to get himself seen buying the ingredients he needs to cut the coke, and he's managed to get himself a mobile home which, get this, he's stripped down the inside of so it resembles some sort of makeshift drug lab."

"Sounds a bit convenient right enough," said Max.

"Exactly what I was thinking, Vince could have us all jumping through hoops, chasing this mobile home all over the city while the drugs are getting cut elsewhere."

"Unless it's a double bluff of course sir," pointed out Max, "and he really is planning on using the vehicle."

Chapter Twenty Nine

"What about the passports?" asked Mark.

"Calm down," replied Jimmy. "I told you I sent the photos by 24 hour Euro delivery. He'll have got them yesterday and we should receive them back today sometime. I gave him Elsie's address, so stop panicking."

"How does he get these fake passports?" asked Liam.

"No idea, it's a side-line of his, one of many. All I know is they're top notch, can't tell them from the real thing, so no worries there."

"How long to go now?" asked Liam, as be paced about the room smoking his third cigarette in a row.

"Still three hours till we phone him, why?" asked Jimmy.

"Why! Because it's doing my fucking head in, all this waiting about shit."

"Calm down for fucks sake, and sit on your arse would you, Liam," said Mark. "Tell you what, I'll skin up a joint, you go and get the beers. Is that all right Jimmy, a bit of Dutch courage?"

"I don't see the problem with having a couple of beers and a smoke, as long as we don't overdo it; now let's look over that map again."

Jimmy unfurled the map on Elsie's dining table.

"Right, we start where, Liam?"

Liam took a mouthful of his beer and pointed to a spot on the map.

"We start off there, the car park at Fountain Place."

"And then?"

"Then you lead him a merry dance around the centre of Loanhead with us following behind on the bike to make sure you're not being followed."

"That's very good, Liam. Now Mark what next?"

"We make our way behind you along the A703, then after checking to make sure you're still not being followed, we bomb ahead, park the bike behind the old byre, and hide ourselves behind the hay bales."

"You've got it. Are the mobiles I bought you fully charged?"

"Check!" said Liam.

"Ditto," said Mark. "One thing bothers me though this may sound daft, but how on earth can we make phone calls from a motorcycle?"

"With these things," said Jimmy.

He threw the two packages on the table where Liam picked one up and read the blurb on the back of the packaging.

"Make, receive and reject phone calls from your mobile phone via voice command," he read aloud.

"The new phones I bought you are programmed with one number, my mobile. We'll set them up with the command 'PHONE,' so once you're on the bike just say the word phone and we'll instantly be in contact with each other," said Jimmy. "We'll give them a test run before we leave."

"This might be a dumb question, but how's this thing going to hear our voice over the noise of the bike?" asked Mark.

"They fit inside your helmet that's what they're made for." said Jimmy.

"That's fucking brilliant!" said Liam.

He turned to Jimmy.

"Can I see you outside a minute?"

They both grabbed a cigarette and went out into the yard.

*

"Why did you pick Loanhead?" asked Liam.

"I used to stay there now and again at my Aunt's."

"So you know the place pretty well then?"

"Most of it, especially around the town centre. My Aunt stays across from the Miners Club."

"The Miners Club?"

"The Miners Welfare Club to give it its full name. They used to be all over the place, in mining towns. They were originally built and run by the miners themselves for the benefit of the community and their families. They were even funded by weekly contributions deducted from the miners' pay. It's more of a social club nowadays though. I've been there a few times with my Aunt, the pints are cheap."

"You seem to know a lot about miners clubs."

"It's all Aunt Judy seems to talk about, mining and the history of the area; she bores the shit out of you sometimes, especially after a drink."

"Is there anything else of interest in the place?"

"Not much really, there's a good scrap car place. I used to go there for spares with Aunt Judy's neighbour. I can't remember his name but he was always fixing cars, every time you saw him he was wearing this oil stained blue boiler suit. I used to help him sometimes. I used to love raking about the scrappies. Mind you, the owner of the yard used to prowl about the place now and again with a big bastard Rottweiler. It used to scare the crap out of me."

"Not much to do around there then," said Liam, "a scrappies and a Miners Club that's it?"

"It's a tiny place, what do you expect?"

Liam let out a sigh.

"What do you really think our chances are Jimmy? I know you've been putting on this bravado thing in front of Mark but this time no bull shit, it's just you and me. Do you think everything will go smoothly, that we'll just ride off into the sunset with a wad of cash?"

Jimmy rubbed his chin.

"I hope so, man. All I know is that I'm sick of this life, living off dole cheques, having to sell a bit of weed now and again for an extra few quid. You and Mark must be the same. Answer me this. If you had a decent amount of money, would you always be stealing stuff? Taking a chance that you might end up in the nick one day?"

"No danger!"

"Well its worth it then isn't it, it's worth taking a chance. If we keep it together and manage to pull this off, we can say goodbye to all that shit and bugger off to Spain with a heap of cash."

Liam patted Jimmy on the back.

"Amen to that brother."

Once back inside, before they could go over the map once more they were interrupted by a knock at the door.

"I'll get it," said Elsie, "that'll be the Chinese food being delivered from Mr Chang's, he's such a nice man."

It wasn't the food, the passports had arrived.

"What did I tell you, Mark?" said Jimmy.

*

Feeling the last few days catching up with him, a tired Buchanan arrived at the flat in Northfield. He'd got Max to park further down the street and they'd walked the rest of the way trying their best to look un-police like. After climbing the stairs to the third floor, Buchanan stifled a yawn and pounded on the door. He shouted through the letterbox.

"Open up! You're busted!"

Rob Bennie opened the door.

"Very funny, Ronnie, get your ass in here."

The flat's decor consisted of peeling paisley patterned wall paper and stained bare wooden floorboards. It was totally empty apart from three plastic chairs, a coffee machine, a small fridge, a flat screened television, a DVD player, and a table in the corner with two monitors attached to a couple of cameras with wide angled lenses hidden in the corner of the paint peeled window frame. The officer at the controls was studying the screen, zooming in and out at various parts of the house across the road.

"Any chance of a coffee?" asked Buchanan, "And an ashtray if you have one."

"Help yourself to the coffee Ronnie, and feel free to use any part of the house as an ashtray, that's what we've been doing."

Buchanan grabbed a coffee and walked across the room to look at the screen.

"I take it that's the motor home you were telling me about? Zoom in a bit son, would you?"

"That's some fucking size," said Max, "plenty of room for a mobile drug lab right enough."

Rob walked over to join them.

"What does this Vince guy look like anyway?"

"There's no simple answer to that," said Buchanan, "he's a big fan of disguises, the only consistency is his height. He's over six foot, quite a big bastard as well, very broad across the shoulders."

"Can I stick on a DVD? It'll pass the time while we're stuck in this shithole," said Max.

"On you go!" said Rob.

Max looked at what was on offer, a couple of crappy old movies and a box set of Columbo.

"Decisions, decisions!" said Max.

"Stick on Columbo" said Buchanan," I love that guy."

"What's so fucking great about Columbo?" asked Rob.

"He's very cerebral," said Buchanan. "Not so much who done it, as how the fuck did he do it?"

"How do you mean?" asked Max.

"Well, think about it, at the start of every episode you see the crime being committed, you know who did it, and it's all about how he cracks the case."

"He's a bit of a scruffy bastard though."

"Ah Max, but that's all part of his plan, the murderer thinks, whose this scruffy useless bastard on my case? He'll never catch me, but underneath the scruffiness is someone very intelligent, with a very astute mind, the scruffiness throws them off, don't you see?"

"He reminds me of you in a way, Ronnie," said Rob.

"You're not talking about my powers of observation here, are you Rob?" said Buchanan.

"No, I'm talking about that scruffy bastard of a suit you're always wearing."

The room erupted into laughter.

Buchanan took a phone call.

"What's his address," he said as he grabbed a pen and a sheet of paper from the window sill. "Do you have a brief description? Cheers Gary, I owe you one."

He turned to the other officers in the room.

"Something's came up lads, I'll be gone half an hour tops."

Buchanan drove to Holburn Street. The phone call had informed him of who Michelle's attacker was, a totally unofficial tip off; the lab knew it was personal. They had found prints on the knife used to pin the warning to the door. They came back to a guy called Tommy Aldridge who worked the doors in various night clubs throughout the city.

*

Driving slowly to make sure he had the right door number, Buchanan parked the car further along the street and walked back to the house.

He knocked at the door and as soon as it was opened, the greasy pony tail hanging from the man's head told him he had the right guy. Buchanan hit him with a vicious uppercut, almost knocking him clean off his feet. The guy was dazed but came back with a wild swing of his own.

"Nice try, son."

 Buchanan caught his fist mid punch, twisted the arm attached to it through a hundred and eighty degrees and put his full weight on the back of the guy's elbow with a loud crack. The guy screamed in pain as Buchanan threw him face first into the nearest wall, his forehead taking most of the impact.

"What do you want with me, you fucking psycho?"

"Partly right son, but I'm not your normal psycho, I'm a psycho with a badge, your worst fucking nightmare."

"You've broke my fucking arm."

"Aye and I'll break your skull next if you don't pack your stuff and get out of here in the next five minutes."

"Ok, ok, I get the message!"

The guy paced about the flat packing what he could with one arm and muttering under his breath.

"I hope your car's automatic, is it?" asked Buchanan.

"Aye it is. What's it to you?"

"Well you'd have a problem driving a manual with a broken arm now wouldn't you? Now get in your fucking car."

"What's this all about anyway?" asked Tommy.

"I'll tell you what it's about," said Buchanan. "It's about your scare tactics earlier and how you frightened a good friend of mine."

Realisation dawned on Tommy.

"Fuck! So you're Buchanan."

"Just get moving, I see you in Aberdeen again anytime soon, you cease to exist, got the message?"

"Loud and clear!" said Tommy as he took off in his car.

*

Returning to the surveillance flat, Buchanan helped himself to a coffee.

"Where did you take off to?" asked Max.

"Nothing important, I needed a break. Anything happening here?"

"A few folk have turned up, foreigners we think, possibly Polish," answered Rob.

"How do you know that they're foreign?"

"The guys in the car heard them talking as they walked past, they could be the guys he's hired to cut the coke."

"Cheap labour right enough," said Max.

"Oh! I almost forgot" said Rob, "we found out he owns a lockup in Mastrick, so we've stuck a car there as well just in case. It could be another possible locale."

"Good thinking Rob. Vince is renowned for switching venues; we should cover all the bases. I'm just off to the loo."

Now he had a bit of privacy, he phoned Michelle.

"Hello love, it's Ronnie, I've taken care of your little problem."

"What you talking about Ronnie?"

"The guy who threatened you, you won't have any problem with him again."

"Ronnie! What have you done?"

"I persuaded him to leave, simple as that."

"How do you know he's gone?"

"Let's just say I helped him on his way, explained how it might be detrimental to his health to stick around Aberdeen."

"You shouldn't be doing that you know, you're supposed to uphold the law, not take it into your own hands."

"Well, sometimes you have to bend it a bit, especially with low lives like him."

"Thank you Ronnie, I'll sleep better tonight now."

"You're welcome love, enjoy your sleep."

He flushed the toilet and washed his hands before heading through to the lounge.

"Right lads, first things first, how's Columbo getting on?"

Chapter Thirty

"One more whisky, then we'll get organised," said Barney. "Whose car do you want to take?"

"I'd rather we took separate cars. They say they'll be watching so they'll no doubt want to make sure I arrive alone. Anyway, you can follow me by tracking my phone, I'll show you how."

"What about weapons?"

"I have my hand gun and the rifle you gave me."

"I mean what about my weapons; I'm not sure what to take."

"What you thinking of taking?"

"You know my weapon of choice back in the day?"

"The pump-action!"

"Yep, scares the shit out of people," said Barney with an evil grin on his face.

Barney bent down behind the bar.

"Come to daddy! Check this out, Vince." He stood up, producing a mean looking weapon.

"The Persuader! These babies are virtual duplicates of the proven Mossberg military 500 models, the only pump-action shotguns ever to pass all stringent U. S. Military standards."

Vince picked up the gun.

"Nice weight. I see you've added a pistol grip to shorten the size. Nice!"

"I thought you'd appreciate it."

Vince looked down the barrel.

"Do you know what I like about these guns?" He pointed the shotgun in Barney's direction.

"You don't have to aim it, just point it in the general direction and it will spread out and hit the target, BANG!"

"Well you can stop pointing that thing in my general direction Vince, that fucking gun's loaded."

"Sorry Barney!"

Barney took back his weapon.

"It's a bit heavy on the recoil but it'll get the job done, and like I said earlier, it'll scare the shit out of people to boot. Give me a couple of minutes to grab some ammo. It's full of light gauge buck shot at the moment, not much use for what we might come across. If these guys are wearing heavy leather jackets for instance it might not even penetrate their clothes. It will, at best, make a nasty wound and probably not penetrate deep enough to incapacitate them for any length of time. No! This job definitely demands something heavier."

*

"Who are these guys we're after anyway, Vince?" asked Barney as he returned with several boxes of ammo.

"Two small time thieves from Dundee, they just got lucky, simple as that. They just happened to break into the courier's car and they came away with four kilos of coke. However, they're travelling with a third guy, I have no info on him, but I've got a feeling he's calling the shots."

"You have to admire their brass necks though, that was a master stroke putting the coke up for auction."

"Who was behind the auction though? Themselves, or are they getting some backup from elsewhere, that's what's bothering me."

"So basically, you're saying we have no idea who is likely to turn up."

"That's the gist of it," replied Vince.

*

The three guys from Dundee checked they had all their

equipment, said goodbye to Elsie, and headed for Loanhead. They planned to get to the car park before calling the guy, so they could watch and make sure he arrived on his own. The night was foggy, with a full moon just visible behind a curtain of fine rain. They turned right and drove along the A703 just as the wind began to pick up and the rain got heavier.

Jimmy tested the intercom.

"Are you picking me up, Liam?"

"Loud and clear Jimmy, how does it sound your end?"

"Crystal clear!"

Next he tried Mark's and asked the same thing.

"Hear you loud and clear!"

He felt the butterflies in his stomach and tried to put them out of his mind. He was pretty sure his plan was fool proof and tried to focus on the end result, picturing himself, Liam and Mark sitting on a sun drenched beach with a cool beer in their hand and a shit load of money in their pockets.

They drove into the car park at Loanhead, parked the car and motorcycle, and made their way to the public phonebox on the corner of the road.

"Right, this is it lads!"

Jimmy picked up the phone, took a deep breath and made the call.

*

Vince answered his phone.

"Make your way to Fountain Place and park in the car park at the corner, flash your lights when you arrive, which I will acknowledge and then you will follow me to the drop. I won't have the drugs on me at that time, so don't try anything funny, and remember come alone. I see you have company, the deal's off."

The phone went dead.

"Was that them?" asked Barney.

"Sure was!"

"So, how do you want to play this?"

"If the situation was reversed, I would arrive first to make sure they had no company. I'd use two vehicles, one to lead and one hanging back to follow for the same reason. Bearing that in mind I think you should go there first, park outside the car park and once I'm on my way, leave about five minutes after. I'll keep in constant contact by phone so you'll know exactly where I am at all times."

"Sounds good Vince, and if we do lose contact I can always follow you on the phone tracker, so, let's go, Buckaroo!"

*

Alone in the car, Jimmy was taking slow calculated breaths trying to calm himself down. Breathe in to the count of eight, hold for four, and release slowly again to the count of eight. He'd always had anxiety issues. He'd learned the breathing technique from a new age hippy friend of Liam's. Her name was Summer. She swore it worked and sometimes it did. Not this time though, his stomach was in knots and cold beads of sweat ran down his face and neck. He pulled down the vanity mirror and stared at his reflection, he looked tired; he hadn't slept much over the past couple of days. Peering out of the windscreen into the gloom, he could just make out Liam and Mark waiting in the corner of the car park, tucked down behind a van next to the motorbike. Liam gave him the thumbs up. He reciprocated the action unsure if they had seen him. They both looked up to him and he'd done his best to convince them his plan would work, but now he was beginning to feel the heavy weight on his shoulders slowly beginning to drag him down. He rubbed his unshaven face and let out a huge sigh as he gripped the steering wheel with more force than was necessary.

The waiting was the worst of it, just as Liam had mentioned earlier.

He wiped the back of his neck with the sleeve of his jacket and opened the window to let some fresh air in. The cooling effect was instant. He started to feel more relaxed and lit up a cigarette, the smoke mingling with his breath in the cold night air slowly seeping into the car from outside.

He turned on the radio, a news reader was telling him about some shooting in Glasgow, not the sort of thing he wanted to hear about at this moment in time so he switched it back off again. He lay back in his seat, controlled his breathing again and half closed his eyes. Then he heard the car and the adrenaline kicked in. Time to go to work!

Jimmy watched as the car entered the car park and flashed its lights. He responded instantly, put his car in gear and prepared to lead the guy to the byre. A few minutes later Liam and Mark followed behind.

*

"You've got two bandits on your tail, they're on a motorcycle, and they left just behind you."

"I thought as much, they're taking me on a tour of the town centre so make sure you hang back a bit."

"Why don't we just take them out, finish this now?"

"Because they don't have the coke on them, or so they'd have me believe."

"Fair enough, we'll stick with the plan then."

*

"Doesn't look like you're being followed," said Liam through the intercom.

"Good, we'll head on to the A701, keep checking for a few miles and then overtake me and meet me at the byre."

"I had a thought though; I'm going to have a good look through his car windows as we pass, just to make sure there's only one guy in the car. Better safe than sorry don't you think?"

"Good idea Liam, keep in touch."

*

235

"We're heading for the main road, looks like we're going towards Peebles," said Vince.

"Five minutes behind you buddy," said Barney.

"Oh shit...!"

"Barney?"

*

The loose empty pallet dropped from the truck in front and came sliding along the wet road towards Barney, spraying water from both sides like a surf board. It caught under his left front wheel destroying the tyre on impact. Barney swerved to the side of the road, and tried to get the truck under control by letting it slow down by itself, he'd had blowouts before and knew the worst thing he could do was to hit the brakes which could send the truck into an uncontrollable spin. Eventually he got the truck under control and pulled over to the side of the road.

*

"Barney?"

*

"I've had a blowout Vince, give me five minutes."

"You're already five minutes behind, Barney. That will make it ten, probably more."

"Look, the longer I sit here talking to you, the longer I'll be. Just let me get on with it!"

Barney jumped out of his vehicle to get on with the job of replacing the wheel with his spare.

Halfway through the job, a grizzled old man suddenly appeared as if by magic at the side of the road.

"Sorry son, I was sure I'd tied that load down safely."

Barney looked up.

"You just about killed me, you old bastard!"

"There's no need to be talking to me like that."

"Look grandpa, I suggest you get yourself back in that truck pronto or I'll be putting this tyre iron to another use real soon."

"Here, let me give you a hand to change that wheel."

"Look I'm in a real bad hurry here, I'm fucking soaked to the bone and I've already told you to be on your way. If you don't get the fuck out of my face and stop holding me back, I'm going to do some real damage to you, you understand?"

Barney tightened up the last wheel nut as the old man shuffled back to his truck occasionally looking back over his shoulder through the rain and muttering away to himself.

*

"Vince, I'm back on track. I'll put my foot down, try to make up some time," said Barney.

"I'm just past Howgate," replied Vince. "Look for a farm track on your left, there's an old gate, a huge rusty one half hanging off at the entrance, you can't miss it. We're heading down there now. Wish me luck."

*

At the end of the track Jimmy got out of his car, narrowly avoiding one of the many rain filled potholes. Vince did the same. The rain was coming down in sheets now and every few minutes, ragged bolts of lightning lit up the night sky. They looked at each other for the first time.

Vince was well over six foot and weighed over two hundred pounds, Jimmy nearer five foot six and thin as a rake.

"Looks like we've come to the end of the line," said Vince "so, what now?"

"Now we go inside and make the trade," said Jimmy.

Vince looked towards the old barn and laughed to himself.

"Ok, I'll go get the money, it's in the car."

Vince, fighting against the wind, opened the passenger door and came out with the bag of cash and a laser sighted hand gun, which he trained on Jimmy's heart.

Jimmy stared at the hovering red dot, something he'd only ever seen in movies up until now.

"Nice try asshole!" said Vince. "Now where the fuck's my coke?"

Chapter Thirty One

Crouched down in place behind the hay bales Liam and Mark were wondering what the hell was going on. They'd arrived ahead of time, they were dressed for the part and they were in the perfect position, armed with their replica shotguns. The plan had been going faultlessly right up until they had heard the two vehicles pulling up outside the byre. What had happened since then was anyone's guess.

"Surely to fuck they should be in here by now," said Liam.

"I would have thought so," said Mark picking strands of hay off his overalls.

"Go and take a look then," said Liam.

"Why me?"

"Because you've always been good at all that sneaking about shit," Mark thought for a moment.

"Aye, you're right enough, I suppose."

He crawled over to the byre's entrance to take a look. Keeping in the shadows so he couldn't be seen from outside, he carefully peered round the ramshackle door.

"Shit!" he exclaimed. "The guy's got a gun on him and he's got it pointed at Jimmy, what the fuck do we do now?"

"We could jump out with our shotguns, just as we planned!" said Liam.

"That's not going to work, he'll just shoot us. We might have got away with it behind the bales in the byre, but in the open air with no cover, forget it."

"Do you have a better idea?"

"I do, actually." With that, Mark pulled down his balaclava and he was off. He climbed through the hole at the back that they'd seen earlier when they'd parked the bike, and sneaked along the side of the byre. Reaching the corner, he quickly dived for cover behind a rusty old piece of farm equipment and crawled along the bottom of the overgrown hedge at the side of the track. Once he'd crawled far enough, he waited until the lightning had lit up the night sky and then, between flashes, he rolled quickly along the muddy path through a deep puddle to come up kneeling behind Vince's car. After making sure he hadn't been spotted, he took a few deep breaths to relax himself.

So far so good, he thought.

*

"So, the coke's in that barn you say?" said Vince, "and you just expect me to walk in there, where you'll probably have some sort of ambush set up? Nice try, Bright Boy, but I think I'll pass. You can get your cronies to bring it out here, while I keep you covered. Now walk ahead of me to the door, try anything funny and I shoot, that's a promise."

Jimmy, visibly sweating, did as he was asked.

"You're way out of your depth here pal, you do know that don't you?" asked the menacing voice from behind.

"It was a chance to make a bit of cash, that's all."

"Well, it all ends here right......"

Vince was cut off mid-sentence, and he dropped to the ground in a heap.

Jimmy, wondering what the hell had just happened turned round to see a soaked, mud covered Mark grinning, with the butt of the replica shotgun in his hand.

"Get the bag of money, leave him the coke and let's get the fuck out of here. I'll slit his tyres so he can't follow us, you go and get Liam. You'll find him shitting himself behind the hay bales in the byre."

Back in the car Liam turned towards Mark.

"Where the fuck did you learn the commando skills?"

"The Discovery Channel, there was an SAS documentary on the other night."

"Well thank fuck you watched it," said Jimmy. "Now let's get back to Elsie's. I really need to get out of these wet clothes and have one of those beers right now."

"Amen to that!" said Liam.

*

Vince woke up soaked and light headed outside the barn, totally at a loss to what had just happened. As he climbed back into consciousness, he saw the holdall lying next to him. He also saw that his tyres had been slashed. He checked the holdall and found his coke.

Well, that's something he thought to himself. Next he checked the tracker on his phone and saw that his money was heading towards Peebles. Just at that moment Barney arrived in his truck.

"Sorry for the holdup Vince, just one of those things. Did you get your stuff back?"

"I got the coke all right, but the bastards cold cocked me, and then made off with the cash." Vince held up his phone. "It's not too big a problem though, I'm on their case."

After removing his rifle from the car and tucking the handgun into his belt, Vince jumped into Barney's truck and they started their pursuit. Once they got as far as the end of the track however they were blinded by headlights cutting through the gloom of the storm.

"What the fuck now?" said Vince.

The old man slowly got out of the truck.

"Not this bastard again!" said Barney, getting out his own truck.

"I tried to be nice to you son, and got nothing but a mouthful of abuse, so I've brought my two sons along, what you going to say to them?"

His two huge well-built sons, both wearing dungarees and scruffy tartan work shirts, got out the truck; each one had a baseball bat in their hands, and looked extremely pissed off.

"I've had enough of this shit!" said Barney. He leaned through the open window of his truck, took out his pump action-shotgun and blew away the truck's two front tyres then followed that up by shooting out the windscreen. The old man's sons' jaws hit the floor as they dropped their baseball bats in unison, and recovered just in time to stop their father collapsing in a heap as he fainted.

"You two fuckers get that old bastard out my face or the next thing I'm shooting is him, and after that you can move that fucking truck."

*

"Here are your beers, boys."

"Cheers Elsie!" said Liam. "We've fucking done it guys, we're rich!" said Jimmy. "By the time we pay Uncle Frank his share for setting the auction up, we should have about seventy grand each."

"That should last us a while in Spain," said Mark, "the cost of living is ten to fifteen per cent cheaper than over here. I saw that..."

"On the Discovery Channel!" said Liam and Jimmy in unison.

"Actually it was on the holiday programme on BBC1."

They all laughed.

"What are you planning on doing with your cash when we get to Spain, Liam?" asked Jimmy.

"I've not really thought about it. For the first few months I just plan on kicking back, lying about in the sun, getting pissed, that sort of thing. After that," Liam shrugged his shoulders, "who knows?"

"We'll have to find somewhere to stay, I suppose," said Mark.

"That's not a problem," replied Jimmy finishing his bottle of beer. "Uncle Frank owns a few properties, he says he'll let us have a flat for fuck all, we can keep it as long as we want."

"That's damned decent of the man," said Liam in a funny accent.

"The money won't last forever though will it?" said Mark. "I mean we'll have to eventually work out a way to earn a living, start a business or something, you know what I mean."

"I take it you've given up on your cheesy script writing then?" said Liam.

"I was just taking the piss man; I couldn't write a script to save my life."

"Aren't we getting ahead of ourselves a bit here lads? Think about it, seventy grand each, no rent to pay, it'll last us bloody ages. Compared to the money we're used to, it's a fortune and besides when the money eventually does run out, I've no doubt Uncle Frank will help us out. He has a few dodgy side lines but a lot of his stuff's legit. He'll find us a job somewhere. So I'm with Liam." Jimmy raised his unopened beer bottle in Liam's direction in salute.

"Chill out in the sun for a few months, skin up a few joints and get pissed."

"I take it, it's still hot and sunny at this time of the year, in Spain I mean?" asked Liam.

"Certain parts," replied Jimmy. "We'll be 'wintering,' Uncle Frank's words not mine, in the Costa del Sol. It's still in the high seventies over there. That's why a lot of old codgers bugger off to that part of Spain at this time of year, saves them paying their fuel bills."

Just as Jimmy leaned over to pick up the bottle opener from the floor, the living room window exploded in a hail of gunfire, several bullets just missing his head.

"Holy shit!" he cried, as the four of them dived for cover behind the settee.

"Oh shit!" said Liam. "It must be him, back for his cash, how the fuck did he know we were here?"

"Quick guys, round the back, we'll hide in the barn, you too Elsie."

Just as they approached the back door, the kitchen window exploded with a huge bang, showering the floor with glass and sending Cyril running for his life.

"Fuck! He's around the back now," said Mark, "how the fuck did he get there so quick?"

"It's not him," said Liam, "he's still outside the front with a huge

243

fucking gun. There must be two of them."

"Follow me!" said Elsie. "There's another way out."

They followed her into a big cupboard in the kitchen where she pushed the wall at the back; it swung inwards with a loud creak. Once on the other side she felt about in the darkness and came out with a torch, which she turned on, casting an eerie light along the damp smelling passage.

"It's another way to the plants. Gerald says he didn't feel safe only having one way in and out, so he dug this passage, just in case he ever needed it. Two months it took him, if we stay here, they'll never find us."

The tunnel felt like a fridge and they could hear water dripping off the roof and feel the damp seep into their bones.

The old woman was shaking visibly, the thin light beam from the torch moving back and forth in her hands.

"Here Elsie, take this," said Mark as he wrapped his sweat shirt around her shoulders. "I'll hold the torch."

"Who are these people and what do they want?" she asked as she snuggled into Mark's shirt.

The three guys from Dundee looked at each other through the low light of the torch. Mark and Liam were waiting for Jimmy to come out with one of his usual made up excuses, but he just shivered and stayed silent.

"Did you hear about the two dead girls Elsie? The ones on the news?" asked Liam.

"Aye, the police were looking for witnesses. Is that why they were looking for you the other day?"

"Something like that. We sort of came in contact with one of the lassies up in Dundee, and I think that's why these two guys are looking for us. They seem to think we witnessed something, that's why we were hiding out at your cottage. We hoped the police would catch them before they found us. But it looks like they didn't, eh lads?"

The other two nodded their heads, Jimmy giving him a wink. Liam knew his explanation was full of holes but Elsie seemed to accept it.

A raised voice suddenly broke the silence.

"There's something crawling on the back of my head, it feels fucking huge," said Mark. "Get it off me."

"Would you shut the fuck up, they'll hear you," said Liam. "Give me the torch."

Liam checked the back of Mark's head.

"It's a spider, it's tiny."

"Get the fucker off me, I hate them bastards."

"Mark if you don't stop freaking out, I'm going to crown you with this torch." He flicked the back of Marks neck.

"There, it's gone."

Mark calmed down.

"Sorry lads, it's not my fault. I've got that agoraphobia. I've always had it since I was a kid."

Jimmy laughed quietly

"That's a fear of open spaces you twat. What you have is arachnophobia, a fear of spiders. Now like Liam says, shut the fuck up, unless you want us all shot."

*

Vince came storming out the living room.

"Where the fuck have they gone?"

"Beats me," said Barney. "I've checked the whole house and that barn round the back. It's like they've completely disappeared."

"Fuck it!" said Vince. "Let's get going, someone probably heard the gunfire so it won't be long till the cops arrive. Anyway I found the cash, that's the main thing."

"Where we heading next?" asked Barney.

"Back to your place, it's been a long day and I could do with freshening up and having a few hours sleep before I drive up to Aberdeen and get rid of the coke."

*

"Guys, I think I hear them leaving," said Jimmy.

"Aye, with all the fucking cash!" said Liam.

"Could be worse, lads. Look on the bright side, if it weren't for Elsie here, we'd probably be shot," replied Mark.

"I'd rather be shot than skint again," said Liam.

"Oh my God, look at the state of my windows, and look at the glass it's everywhere," said Elsie, "and look at my settee, its shot full of holes."

"We'll board up the windows for you," said Liam. "We'll need a hammer and some nails and a few big boards."

"We have some boards but they're stored in a barn a couple of miles from here, on old Mr Simmons farm," said Elsie.

"No problem. Just give me the directions and me and Liam will go and get them. Mark can stay here and help you clear up."

*

Halfway into their journey they got a puncture, and just as they got out the car to fix it, the heavens erupted once more.

"Fucking great, soaked again!" said Liam. "I've had enough of this shit; I'm going for a piss."

Just when Liam thought things couldn't get any worse they did. After zipping himself up, he slipped on a wet pine cone and went tumbling down the steep embankment at the side of the road. Unable to stop himself, he slid down about thirty feet of wet mud and sharp brambles, coming to an abrupt stop at the bottom.

"Jimmy! Jimmy!" screamed Liam.

"Where the fuck are you?" answered Jimmy.

"Down here," came the voice from below. "Throw me down the torch; I can't see a fucking thing."

Jimmy did as he was asked. Liam turned on the torch and tried to find his bearings.

The area all around him looked the same in all directions. He was surrounded by bushes, huge ferns and trees and the beam from the torch wouldn't penetrate the darkness far enough to show him any means of escape.

"Fuck, I've fallen into the Blair Witch Project," he said aloud.

He heard a high pitched shriek in the distance and it sounded like it was getting closer.

"What the fuck was that?"

He squeezed himself through one of the thinner looking bushes, carefully shielding his face from the whip of the thin branches whilst frantically looking for a way back up that didn't look too steep.

"Can you see me from up there, Jimmy?" he shouted.

"Not really, I can just see the light from the torch every so often shining below the trees," came the voice from the distance. "Fuck! Can you manage to get down?"

"Hold on, I'll get that rope Elsie gave us, see if I can lower myself down. Give me two minutes."

Suddenly Liam heard a heavy rustling from the foliage on his left and two bright eyes suddenly appeared reflecting the beam from the torch.

They stared at each other for what seemed to Liam to be an inordinate amount of time before the fox slunk back into the undergrowth.

"Jesus!"

He stumbled backwards, tripped over some tree roots and landed on his rear on a wet boggy patch of ground.

As the foul smelling water seeped into his jeans, he slowly got to his feet, recovered his breath and while he was wiping the sweat from his brow he felt the hand on his shoulder. He let out an uncontrollable primal scream.

"Whoa! Calm down man! It's me, Jimmy."

"Fuck man, I just about shit myself. You could have given me some warning you were here, Jesus!"

"Sorry Liam, I just saw the torch beam and it led me straight to you."

"There's somebody getting murdered down here, at least that's what it sounded like."

"Wise up man, that's a female fox, they make some freaky noises. I heard it as well."

"That could be it; I did see a fox right enough."

Jimmy pointed straight ahead.

"What's that shining over there?"

"Where?" asked Liam.

Jimmy pointed again.

"Over there, next to that big tree, shine the torch in that direction."

Liam did as he was asked.

"I can't see anything."

"There's definitely something over there, go and have a look."

"Why can't we both go?"

"Because I need a piss. You go on ahead I'll catch you up. Or do you want me to hold your hand?"

"Fuck off!"

Sweeping the torch from side to side the beam did eventually flash on something. It was the front grill of a car. The vehicle was badly damaged, the front end practically destroyed by the huge oak tree in front. He tried the driver's door but it was held fast by a huge branch that must have fallen off the tree due to the impact of the crash. Liam shone the beam through the cracked windscreen and in the driver's seat he saw the body.

"Jesus Christ" said Liam. "Jimmy, get your arse over here."

After a few minutes Jimmy joined Liam.

"I've found a car!" said Liam.

"Good for you, but I've seen one before, let's get back."

"Here," he handed Jimmy the torch. "Take a look inside."

The corpse sat with its hands still gripping the wheel, its mouth was open in a silent scream, its milky eyes staring straight ahead at the oak tree outside.

"That's some creepy shit," said Jimmy. "What's in that bag?"

"What bag?"

Jimmy pointed the torch at the passenger seat.

"There, look!"

Liam walked round to the other side and opened the passenger door. The sickeningly sweet odour of decomposition assaulted his sense of smell instantly. Covering his nose and trying not to retch he looked in the bag and gave Jimmy a huge grin.

"You're not going to fucking believe this!"

248

He threw the bag to Jimmy.

The bag contained individual bundles of cash, twenty five of them, the sleeve holding each bundle together was marked ...Bank of Scotland-£10,000..!.

"Two hundred and fifty grand, that's more than the money we got for the coke" said Jimmy.

"But what the fuck's it doing here out in the middle of nowhere?" asked Liam.

"The bank robbery, remember, the one in Edinburgh, they only got half the money back, it was on the news. They reckoned the other guy had got clean away. I don't think he did. I think this must be him, look at the front of the car it's bashed to fuck. I think he must have swerved to avoid something on the road, careered down the steep embankment and ended up down here head first into that tree, dead as a fucking door nail!"

"Poor bastard," said Liam, "but you know what they say, waste not, want not!"

Liam picked up the cash.

"It looks like we're going to Spain after all. Way-hey!"

Chapter Thirty Two

Buchanan tossed and turned in bed, he couldn't sleep. He was back at home with Michelle, he'd hoped to catch up on a few hours shut eye, but his mind couldn't let go of the fact that Vince could arrive at any time. Arrive where? He thought to himself. He turned on the bedside lamp and carefully reached over Michelle to pick up his notebook off the bedside cabinet. After quietly getting a pen out of the drawer, he began to jot down some notes.

3 possible venues
Mother's house
Motor home
Lockup
When would Vince most likely arrive in Aberdeen tonight or tomorrow?

Carefully getting out of bed, he went to the loo and then headed on through to the sitting room. He picked up the phone and proceeded to call Rob at the surveillance flat.
"Where's Tony?" he asked.
"He's still at home, the motor home's still parked up outside. I thought you were going to catch up on some sleep, you looked like you needed it."
"Plenty of time to sleep when this is all over," said Buchanan.
"Any word on the lockup yet?"
"The officers have just radioed in. No one's been near the place;

it's a dead end if you ask me."

"Well, phone me the minute anything happens, regardless of the time. Cheers Rob."

He returned to the bedroom.

"Try and get some sleep will you, Ronnie," said Michelle.

"I can't sleep; I've got too many things on my mind."

"Like what?"

"This guy we're after, Vince, he's coming up to Aberdeen."

"When?" asked Michelle.

"Could be anytime tonight or tomorrow, we're not sure exactly. What we do know though, is that he needs to get a load of drugs cut and sold before he flees the country."

"Where is he getting the drugs cut?"

"That's the thing, we're not exactly sure. We're pretty sure we know who's doing it for him though, a guy called Tony. Vince has used him before."

"I thought you had his place staked out?"

"Yeah, we do but he's got himself a mobile home and a lockup, add that to his mother's place and it could be any one of the three."

"So, it could be any one of three places. I take it all three are being watched?" said Michelle.

"Yes they are!" said Buchanan.

"Then what's the problem?"

"The problem is I want to be there, I want to be the one who collars the bastard."

"Why's that so important to you?"

"Why?" said Buchanan. "Well let's see, maybe the fact he pulled a gun on me, or how about him getting that guy to put the frighteners on you."

Michelle shook her head, let out a huge sigh and got out of bed.

"Right come on you, through to the kitchen. I'll stick on the coffee maker and you can tell me what you've found out about this Tony guy."

*

Sitting in the kitchen with their freshly brewed coffees, Buchanan told her all they had on Tony. He told her about the customised mobile home, how he'd been seen buying the baby milk and various other materials commonly used for cutting coke, and about the Polish folk that had been seen arriving at Tony's house. Michelle mulled it over for a couple of minutes and took a large drink of her coffee.

"My money's on the lockup!"

"What makes you say that?" said Buchanan.

"Well this guy Tony, he doesn't physically have to be there himself to cut the drugs, does he?"

"I don't suppose so."

"Well, maybe his job is simply to organise things, set up the cut and then act as a decoy," said Michelle. "Think about it Ronnie, why would a guy shopping for materials to cut drugs with make a big display of buying it from a cash and carry? I know I wouldn't, I'd go and buy it online. He could use any of the major supermarkets and have it delivered the next day."

"I see where you're going with this," said Buchanan.

"The same with the foreign guys, why have them coming to the house in dribs and drabs when he could just meet them all somewhere and drive them all to wherever they're cutting the drugs at the same time?"

"The bastard's playing us for fools, he knows we're watching him, he's putting on a show. I had a similar idea myself; Max and I were discussing it earlier."

"He's not putting on a show everywhere though, is he?" said Michelle. "Think about it Ronnie, you've seen him using the mobile home to pick the ingredients up and you've seen the folk arriving at his house but have you seen anything going on at the lockup?"

"No, there's bugger all happening there apparently."

"That's because he's purposely keeping away from there, and that's why I think that's where Vince will go to get the drugs cut."

"Michelle, you're a fucking genius," said Buchanan giving her a quick peck on the cheek.

"Well one of us has to be. Are you coming back to bed now?"

"No, sorry love, I'm going to check out this lockup."

With that he quickly finished his coffee, got himself dressed, grabbed his coat and left the house.

*

After parking his car at the end of the road, Buchanan had a quick look around and then got into the back of the unmarked police car.

"Morning, gentlemen!"

"Hi Ronnie, what are you doing up and about at this time of the morning?"

"I couldn't sleep!" answered Buchanan. "What's been happening then?"

"Bugger all! No one's been near the place."

"Any of you two know how to pick a padlock?"

"Haven't got a clue," they both replied.

"Just as well I'm here then, isn't it? Give me a shot of that torch, son."

One of the officers passed the torch to Buchanan and he left the car heading for the lockup.

Holding the torch in his mouth Buchanan inserted the torsion wrench into the padlock. He eased it back and forth till it sat tight. Next he used the lock pick, moving it around carefully whilst applying pressure to the wrench. After a couple of minutes he heard a satisfying click. He put away his tools, carefully removed the padlock and quietly opened the doors of the lockup.

*

Vince decided he might as well get up. He'd tried to sleep, but things kept turning over in his head. He pulled back the duvet, got out of bed, showered and poured himself a strong coffee. He'd already checked in with Tony, things were going to plan. As suspected, the cops were on Tony's tail, he had one lot following his every move while another lot watched his house from a derelict flat across the road. Well they can watch all they want, they didn't know about the lockup, thought Vince.

After another coffee he checked his weapon was loaded, grabbed the holdall full of coke and prepared to leave for Aberdeen.

"Where the fuck are you off to?" said Barney blocking Vince's exit.

"I told you earlier, I'm off to get this coke cut and sold, I'm heading for Aberdeen."

"I'm coming with you then."

"You don't have to," said Vince.

"I know I don't have to, I want to. I'll feel better when I know you've got rid of that shit and you're on a plane safely out of here."

"In that case, let's go my friend," said Vince.

*

Buchanan fumbled about in the darkness until he found a light switch; he turned around making sure to shut the doors behind him before switching it on. The lockup up was instantly flooded with a bright clinical light and he could see the space was vast. Tony had knocked down the dividing wall between this lockup and the one next door, the walls were whitewashed a brilliant white and the place was scrupulously clean. It looked more like a medical laboratory than a lockup thought Buchanan. The back wall had a large wooden bench equipped with four sets of digital scales. There were half a dozen folding tables stacked up at the sides and boxes and boxes of various sized ziplock bags were piled up in the centre of the floor. A cupboard on the left hand side contained large amounts of dried milk, talcum powder and dried vitamin C.

Well done Michelle, thought Buchanan, you're a fucking genius. After closing up and relocking the padlock, Buchanan returned to the car.

"I don't suppose either of you two officers spotted any CCTV cameras around here anywhere did you?"

"Aye, down the road a bit, at the local Community Centre," said one of the officers.

"Get on to the council," said Buchanan, "see if we can get hold of the keys."

*

The guy turned up with the keys an hour later. He wasn't too pleased about being called to the premises three hours before he normally started his work for the day. He unlocked the heavy gate in front of the car park, and then opened the centre. After moaning for a bit he offered to give Buchanan a quick run through of the cameras controls.

"No need for that, son," said Buchanan patting the man on the back. "Just point one towards those lockups and zoom in as close as you can get."

The man did as he was asked.

Buchanan picked up the phone and called Rob.

"It's the lockup Rob. I'm sure of it!"

"What makes you say that?"

"I had an unofficial look around; it's all set up to cut the coke."

"Flipping heck, I'll send another couple of cars over there, we'll keep watch this end, just in case."

"Send the cars to the Valley Community Centre then. I'm there now. It's got a great CCTV system. I'm a bit worried that Vince or one of his cronies might scout the area for surveillance vehicles, so I think we're safer watching from here. I've already arranged for the place to close for the day so we can use this as our base."

"Sounds good, Ronnie!"

Just then, Max walked in, yawning and rubbing his eyes.

"Morning, sir."

"Jesus Max, you look about as knackered as me, what the hell are you doing here at this god-awful time in the morning anyway?"

"Michelle phoned me, she wants me to keep an eye on you, sir."

Buchanan shook his head.

"She means well."

"I heard you picked the lock to get into the lockup, sir. How did you learn a skill like that then if you don't mind me asking?" Buchanan took a sip of his coffee.

"I learned it from my Uncle Tommy. Do you know the locksmith across from the station, the shop with the red sign and the old style gothic writing?"

"Of course I do, I see it every day on the way to work, why?"

"What's the name above the door?"

"Buchanan. You mean..."

"Exactly, that was my uncle's shop. He ran it for twenty five years. It's still family owned; my brother Davie runs it nowadays. He bought the business over when my uncle retired."

"I never even knew you had a brother, let alone one that works across the road, you never mention him."

"We don't talk much, we fell out years ago. Anyway, back to my lock picking skills. My uncle's party piece was picking locks, usually handcuffs. He would challenge anybody to bring in their own handcuffs, and remember, because of where his shop's situated, he knew a lot of people with handcuffs. He'd get them to secure him with his hands cuffed behind his back and then bet you he could escape in a certain time. He was a regular Houdini!"

"How did he manage that?" asked Max.

"He'd hide a small piece of wire, usually in the cuff of his shirt sleeve and proceed to escape in less than thirty seconds. He'd even make you time him. Anyway he seemed to see it as some sort of skill that needed handed down for posterity. He had no kids of his own so it fell to either me or my brother. Davie never showed an interest so he passed it on to me."

"Could come in handy, I suppose," said Max.

"It's came in very handy through the years," said Buchanan tapping the side of his nose.

Chapter Thirty Three

Vince and Barney had made good time and they approached Aberdeen just before six am. It was still dark as they crossed the River Dee. They turned right, drove up Holburn Street then headed straight on to the town centre. Turning left at the crossroads, they parked the car in the underground car park just past Union Terrace Gardens. They walked slowly back towards the Rendezvous Cafe, accompanied by the sound of the seagulls crying from above.

Barney stopped at the statue across from His Majesty's Theatre.

"Who's that?" he asked.

"William Wallace!" said Vince.

"It looks fuck all like Mel Gibson, does it?"

Vince stopped and gave it a good look.

"Nah, bugger all like him. But then again Mel is only about five foot nine and they reckon Wallace was at least six foot six, maybe even seven foot tall. You should go and look at his sword in Stirling if you ever have the time, it's huge. Mel Gibson probably couldn't even pick the fucker up."

They crossed the eerily quiet road. Vince lit up a cigarette and offered one to Barney.

"I don't smoke much nowadays but what the hell."

They both sat down on a wooden bench taking the weight off their feet for a few minutes.

"I haven't been in Aberdeen in years," said Barney. "I remember that park though. It looks like a smaller version of the one in Princes Street."

Vince looked down.

"Union Terrace Gardens, take a good look while you can Barney, it'll soon be filled in."

"Why the fuck would anybody want to fill that in? It's a nice tidy little park, well cared for by the looks of things."

"Aberdeen City Council wants to redevelop it and turn into some sort of modern cultural centre. The Granite Web they're calling it."

"Surely not!"

"It's going ahead even though a lot of locals aren't happy about it. They got a chance to vote for either the new project or to keep the gardens as they are. The vote was very close. The whole thing's caused a divide across the city."

"Bastards!" said Barney.

"I've seen the plans for the new design," said Vince. "I'm not impressed, and get this Barney; they reckon it's going to cost £140 million."

Barney whistled.

"£140 million, that'll be the starting figure, but you know as well as I do these figures have a way of creeping up. Look at the trams back in Edinburgh."

Vince stopped walking.

"Don't start on the trams, Barney. Jesus!"

Barney laughed and took another look at the gardens and shook his head.

"Why can't folk just leave things as they are nowadays? They're always changing things for the worse and giving them stupid fancy ass names."

They entered the old fashioned cafe where they ordered the full breakfast and a pot of coffee each, before taking a seat at a table near the window.

"I used to come here quite often when I was a kid," said Barney. I had an uncle who lived in an old cottage at Fittie."

"Where's Fittie?"

"It's an old fishing village at the east end of the harbour, the official name's Footdee but he always used the local name, Fittie.

He used to take me and my brother for long walks along the beach. I used to love all that shit when I was a kid, collecting sea shells and poking around rock pools looking for crabs. By the way, what are we doing after breakfast?"

"There's still a few hours to kill," replied Vince. "I know a bar in Loch Street that opens at seven. I'm meeting a friend of Tony's there. We'll go for a pint."

"Sounds good to me," said Barney. "It's never too early for a beer, I always say."

*

They decided to leave the car and walk to the meeting place.

"Are those seagulls following us?" asked Barney. "I'm sure that's the same big bastard we saw earlier."

"It's Aberdeen, get used to it, they're fucking everywhere."

"Fucking noisy as well aren't they?" said Barney, staring at the grey sky above him.

*

They arrived at Loch Street just as the sun was rising in the cold grey Aberdonian sky.

Aberdeen was a strange city at times, thought Vince. The silver city it's sometimes called, due to the fact that in the summer it almost glowed due to the reflection of the sun in the numerous granite buildings. However in winter, due to the low lighting, the whole place reflected the grey sky which could make the whole town look very dreary. It was almost like the sea in a way, either reflecting a warm summer sky or the grey overcast shadows from above. The voice behind him brought him out his reverie.

"It's fucking freezing!" said Barney rubbing his hands together. His breath was visible in the chilled morning air as they crossed the road to the pub. As soon as they opened the door the welcoming warmth hit them. The bar was small but surprisingly busy considering it was just after seven am. Vince and Barney carried their drinks over to the corner and squeezed through the crowd until they found an empty table.

"Jesus, this place is mobbed Vince. You wouldn't think a pub would be so busy at this time would you?"

"I've been here a few times when it's just opened for the day; it's always the same, a real hodgepodge of people. I imagine it's mostly a mixture of night workers just finished their shift, hardened drinkers in need of a quick one to start the day, or maybe even the odd student still going strong from the night before."

Barney took in his surroundings.

"Aye it's a strange mixture of folk right enough."

He gave Vince a nudge.

"Bandit at two o'clock!"

Vince saw the man approaching them through the crowd.

"Are you, Vince?"

"What makes you think that?" asked Vince.

"Tony said to look for a big bastard in a sharp suit."

Barney laughed into his pint glass, the beer coming out his nose.

"Yes. I'm Vince and laughing boy here is Barney, a good friend of mine. Grab a seat."

The man sat down.

"So how are things going?" asked Vince.

"Everything's ready, the guys will arrive about ten. Once you deliver the stuff, it should all be done and dusted in about half an hour."

"I take it there's no police presence at the lockup?"

"Nope, checked it out myself on the way here, everything is sound."

"What about the money?" asked Vince.

"It's all been collected, some of our clients were a bit funny about handing it over before receiving the goods but what choice did they have? There's a bit of a drought on and yours is the only stuff going."

"I'll be there just after ten then. Are you staying for a drink?"

"Aye, cheers! My name's Simon, by the way."

He offered his hand to Vince and Barney.

"I'll have a pint of heavy seeing as your offering."

"Pardon me for interrupting Vince," said Barney, "but why not just give this guy the coke now. Take yourself out of the equation, there's less risk that way."

"This is my last job Barney, I want to see it through, and I'm going to see it through. I'll be in the lockup for half an hour tops, once it's cut I'm going to deliver it to Tony and get my money."

That could be a big mistake, Barney thought to himself, as Vince stood up and headed for the bar.

*

"Tea or coffee anyone?" asked Buchanan as he walked into the Janitor's room at the Community Centre, with a tray full of cups and a huge flask of hot water in his hands. The room was full of plain clothes police officers all standing around the half a dozen camera monitors, except for Max, who was seated in front of the camera controls.

Buchanan looked at the notice board on the nearby wall.

"Have you seen some of the shit on here, Max?"

"Look at this one. 'Wanted - Walking Co-ordinators,' what the fuck's that?" Buchanan put on a high voice. "Ladies and gentlemen, my name is Phyllis and I'll be your walking co-ordinator for today. The sun is shining, the best kind of weather for this activity, so if you could just put one foot in front of the other and keep going, I'm sure you'll pick it up."

Max laughed.

"And check this one. 'Healthy Eating Club' - 'Come and join us every Wednesday afternoon, cook some healthy meals and find out about good nutrition. Contact Gordon.' There's a picture of him here. It doesn't look like Gordon's been dodging many meals lately; he looks about twenty four stone. Maybe it's just me, Max, but if someone was trying to convince me to eat more healthily, I'd rather he didn't look like he'd just stuffed his face with three pizzas before pontificating about healthy living."

"Stop it, sir, you're making me crack up and I'm trying to

concentrate on these cameras."

Buchanan sighed. He was off on one and he couldn't stop himself. "Even this place in itself is a bit of a joke, it's a Community Centre right, but there's no sense of community anymore, you must have noticed that being in our game. Old folk lie dead in their homes for weeks and no one notices. People get their premises broken into and low and behold, nobody's seen anything."

"No sense of community, that's a bit cynical, sir?"

"Well, granted Max there are wee pockets of people here and there that look out for each other, but the majority are too busy looking after number one."

"I take it you're not a fan of Cameron's Big Society thing then?"

"Don't make me laugh son. They aim to encourage people to take an active role in the running of their neighbourhood, right?"

"So I believe, sir."

"So they plan on moving power away from Central Government and giving it to Local Communities and individuals. Mostly volunteers I've heard."

"What's wrong with that?"

"Who can afford to volunteer, Max?"

"Anyone with some spare time on their hands I would imagine."

"No Max. Rich people. Rich people who already have a shit load of money in the bank and therefore don't have to go out and earn a wage like most of us do. So that means everything from libraries to places like these, will be run by rich toffee nosed twats. They could end up with complete control of how every penny that's been allocated is spent in your area. THAT is why I don't like this Big Society idea!"

"Jesus sir, I never knew you felt so strongly about it. I think you better cut down on the coffee, and maybe get some sleep."

"Aye, you're probably right. I am feeling a bit jittery."

"Anything happening at all?"

"Apart from that mini bus full of old folk that just turned up," said Max pointing to the screen, "there's been nothing of interest since that guy cased the place out earlier."

"What about the Armed Response Unit?"

"They're sitting a couple of streets away, one phone call and they'll be here in two minutes."

"So!" said Buchanan. "It's just a case of waiting then. Anyone bring any cards?"

Just then an old woman entered the room. She looked at each of the officers in turn.

"Where's the Janitor? Our room's not been opened; we can't have our game of dominos."

"Sorry, Madam," replied Buchanan. "The centre's closed for the day."

"I didn't see any signs up."

Sighing, he pointed to the screen showing the camera trained on the front door.

"What's that?"

"It's a sign," said the old woman.

"And what does it say?" asked Buchanan.

The woman opened her bag, removed her glasses and after breathing on them for an inordinate amount of time and giving them a thorough clean she finally put them on.

'Closed until further notice.' "But it can't be closed! We have a tournament organised. Nan won't be pleased."

"Who is Nan when she's at home?" asked Buchanan, beginning to lose his patience.

"She's the organiser of our fifty plus group."

"Well I'm sorry," said Buchanan, "but you'll have to tell her to reschedule it for another day."

The old woman shook her head. "You don't want to annoy Nan," she said as she shuffled off muttering under her breath.

Buchanan watched her on the CCTV screen as she slowly hobbled over to the car park to join the rest of her cronies beside the mini bus.

"Jesus, look at the age of them, fifty plus my arse, there couldn't be one of them under eighty."

Then, from out of the group approached a heavy set bull of a woman, she stormed towards the centre rolling her sleeves up as she approached the door.

"Jesus!" said Buchanan. "That's got to be Nan, you deal with her, Max. I'm off to the loo."

"What!"

By the time Max looked round, he was gone.

*

For the second time in three days, the three guys from Dundee woke up with huge hangovers.

"What the hell is that banging noise?" asked Liam.

"That would be either the Glazier or the Joiner," said Elsie giving them each a strong cup of tea and some warm buttered toast.

"I'll pay for that, here," said Jimmy as he handed Elsie a couple of grand.

"It won't cost all that," said Elsie.

"Don't worry about the change. Buy yourself a new suite or something."

"So, you boys are leaving then?" said Elsie tucking the money into the front pocket of her apron.

"Yep, we're off for a new life in Spain. By this afternoon we'll be wearing sombreros and sitting on the beach enjoying a cold beer," said Liam. "Which reminds me, take this," Liam handed Elsie another pile of money. "This is for your son, to replace the beers we drank."

"There's no need for that!" said Elsie.

Just then Mark walked downstairs with Elsie's son's laptop, which he'd borrowed earlier.

"There's a flight to Malaga at ten or twelve thirty."

"Make it ten will we?" said Jimmy.

The other two agreed.

"Oh! And make it first class, let's spoil ourselves."

"Sounds good!" replied Mark.

"What time do we arrive there?" asked Liam helping himself to a second helping of Elsie's hot buttered toast.

"It arrives about one."

"Perfect!" said Jimmy. "Now, let's have a couple of beers and one of Elsie's joints before we go. I'll phone Uncle Frank."

"Frank, it's Jimmy."

"Hi Jimmy son, how did it go?"

"Not exactly as planned but I'll tell you all about it when we get there, we're arriving about one o' clock."

"You got the money though, didn't you?"

"Oh yeah, we got the cash all right."

"Good, I'll send a car to pick you up at the airport and I'll have the barbecue going by the time you get to mine."

"Sounds good Frank, we'll see you there".

Jimmy ended the phone call and took a large, very satisfying mouthful of his beer. He looked at the label at the back and laughed to himself.

- 'Made In Spain'-

Chapter Thirty Four

They watched on the monitor as the car pulled up and the four men got out. Three were wearing boiler suits, one wore a suit. The guy in the suit opened the lockup, let the other three in, glanced left and right then pulled the doors closed behind him, totally unaware he was being watched from the Community Centre along the road.

"Now we're getting somewhere," said Buchanan.

*

Barney drove his old bashed up truck, with Vince in the passenger seat, towards Northfield. They'd both been silent for the last ten minutes, both quietly pondering on what might lie ahead.

"I have a bad feeling about this, Vince," said Barney breaking the silence.

"So you keep saying," answered Vince. "Don't worry about it, it'll be cool. Just drop me off at the lockup and find somewhere to park and keep watch. Any sign of trouble you come and get me, if that's not possible, just take care of yourself."

They drove up slowly looking out for any police presence and making sure no one was hanging about the myriad of small lanes and alleys that lead to the lockups.

After convincing himself that they weren't being watched, Vince got out with his bag of coke, banged on the side of the truck and Barney drove away, still trying to shake off his bad feeling.

After a last look around Vince knocked on the lockup door and the guy in the suit let him in.

*

"That!" said Buchanan pointing to the screen "is Vince!"
He radioed the Armed Response Unit.
"Be ready to move any minute now, await my call."
"How long should we give him?" asked Max.
"Not too long, five minutes maybe. It'll give them time to start cutting the coke, we can catch him red handed."
Five minutes passed.
Buchanan picked up the Radio.
"Go, go, go...!"
They all left the community centre and approached the lockup just as the armed police arrived.
"Open the door and come out right now, with your arms above your heads."
The lockup doors opened, out came the guy in the suit followed by three naked men all with their hands above their head.
"What's been going on here then, an orgy?" asked Buchanan.
"Where's Vince?" asked Max, beginning to panic.
Buchanan went to look in the lockup just as the hand gun was thrown out.
Vince was sitting on a stool, a bottle of beer in his hand staring outside at the officers.
He raised the bottle to Buchanan in a gesture of cheers.
"Well done Inspector, you were one step ahead of me, something no one else has ever been. Tell me, how did you find out about Tony's lockup?"
"You were unlucky. If it wasn't for the fact that the young police officer who did the check on Tony was so thorough, we would never have known about it. He took it upon himself to check on Tony's father's holdings as well."
"He deserves a medal." said Vince.
"Let me check you for weapons," said Buchanan as he walked

into the lockup, escorted by one of the armed police officers.

Vince complied and raised his hands.

After making sure he was clean, Buchanan cuffed him and lead him outside.

"What's with the naked guys, Vince?"

"Simple, they can't steal any coke if they've no place to stash it, can they?"

Buchanan approached the other armed officers. "We'll take it from here lads, thanks for the help. We'll catch up with you at the station. I want to take this bastard in myself."

The Armed Response Unit left, followed by two unmarked cars and the police van full of naked men. Leaving Vince with Buchanan, Max and two other uniformed police officers.

*

Barney watched the whole thing from his vantage point at the end of the road. As far as he could see, Vince was fucked, pure and simple. A few coppers he could deal with, but the ARU that was a whole different ball game. He was just about to go, and then he changed his mind. He changed his mind because the armed guys were leaving, he couldn't believe it.

Vince you lucky bastard, he thought to himself.

He put on the balaclava, chose some appropriate music, put his foot down and raced towards them; his truck took out the first car containing the two uniformed police officers, sending it rolling sideways against the lockups. He jumped out with his shotgun in hand, used the butt to break the driver's side window on the second car and pointed both barrels straight at Buchanan's head.

"Open the fucking door and let my friend go!"

Buchanan, quickly deciding he had no choice in the situation, did as he was asked.

"Give me the keys to the cuffs,." said Barney.

Again Buchanan complied.

Vince got out the back seat, turned round with his back to Barney, so he could get the cuffs off and stared at Buchanan.

"Nice try Inspector, you almost got me. Give me two seconds!" he said to Barney.

Vince leaned into the car and took out the coke they hadn't cut yet from the back seat where Max had put it. It amounted to just over three quarters of the original amount. He thought about ing up all the smaller bags that had been cut but judged that he didn't have the time to spare. He put what he had back in the holdall.

"Vince, would you hurry the fuck up!"

"I've lost this shit once already Barney, I'm not losing it again."

He left the car, took the time to salute Buchanan and jumped into Barney's truck.

"Let's go, Buckaroo!" said Barney as he took off at great speed.

*

Within seconds Buchanan was on the radio.

"I want all cars on the lockout for a black pick-up truck, registration SK03 XZV, driver believed to be armed."

He turned to the other officers, who were half dazed thanks to the collision.

"Wait here you two, and guard the lockup until forensics get here. Max, you come with me, they can't be far. Try the main road."

A voice came over the radio.

"Getaway truck has been found abandoned on Provost Fraser Drive."

"Shit!" said Buchanan, "That didn't take them long. Head for the Drive, it's just around the corner, they must be around there somewhere."

They arrived at Barney's abandoned truck and approached the two police cars parked either side of it.

"Any sightings?" asked Buchanan.

"Sod all!" said the young PC.

"Check the truck Max, see if they've left any clues as to where they're heading."

Buchanan crossed the road, sat down on the grass verge and lit a cigarette.

"I saw where they went."

Buchanan turned round to face the voice from behind.

An old man approached him.

"I said I saw where they went."

"What did you see?" asked Buchanan.

"They got out that black truck over there, flagged down a red car and forced the driver into the boot at gunpoint."

"What kind of car?"

"Not too sure, some sporty looking thing but I wrote down the registration, just bear with me a minute."

The old man emptied both his pockets which contained everything from old chewing gum wrappers, various loose sweets, two broken lighters and some pieces of paper which he proceeded to go through one by one. After what seemed like an age he handed a crumpled piece of the paper to Buchanan, who threw away his half-finished cigarette and ran over to Max.

"Back in the car Max, the game's afoot."

"What?" Buchanan picked up the radio and gave the description and registration for the new getaway car.

"We need a chopper so we can keep an eye on this bastard. He's heading down Provost Fraser Drive towards town."

"How the hell did you find that out?" asked Max.

"An old guy out walking his dog told me, now come on Max, put your foot down."

*

"Put your foot down Barney," said Vince. "We need to get to the city centre, head for the Shopping Centre in Union Street. I'll give you directions; they have an underground car park. Once we get in amongst the crowds, we'll be safer."

Barney increased his speed, overtaking the car in front.

"We should split up," said Vince. "It'll be better for you; they don't know what you look like."

"They have my truck though, don't they?"

"Report it stolen when you get back to Edinburgh. Get one of your cronies to give you an alibi. Say you've never been near Aberdeen and you'll be okay."

"What about the gun?"

"Wipe it down and leave it in the car. I take it that it can't be traced back to you."

"How stupid do you think I am, Vince?"

"Shit!" said Vince as he looked in the rear view mirror, "we have a cop on our tail."

"I see him," said Barney. He looked towards the back of the car. "What the fuck's that noise?"

*

Hello! HELLO!

The driver who had recently been thrown in the boot of his car by the man with the gun, was being thrown back and fore from pillar to post. The boot was small and claustrophobic and he was beginning to panic. What if I suffocate? He thought to himself as he banged once again on the roof above him to no avail. Then he had an idea, his mobile, it was in his jacket pocket. After almost dislocating his shoulder he managed to reach it. He pushed the button to bring it out of standby mode. The screen was black, he'd forgotten to charge it the night before. "Fuck!" he screamed, as he was once more thrown violently to the side.

*

Turning on his lights and siren the young constable picked up his radio.

"We've spotted them on Midstocket Road, we're in pursuit."

*

The Aerial Support Unit received the call and was up in the air within five minutes.

271

The pilot picked up his radio.

"Could you give us a better description of the car, other than a red sporty thing?"

"Hold on."

The radio crackled then went silent.

"It's a red Subaru Impreza WRX four door saloon last seen heading towards Midstocket Road."

"Nice motor," said the pilot. "Top speed up to a hundred and twenty miles an hour, depending on the model of course."

"Don't bore me with the details Jim, just catch the bastard."

"I'm on my way!"

He turned to the camera controller.

"Did you hear that Helen? You're looking for a red blur!"

*

"Oh fuck! Roadworks, that's all we need."

Buchanan wound down his window and held out his warrant card.

"Get that fucking lollipop thing turned to go."

The pissed off guy with the stop sign did as he was asked and then stuck up his middle finger as they passed.

Buchanan watched the action in the rear view mirror.

"Charming!"

Max laughed.

"You weren't exactly polite to him yourself, sir."

"Shut up Max, and put your foot down."

*

The red headed cyclist dressed in his skin tight clothing approached the main road from the quiet side street. He was trying out his new £500 bike he had bought that very morning. He had a good look to either side before turning left and being thrown ten feet in the air by the speeding car which had appeared from nowhere. He escaped a concussion thanks to his fancy helmet but that didn't protect his legs, they both fractured on impact with the road, his new bike ending up a mangled mess at the other side of the road.

"Oops!" said Vince.

"Fuck him!" said Barney. "I can't stand cyclists. I especially hate the ones that wear that clingy, obscene lycra shit."

Barney put his foot down hard on the accelerator, watching the lights change to red at the approaching crossroads.

"Go straight through!" said Vince. "Move it!"

Barney swerved to avoid the screeching traffic and just made it through by the skin of his teeth. The pursuing police car wasn't so lucky, it hit the side of a bus and ended up on its roof in the middle of the road, spinning three hundred and sixty degrees, the spin giving the siren a strange other worldly sound.

*

"Where the fuck's the chopper you promised us?" Buchanan asked the voice at the other end of the radio.

"Should be with you any minute now, keep your eyes peeled."

*

"We're not going to make it," said Barney.

"Of course we are," answered Vince. "Turn right at the next crossroads and its five minutes straight ahead."

The crossroads however were blocked by two police cars.

"We're fucked now!" said Barney.

"Maybe not, look to your right."

"I see it!" said Barney.

*

"Do you have it in green?"

"What the fuck do want it in green for?" asked the extremely pissed off man who had been shopping for kitchens with his wife all morning. "It won't go with the wallpaper."

273

"We could always redecorate?" answered his wife.

The husband slapped himself on the forehead letting out a huge sigh.

"Yes we do have it in green act......"

The salesman was interrupted mid-sentence by the sight of the car heading for the kitchen showroom's window.

He just had enough time to physically throw the man and his wife out of the way before it reached them.

The car flew through the window like a bullet, as glass flew everywhere. It ploughed through the display cabinets and came out the other window that was situated ninety degrees from the first, totally negating the road block.

Barney did a hand brake turn, narrowly avoiding the drunken man trying hard to cross the road, and continued at great speed down Rosemount Viaduct.

"Almost there," said Vince.

Suddenly a police car appeared from a side street and drew level with Barney's car, trying to force it off the road.

"Where's the shotgun?" asked Vince.

Barney handed it over and Vince half climbed out the window resting the pump-action shotgun on the roof of the car.

"Try and get slightly ahead of him, Barney," shouted Vince, his voice barely audible above the roaring of the high powered engine.

Once Barney got ahead, Vince steadied his aim as best he could in the situation. He targeted the pursuing vehicle's front tyre, sending it spinning off the road onto the pavement where it crashed head first into a post-box.

*

The police helicopter approached Rosemount.

"We have a visual; they're heading towards Union Terrace. All vehicles in the vicinity respond, but be warned, they have a firearm and they don't seem shy about using it."

"Where the fuck did this other guy come from?" said Buchanan. "He's a fucking maniac."
"No idea! But you've got to admire his driving skills," replied Max.

Barney ignored the lights again at the crossroads in Union Street and sent the pedestrians, who had just been informed by the green man that they could cross, running and screaming in all directions. He tore down Bridge Street heading for the underground car park.

The middle aged man stood in the middle of the road with his small band of protesters. They all wanted the same thing. They wanted the city centre pedestrianised. They all carried their own handmade placards declaring what they were after. His sign was emblazoned with the words, 'Cars Cause Accidents-Someone could get hurt!' He must have been psychic. He was just too slow as Barney ploughed into him sending him flying across the roof of the car.
"You were aiming for him on purpose, weren't you Barney?" said Vince as he looked out the rear window.
Barney gave out an evil chuckle.
"We're almost there! Turn left," said Vince.
Barney spun the steering wheel hard to the left and the car flew through the automated gate, smashed through the red and white barrier, sped up the ramp and came to an abrupt stop in the car park. They both jumped out, wished each other luck and after letting the visibly shaken car owner out the boot, Vince grabbed his bag of coke and they went their separate ways.

The chopper pilot radioed in.

"We've lost them, I repeat; we've lost them. They've gone underground into the shopping centre car park."

*

"Shit!" said Buchanan, "That place is always fucking crowded." He picked up the radio.

"All available officers make their way to the Trinity Centre. I want all entrances and exits covered, including the car park."

Chapter Thirty Five

Vince knew exactly where he was going and he knew he'd have to be quick. As usual he'd planned his getaway with precision, just in case something went wrong. He took the steps from the car park two at a-time, entered the shopping mall, and headed for Jacksons Work Wear, getting there just before the police flooded the mall. He bought a set of overalls, a pair of work boots and a hard hat, a pair of safety goggles, some ear protectors, and a toolbox.

While the assistant was serving the next person in line, he went into the changing room and put on his new purchases. Once done he put the suit and shoes he'd taken off into the toolbox and left the store.

Walking straight past the two police officers outside the shop, he headed for the back entrance to the centre, whistling to himself, like he didn't have a care in the world.

Vince knew he couldn't do much about disguising his height but then again he thought, didn't everyone look taller in a hard hat. He had picked the shopping centre for a reason. Out the front entrance on Union Street he could get a bus to anywhere in the city. Across the road, next to St Nicholas Churchyard, was a taxi rank. And out the back entrance, straight across the road he could get a National bus to anywhere in Britain, the same as he could a train at the station next to it. Four different ways of escape, the police couldn't cover them all.

However, Vince wasn't going for any of those, he had a fifth option in mind.

Buchanan had acted quickly, he had two officers situated at each exit, and he'd sent Max off to the centre's CCTV office. Another half a dozen officers were patrolling the centre and as much again at the nearby bus and train stations. They had all been given a description of their quarry.

"Any sign of them, Max?"

"Not so far no, we're getting a few complaints though, about no one being allowed to leave."

"Get on to the officers guarding the exits, tell them they can let folk out. One at a time mind, and tell them to have a good look at who they're letting out, especially the ones leaving the car park."

"Ok, sir."

*

PC's McKay and Kennedy held the crowd back at the rear entrance.

"I've got a bloody train to catch in ten minutes," said the businessman in front.

"Shouldn't be long, sir," said PC Kennedy.

"It better not be long because if I miss my meeting, I'm holding you personally responsible."

PC McKay came off the radio.

"We can let them out now, one at a time though."

"About bloody time!" said the businessman, shoving his way through to the outside

"What a jerk!" said the tall workman in the blue boiler-suit and hard- hat.

"You get used to it in this job," said McKay as he let the man through.

Vince crossed the road. He walked past the train station, continued on past the bus depot and crossed the road to Aberdeen Harbour. He walked along the dock for a while, yet again accompanied by the cry of seagulls. Thanks to his work clothes, he never received as much as a glance from the many workmen going about their duties. Screwing up his eyes to protect them from the low winter sun dazzling off the water, he lit a cigarette and hung around the loading area where half a dozen lorries were shedding their loads onto a couple of oil rig supply vessels.

Carefully taking in his surroundings he saw what he was looking for and walked nearer the edge of the dock. He offered the driver a cigarette which was gratefully received.

"You're almost unloaded?"

"Aye, not long now," said the driver.

"Where are you heading next?"

"Back to Newcastle once I'm reloaded. I'm taking a couple of valves back to be fixed."

Perfect thought Vince, discarding what was left of his cigarette into the cold grey water.

"Is there any chance of a lift?"

"I'd like to help you out mate but it's against company policy."

"There's two hundred quid in it for you," said Vince, giving the guy a wink as he put the cash into the man's top pocket.

The driver looked around.

"Get in then, but stay in the bunk at the back of the cab until we hit the road."

"You're the boss!" said Vince.

*

"Where the fuck are they?"

Over an hour had passed and Buchanan was worried. There was no sign of either of them. He now had his men checking out individual shops, but didn't hold out much hope. It looked like Vince had beaten him again.

Max and a young woman entered the surveillance booth.

"You have to hear this, sir!"

The woman told him about the tall man who had come into her shop and bought work clothes. When he thought she wasn't looking, he had made his way to the changing rooms and changed

279

into them, and then left the shop.

"Did he leave his old clothes in the changing room?" asked Buchanan.

"I had a look," said the girl, "but there was no sign of them. However he did also buy a tool box, perhaps he stashed them in there."

"Thanks Miss...?"

"Todd, Hazel Todd."

"Thanks Hazel," said Buchanan.

He picked up his radio.

"Everyone be on the lookout for a tall guy wearing blue overalls and a hard hat."

Two minutes later a rather sheepish looking Police Officer entered the room. He removed his hat and averted his eyes, looking everywhere except at the DI.

"I thought I'd better come and see you personally, sir. The description you just gave out, the tall guy in the blue boiler suit, we let him out the back entrance about half an hour ago."

The silence in the room was palpable and after what seemed like an age Buchanan stood up.

"Get the fuck out of my face son, and get yourself home I don't want to see you for the rest of the day!" screamed a red faced Buchanan.

"Well that's it Max, he's beaten us yet again!"

Max stared at Buchanan.

"Wasn't that a bit harsh, sir? You can hardly blame the guy. A blue boiler suit and hard hat is hardly the description we gave him to look out for now, is it."

"You're right enough Max," said Buchanan beginning to calm down. "I'll go and have a word with him."

Just then his phone rang.

"Ronnie, its DI McLean, we have something at our end, don't know if it's any help but....."

*

Vince was on his way to Edinburgh, another hundred bucks had convinced the driver to take a detour on his way to Newcastle. He picked up his phone.

"Barney, did you make it?"

"No problems Vince, I hung around till they started letting us out the shopping centre. I just removed my baseball hat and leather jacket then crossed the street and caught a train. I'm on my way home already."

"Fuck! I've never seen you without the baseball hat. I always assumed you slept with it on. Anyway, remember to report your car as stolen." said Vince.

"I already have, well, one of my employees has. They can't come to take my statement until tonight, which suits me. I'll be home by then."

"Glad to hear you made it," said Vince. "I'll be in touch."

Next he phoned Tony.

"Tony! Bit of a problem, we were busted. I only managed to escape by the skin of my teeth."

"Shit!"

"It's not all bad though, I managed to save three quarters of the merchandise, and I've stashed it in the boot of a black Volvo estate that I planted earlier at the mall. You'll find it on the first floor of the car park, section B. I'll let you have it half price, a hundred grand and it's yours, you can get it cut yourself, keep all the profit."

"Cheers man, how do you want the money?"

"I'll text you a bank account number, just stick it in there as soon as you can."

"Sure Vince. Take care of yourself."

Vince gave a big sigh of relief.

"Busy day?" said the driver raising his eyebrow.

"You wouldn't believe it" said Vince, "I'm fucking knackered!"

"Get your head down for a while," said the driver. "Catch up on some sleep. I'll give you a shout when we reach Edinburgh."

"You know what? I think I'll take you up on that offer," said a weary Vince as he climbed into the bunk at the back of the cab.

Chapter Thirty Six

Vince sat in the corner of the bar staring at his laptop. He was totally burnt out. He rubbed his eyes with the back of his hands.

"I'm getting too old for this shit!" he muttered to himself. He was looking for flights to mainland Europe, anywhere would do, preferably one leaving in the next couple of hours. He found a seat on a flight to Amsterdam, leaving that evening.

What identity should he use, he thought to himself?

Vince opened one of the many password protected folders on his desktop. It contained a dozen photos of Vince in various guises. He decided to go with Jacob Crawford. All he needed now was the long dark wig and the grey tinted contacts, that and Crawford's passport. All these items were inside his holdall in the hotel's safe. He pressed enter and confirmed his booking under his newly adopted name.

For the second time since he'd come in, the television above the bar was replaying the interview with Buchanan. He stood outside the back entrance of the shopping centre back in Aberdeen. He looked flustered.

"Could you give us a brief description of the men that caused so much havoc in the centre of town today, Inspector?"

"One of the men we don't have a name for, all I can tell you is that he's heavy built and was last seen wearing a brown beat up leather jacket and a grey baseball hat. We know he's armed, so I would advise the public not to approach him, just give us a call."

"It's not much to go on is it?"

Buchanan glared at the woman.

"The other man is Charles Vincent Mackie. He's over six foot tall, stocky and he has a penchant for changing the way he looks. He hauled out a sketch of Vince's latest appearance with the shaved head and short goatee. This is a picture of Vince as he was last seen this morning. Our Forensic Artists are putting together a group of pictures of what we think he could possibly look like now. Again, this man is dangerous and we would strongly advise people to stay away from him. If you see him, just phone us."

"Grampian Police have set up a hotline for this incident. Anyone with any information on these men, please phone the number at the bottom of your screens. Thank you Inspector."

"One other thing," said Buchanan. "He was last seen wearing a blue boiler suit and a hard hat and carrying a tool box."

"Fuck! They're looking for Bob the Builder!" cried an onlooker. Vince laughed to himself and raised his glass to the screen. The sketch didn't bother him one iota. He'd already been to one of his numerous safe houses, and changed into a pair of jeans and a hooded sweatshirt. He'd also put on a baseball hat and removed the beard. He looked bugger all like their sketch.

*

At last, thought Vince as he stood outside the hotel in Princes Street. He bowed silently to the concierge on the way in and went through to the bar to meet his father. He paid no heed to the unobtrusive man sitting in the corner behind that day's copy of the Scotsman.

"You look like shit son, if you don't mind me saying."

"Cheers dad, let's just say I've not had the best of days and leave it at that shall we," said Vince.

"Do you fancy something to eat, son?"

"I do actually. I'm starving but I think I'll just have a quick whisky and jump in the shower first."

"No problem son, meet me down here when you've spruced yourself up a bit and then we can go to the restaurant. I'm getting used to all this fancy eating."

Vince, laughing, took the key from his father and headed off to his suite.

*

After five minutes under the shower he felt better. He towelled himself dry, had a shave, put on some aftershave and walked naked into the bedroom to put on some clean clothes. He looked in the wardrobe mirror and froze, then turned round to face his nemesis.

"This naked thing must be catching, first the guys in the lockup and now you. Cover that thing up before I'm forced to shoot it," said Buchanan.

Vince turned around to find the DI sitting on the bed with Vince's handgun pointed at a particular part of his anatomy.

"Do you ever fucking give up?" asked Vince.

"Not when it's personal, and you made it personal."

"How did you find me?" asked Vince.

"Your father! He couldn't keep his mouth shut at the bar. The cops at this end posted your prison mug shot in the paper, he got pissed last night and started telling everyone how you were set up, his son wouldn't do the things they were saying he had. He told anyone who would listen, 'he'll be back tomorrow anyway, he'll soon put things right.' So the barman phoned the tip line and told us you'd be back here today. DI McLean phoned me in Aberdeen, so I got Max to drive me straight here."

"So you just had to come and make the arrest yourself."

"It's not just me, there are half a dozen armed cops just outside the door, make a run for it if you like; go down in a hail of bullets. Like Clint says, make my day punk!" Buchanan pointed the gun at Vince's head.

"Ok, you win." Vince turned around to let Buchanan cuff him.

"Are you a betting man, DI Buchanan?"

"I like a flutter now and again," said Buchanan. "Why?"

"Whatever you do don't put money on me doing more than a

284

couple of months because I'll figure a way out, I always do. And when I do, I might just come pay you a visit."

*

"Mr Buchanan!"

Buchanan turned around; it was the reporter who had accosted him in the hotel bar earlier.

"Thanks for the call Ronnie, I appreciate it."

"You owe me one. Next time I need some information that I can't find through the normal channels, I may just give you a call."

"Anytime, Inspector!"

"What now, sir?" asked Max.

Buchanan rubbed his hands together.

"We caught the bastard Max, that's all that matters. We'll leave the plaudits to Lothian and Borders. Anyway, I'm in need of some lubrication."

"Can I buy you a Guinness, sir?"

Buchanan put his arm around Max's shoulder.

"Yes you can Max. Why not try one yourself; put some iron in your blood, you're looking a bit peaky?"

Epilogue

Two Months Later

Vince was sitting inside the cell in the back of the prison van, escorted by two security guards. He was already facing a long jail stint to make up for the sentence he'd never served fully last time thanks to his escape, and today was to be his first official trial appearance on the charge of attempting to supply drugs.

So, adding all that together, he was going away for quite a few years.

Or, perhaps not! As soon as he'd found out the date of his trial, he'd bribed a prison guard to smuggle out a letter addressed to Barney stating the time and date of his short trip from the prison to the court. In the letter he also included a detailed map of the prison van's route, also obtained through a bit of bribery.

Vince's freedom now lay in Barney's capable hands.

"You'll be going away for a long time," said one of the security guards making conversation.

"I wouldn't bet on that," remarked Vince under his breath.

The driver as always took his usual route sticking to the smaller side streets to avoid the morning rush hour traffic.

At the end of one of the streets however he found his exit blocked by a huge bright yellow cement truck. He repeatedly pressed his horn to no avail. The way the truck was parked it was impossible to see into the cab. This driver was either deaf, or not there at all, thought the prison van driver to himself, as he opened the small hatch into the back of the cabin.

"Fuck it! I'll have to reverse. We're blocked in by some asshole in a cement truck," he said to the two guys in the back.

Looking in his rear-view mirror however, he realized reversing was also out of the question, thanks to the forklift approaching from behind.

"I don't like the look of this," he said to his workmates. "We're blocked in at the front and there's a huge fucker of a forklift approaching us from behi…" The driver was interrupted mid-sentence by the grating metallic sound of the van's rear door being pushed in by the forks of the forklift.

"Trouble, lads?" asked Vince carefully steadying himself on the bars of his cage.

With a loud clang the door eventually broke its hinges trapping one guard underneath and barely missing the other.

While the driver quickly radioed for police backup, a guy wearing a baseball hat and carrying a shotgun entered the van.

"Which one of you fuckers have the key to this cage?"

"We don't have keys, there's an electronic button on the wall there," he said pointing to the panel on his left.

Barney hit the button and the sound of the electronic lock opening on Vince's cell door was music to his ears.

"Let's go, Buckaroo!" said Barney.

*

At about the same time as Vince was making his getaway; just over a thousand miles away in Spain, Liam and Jimmy were walking along the beach under a brilliant blue sky. They were dressed in shorts, bare chested and wearing sun glasses. They had a cooler full of beer and Jimmy had a big fat joint in his mouth.

They walked over to the three sun loungers under the shade of a huge palm tree. Jimmy passed the joint to Liam and cracked open an ice cold beer from the cooler.

"Where did you say Mark had gone?" asked Liam.

"He said he had to see a man about a dog, says he'll see us here later."

"Oh, oh!" said Liam. "Are you thinking what I'm thinking?"

"Yeah, more like a man about a pig."

"Hey guys!"

They both looked round in the direction of Mark's voice.

And there he was, walking down the beach looking as proud as punch with a pig on the end of a lead.

Other folk on the beach were staring at him but Mark cared not a jot.

"It took me a couple of months but I've eventually found one. Guys, meet Elsie!"

Torn Edges by **Brian McHugh** is a riveting mystery story linking modern day Glasgow with 1920's Ireland.

When a gold coin very similar to a family heirloom is found at the scene of a Glasgow murder, a search is begun that takes the McKenna family, assisted by their Librarian friend Liam, through their own family history right back to the tumultuous days of the Irish Civil War. The search is greatly helped by the discovery of an old family photograph of their Great-Uncle Pat in a soldier's uniform.

The McKennas quickly realise that despite their pride in their Irish origins they know remarkably little about this particular period of recent Irish history. With Liam's expert help, they soon learn that many more Irishman were killed, murdered, assassinated or hung during the very short Civil War than in the much longer and better known War of Independence. And they learn that gruesome atrocities were committed by both sides, atrocities in which the evidence begins to suggest their own relatives might have been involved.

Parallel to this unravelling of the family involvement of this period, Torn Edges author Brian McHugh has interwoven the remarkable story of the actual participation of two of the McKenna family, Charlie and Pat, across both sides of the conflict in the desperate days of 1922 Ireland.

"Torn Edges is both entertaining and well-written, and will be of considerable interest to all in both Scottish and Irish communities, many of whom will realise that their knowledge and understanding of events in Ireland in 1922 has been woefully incomplete. Torn Edges will also appeal more widely to all who appreciate a good story well told."

TORN EDGES can be purchased on *www.ringwoodpublishing.com* for £9.99 excluding p&p or ordered by post or e-mail for the same price.

The e-book version is available for £7.20 from the Kindle Book Store or Amazon.co.uk from October 2012.

Paradise Road by **Stephen O'Donnell** is the story of
Kevin McGarry a young man from the West of Scotland, who as a
youngster was one of the most talented footballers of his generation in
Scotland. Through a combination of injury and disillusionment, Kevin
is forced to abandon any thoughts of playing the game he loves,
professionally. Instead he settles for following his favourite team,
Glasgow Celtic, as a spectator, while at the same time resignedly and
with a characteristically wry Scottish sense of humour, trying to eke out
a living as a joiner.

It is a story of hopes and dreams, idealism and disillusionment, of growth
in the face of adversity and disappointment. Paradise Road examines
some of the major themes affecting football today, such as the power and
role of the media, standards in the Scottish game and the sectarianism
which pervades not only football in Glasgow but also the wider
community. More than simply a novel about football or football fandom,
the book offers a portrait of the character and experiences of a section of
the Irish Catholic community of the West of Scotland, and considers the
role of young working-class men in our modern, post-industrial society.

The road Kevin travels towards self discovery, fulfilment and maturity
leads him to Prague, enabling a more detached view of the Scotland that
formed him and the Europe that beckons him.

*"Written in a thoughtful, provocative yet engaging style, Paradise Road
is a book that will enthral, challenge and reward in equal measure. It
will be a powerful addition to the growing debate on some of the key
issues facing contemporary Scotland"*

Paradise Road can be purchased on *www.ringwoodpublishing.com* for
£9.99 excluding p&p, or ordered by post or e-mail for the same price.

The e-book version is be available for £7.20 from the Kindle Book Store
or Amazon.co.uk

Whisky From Small Glasses by **DA Meyrick** is a stunningly impressive crime novel. Set in a small Scottish rural town, it reveals the seething cauldron of sex, drugs, violence, corruption and murder that lies beneath the dour surface of Kinloch life. It starts with one body found in the sea. Two more bodies are quickly added as it becomes clear a serial killer is at large. Further ramifications include police and harbour staff corruption and the involvement of a Latvian drugs smuggling ring. The book introduces Chief Detective Inspector Jim Daley who is destined to join the ranks of outstanding Scottish fictional detectives. Daley's complex relationships, with his bosses; his colleagues; and his unfaithful but passionately loved wife, drive the story of **Whisky From Small Glasses** forward to a dramatic and almost unbearable conclusion.

Whisky From Small Glasses is a book that is likely to endure, and will be the first in a series of crime novels set in rural South West Scotland that will transcend their genre and will comment on how such rural communities are coming to terms with 21st Century life and all its complexities.

"Whisky From Small Glasses is well named. It can be savoured and enjoyed just like a fine measure of the hard stuff. It engages and rewards as it thrills and delights. Like all the best crime fiction it transcends its genre as it enlightens the reader about the realities of a community that at first sight is stuck in a mid20th century time warp but underneath the veneer of stability is struggling to cope with the influx of modern values and modern, and not so modern, vices. The relationships around the chief character CDI Jim Daley are wonderfully drawn and are used to drive the story line forward relentlessly to a powerful conclusion, that leaves the reader anxious to follow the main character in his next adventure".

Whisky From Small Glasses can be purchased on *www.ringwoodpublishing.com* for £9.99 excluding p&p, or ordered by post or e-mail for the same price.

The e-book version is available for £7.20 from the Kindle Book Store or Amazon.co.uk